To Serve
& Protect

To Serve
& Protect

A Novel By

JAMES K. MAGEE

Keene Publishing
Warwick, New York

KEENE
PUBLISHING
P. O. Box 54
Warwick, New York 10990
www.KeeneBooks.com

Library of Congress Cataloging-in-Publication Data

Magee, James K., 1969-
 To serve and protect / James K. Magee.
     p. cm.
  ISBN-13: 978-0-9766805-7-4 (alk. paper)
  ISBN-10: 0-9766805-7-2 (alk. paper)
  1. Police—New York—Goshen—Fiction. 2. Serial murders—Fiction.
  3. Politicians—Crimes against—Fiction. 4. Washington (D.C.)—
  Fiction. 5. Goshen (N.Y.)—Fiction. I. Title.
  PS3613.A3427T63 2006
  813'.6—dc22   2006007236

For Mom, Kelly, and Reggie.

—J. K. M.

Author's Note

Many of the settings in this novel are based on actual locations in Goshen, N.Y. and Washington, D.C. As with so much in life, the work of others is a vital component of success and I am grateful for the help of so many, but would like to single out a few.

Although I tried to remain as faithful to their advice as the story-line would allow, this is a work of fiction and any errors are purely my mistake or the result of literary license.

To my publisher, Diane Tinney, for taking a risk and making this dream a reality, Managing Editor Melissa Browne for all the editorial guidance, Allison Tevald for early publicity advice, Beth Thomas for helping me polish the manuscript, and Peggy Gavan for the final proofing; Thomas Lopez, City of Middletown Police Chief, retired; Judge Michael Kavanaugh, former Ulster County District Attorney; Matthew Light, formerly of the New York State Police; The Washington D.C. Police Department, the Washington D.C. Office of Tourism, the staff of the United States Library of Congress, and the staff of the U.S. Capitol Building; The late William Gold, for the communication and computer information; Mayor Scott Wohl, The Village of Goshen, Detective Dan Henderson, The Village of Goshen Police Department, and the Village of Goshen employees and residents; Agent Kevin Danko of The Federal Bureau of Investigation, for an insider's POV and the realism advice; Dr. Richard Varbero and Dr. Loyd Lee, State University of New York, New Paltz, for demanding so much from me and my writing; Professor Paul Basinski and Dr. Eldridge, Orange County Community College, for the political Q & A; Veronica Conte, for sifting through the early version of the book and seeing a gem when no one else did; Lawrence Sanders, novelist, for the encouragement and inspiration; David McElroy; To God, who makes all things possible.

For more information on *To Serve & Protect* as well as my new projects visit www.JKMagee.com.

1

Jean Black could see the Washington Monument looming off to his left, and could feel the warmth of the rising October sun on his exposed face, as he made his way from Constitution Avenue to the Lincoln Memorial. The cold, damp air whipped his thick brown hair and he thrust his hands deep into his jacket pockets, his fingertips sliding across the dimpled grip of his 10mm Colt.

A man in navy pinstripes was leaning against a thick pillar of the memorial, engrossed in a *Washington Post*. Black pulled the collar of his leather jacket tight around his neck, watching for the paper to lower, waiting for their eyes to meet. It was Forest, and once he saw Black, he folded the paper, stuffing it into his pocket while he moved down Lincoln's marble staircase.

"Mr. Dresden," Forest acknowledged as he extended a mammoth hand.

Black took it. "Mr. Forest," he said, thinking about how long ago the name game had worn out its excitement.

"It was awfully good of you to come on such short notice," Forest said as they moved away from the memorial, and headed toward the cherry trees running the length of the reflecting pool.

"I was surprised to hear from you so soon. We generally don't handle things this way."

"I apologize for that. I figured you might be hesitant, but this seemed worthy of your time. This is why you pay me," he said, confident of his intentions.

"I'm a creature of habit, Calle. Change is not something I enjoy—"

"But you're here," Forest interrupted.

Black paused to consider the man and his interjection.

They were compatriots but opposites in every sense. Although Black was tall, about six-foot-four, Forest was a giant. Where maturity and purpose had etched several lines in Black's solid face, youth made Forest look smooth and plump. "No matter how hard I try, I can't get my curiosity under control. It'll be my undoing. You've never steered me wrong, so I came. What's so important?" Black asked.

"A senator."

"I might be interested," Black said, pausing to groom his moustache with his fingertips. "The client?"

"Seems as clean as can be expected," Forest said.

Black hesitated. "To be honest, I've had retirement on the brain lately."

"You?" Forest said, his tone catching Black off guard.

"That surprises you?" he asked, but got no response. "You thought I was going to do this forever? Well, I'll tell you a few things. I'm growing a little long in the tooth for this line of work. Plus my conscience is attempting a resurgence, which isn't exactly a comforting thought."

"I guess it's time then," Forest said.

"So tell me more about this senator," he said, looking across the solitude of Constitution Gardens, as it began to give way to early morning joggers and pet owners.

"It's West Virginia Senator Byron Mitchell. He's an old geezer, lives with a younger woman and a butler. Been over there forever," Forest said, staring past the slender monument and in the direction of the Capitol Building.

"Can the client afford it?"

"Easily."

"I'm staying at the Hyatt Regency on New Jersey under the name Dresden. I'll be there one night. Have them send an information packet on Mitchell, then leave it at the front desk for me. I won't wait around, so make sure they understand it must arrive by tonight," Black said, and moved away.

———

Beyond Black's reflection and the heavy rain sheeting across his hotel room window was New Jersey Avenue and its inching traffic. He was trying to talk himself out of killing again. He was losing the argument. A single legal folder labeled *West Virginia* lay on the bureau next to him. Inside were a photograph, an accompanying personal description document, an instruction page, and a set of keys to a Dodge waiting for him at the Hotel Washington.

The photograph was of Byron Mitchell. The short typewritten page fastened to the photo gave addresses, telephone numbers, vehicle types, plate numbers, and more than enough background information. "Eliminate West Virginia" emblazoned the top of the instruction page, which included several very specific questions the client needed answered, as well as a list of evidence the client wanted him to find.

A wicked grin appeared at the corners of his mouth as he pictured himself as an evil Sherlock Holmes. The addition of snooping to his repertoire was not unusual; in fact, it had become one of the reasons clients chose him. It hadn't always been; clients had only been interested in the who, and how much, at the onset of his career. Now they wanted the why, and Black had a talent for eliciting answers, through force and snooping.

The only obstacle left to dissuade him was the conversation with the client. Forest was nothing more than a locator and a courier; in the end it was his choice. And he never made it without following all precautions, the last being the conversation.

Black spent a few minutes disconnecting the hotel telephone and replacing it with a Motorola unit he kept in a small attaché case. The land-line was produced for the intelligence community, and it had two features of interest to Black: a source scrambler, and voice camouflage. It was 10 PM when he sat on the edge of the bed listening to its pulsing rings.

An edgy voice answered. "Hello?"

"Mr. Scaffiotelli?"

"Yes?"

"This is Mr. Dresden."

"I was beginning to think I wouldn't hear from you today. Mr. Forest said I would. I was ready to give up. It's getting late." Scaffiotelli sighed.

"I haven't committed myself. Your relief is somewhat premature."

"I'm sorry, I've never done this before."

"Most have not."

"What can I say to convince you?"

"Are you sure this is the proper course for you?"

"Yes."

"Mr. Forest seems to have faith in you. In your financial ability."

"We didn't discuss that," the man said.

"Account number A-118-64, United Bank of Switzerland," Black stated. "The price is five-hundred-thousand dollars. Nothing will happen until I get confirmation the money is there. Once I'm certain, I'll help you."

"I will transfer the money immediately," Scaffiotelli said. "When can I expect it?"

"I'll be leaving Washington Tuesday, October twenty-seventh, so between now and then."

"That's awfully vague, and it's a week away —"

"I was led to believe that urgency wasn't an issue, so nothing here is negotiable."

"Of course. Within a week's time then?"

"And yours is up," Black said, and replaced the receiver.

Byron Mitchell considered himself a passionate man, and his feelings covered the spectrum from ardent hatred to enthusiastic love. He was an elderly conservative who barked his commands within the stone walls of Capitol Hill, and they rarely carried an importance demanding public awareness. However, for the last several weeks Mitchell had drawn the media spotlight, and seemed to be on the television every time there was a commercial break.

The media held a special place in Mitchell's heart, because he couldn't recall anything he despised more. Their newfound interest in him stemmed from his speaking out against the federal government funding abortions. The surge in favor of government intervention was at an all-time high, and Mitchell stood against it. In fact, he was the most vociferous critic in Congress. His opinions were unpopular, ridiculed, and the media was capitalizing on the fervor.

Although he had spent most of the day chairing a Select Committee meeting on abortion, his thoughts were not focused on legislative ideals or the unborn. They focused instead on the dinner his wife was hosting that evening for his constituency in West Virginia, and about a certain female intern he had befriended—but more so on the intern. She was petite, brilliant, and blonde, a lethal combination, he knew. He also knew he was acting like a schoolboy stricken with a case of puppy love. It baffled him how such a young girl could turn him, the harsh old man of Washington, into such a kitten. He needed to spend time with her before she left the Hill, devoting her full attention back to graduate school, and before his wife returned to Washington.

It was late when Mitchell reached his Capitol Hill office and started packing up for the day, preparing for his journey home. While he mused about how an evening with her might progress, he pulled a set of keys from his suit coat and got into his blue Mercedes which had been a reliable companion for twenty-eight years.

By Monday, October twenty-sixth, Black was growing tired of Washington and was more than ready to kill Mitchell. Toting a heavy-duty duffel bag, he got off the elevator at the parking sub-level of the Hotel Washington. It was deserted. Dressed in a leather jacket, dark navy denims, thin leather gloves, and soft-soled shoes, he made only the slightest sound, which the cement floor amplified and ricocheted. The key ring tag designated the car was tucked into slot 40, and a white Dodge Charger Daytona was waiting for him. He set the duffel on the hood of the car, unzipped it, and withdrew a retractable mirror, flashlight, and an electronic device no bigger than an MP3 player. He placed the device on the roof of the car and flipped a toggle switch. A dim screen warmed and displayed the words *SYSTEM RUNNING*.

Black knelt on the cement amid oil stains and glass debris and extended the mirror, searching the undercarriage with the aid of the flashlight. It was clean. No monitoring devices, and best of all, no explosive surprises. The small screen flashed the words *SYSTEM FREE*, concurring with his finding. He replaced the equipment and got into the sports coupe.

Once outside the city, and away from the tourists who were calling it quits for the day and most likely looking for a restaurant, he headed for Georgetown. The Dodge was one of those American testosterone monsters, all engine and gas tank. Black inserted a compact disc into the player, and began to tap his fingers to the ivory gymnastics of Thelonious Monk.

Senator Byron Mitchell lived in a ten-bedroom brick estate on R Street, and the sprawl of his residence mocked the packed homes of his neighbors.

The house roosted on a rising slope of green property where hawthorns, maples, pines, and birches were strategically placed to lend to a wealthy image. In Black's opinion the plot had succeeded. A brick wall encircled the entirety, and the driveway was a fifty-yard climb past a black iron gate.

The sky was turning prismatic as the five o'clock hour rolled around, and R Street began turning a shade of tangerine. Across the street from Mitchell's home, a sprinkler system began spraying a burnt lawn.

Black parked the Dodge opposite the senator's home in an alleyway, inches from the burnt lawn. Sitting behind the steering wheel of the car, he studied the estate's windows with the aid of a hand-held light gathering scope. He'd been here many times over the past week, studying Mitchell and his estate. Although the house was concealed by abundant foliage, he could see a servant through an upstairs window. According to the information provided him, the wife was in Charleston, West Virginia, throwing a campaign contributor's victory dinner. It was too easy, but he'd spent a week making sure.

Throwing the duffel over his shoulder, he crossed R Street and ran along the walkway to a corner of the senator's property where he'd be unseen by neighbors, and negotiated the brick wall. From the shadows of a large maple he watched for dogs or signs of a perimeter alarm system. There was nothing.

His research had gleaned that the house was equipped with an adequate security system, and that the senator never engaged it. But research and hands-on experience were sometimes two different things. He sprinted to the rear wall of the house where an open window was providing the dining room with fresh air.

Black slid his switchblade down the center of the screened window and stepped through.

He made his way out of the wood laden room, long polluted by the stink of national self importance and tobacco. Once upstairs, he homed in on a vacuum's humming. The butler was turned away, cleaning, as Black reached for his Oplus-XT. The tranquilizer pistol was loaded with a sedative/memory agent combination, that would knock the man out for a good long time, only to awaken with a severely confounded memory. When Black cleared his throat, his oblivious prey reeled right into the dart's trajectory. The man fell on a plush cream carpet with no blood, and no pain.

Black had been generous.

Life was pain as far as he was concerned, and it wasn't meant to be escaped. Black got paid to impart pain, and he considered it his duty to make sure it wasn't avoided. But he hadn't been paid to visit the butler, so the man got a pass.

"No freebies," Black said, and deposited the man in the masterbath tub.

In time, the distinct sound of a German diesel engine could be heard climbing the driveway. Its purr echoed as it entered a detached three-car garage, and was eventually followed by a slamming door and a throaty West Virginia accent calling for Leonard, the servant.

He can't hear you, Black thought. It rolled through his mind as though it were a line to a song. He retreated into the master bath, concealing himself in darkness, his silenced 10mm pointed at the room's door.

The seventy-year-old man lumbered to the second floor and

down the bright hallway leading to his bedroom door.

"Let the games begin," Black mumbled.

Inside, Mitchell switched on a light, threw his suit coat on a brown armchair, kicked off his shoes, and sat on the edge of the bed to massage his eyes.

Black stepped from his retreat and stealthed toward Mitchell, unnoticed until he was on top of the man. The dark shine of an automatic pistol caught Mitchell's eye as it struck him in the temple. He fell hard on the floor.

Leaning down, Black picked him up by the collar of his long-sleeved cotton shirt and threw him into the heavy brown armchair as if he were weightless. He withdrew three pairs of handcuffs and bound Mitchell's wrists behind his back and his legs to those of the chairs. It was an old routine for him. Mitchell regained consciousness with enough energy to begin screaming commands as though he were in charge of a Congressional debate. Black's leather-clad fist landed on his lips and split the lower one. Now the eye and mouth had small red rivers flowing from them.

"You're making this so much worse for yourself than it has to be," Black whispered in his ear.

"Who are you?"

The switchblade knife caught the senator's cheek and provided an answer, while creating another stream of blood. The old man's scream was almost deafening. "You'd be better served to consider the position you're in. Now, then, the people I work for need to have certain questions answered, and this is what you should be worried about," Black said, staring directly at the man, his face no more than six inches away.

"Why don't you kiss my ass," Mitchell said.

Black took his time, and without expression, began to throw punches that rocked the old man's head from side to side.

"Enough, enough. What do you want?" Mitchell screamed.

"What do I want?" Black asked, as though the comment insulted him. Two hard downward punches landed on the old man's chest, making kindling out of his sternum and two ribs. Mitchell was wheezing. The lung hadn't been punctured, but was bruised. "And it's enough when I say it's enough," Black said after a short pause, his voice calm, but piercing.

"All right, for Christ's sake," Mitchell moaned in submission.

Black pulled a chair up and sat before one of the most powerful men in America. He didn't stare at Mitchell as he eased into the seat but concerned himself with getting comfortable.

The sight of his leisurely behavior sent a tremor through Mitchell, and Black couldn't help but crack a wide grin. "Now we're going to have a discussion of sorts. If I may make a suggestion, you should take into consideration whether you want this to be easy or difficult." There was no response. "If you were having money problems, you should've come to us. This could've been avoided."

Mitchell's tone brimmed with realization. "Are you going to kill me?"

The question sickened Black. He'd held up no better than a young boy or a woman. Although he did, in the past, have people die on him at this stage of an interrogation, he despised Mitchell all the same. Most people just give up.

Black moved forward in the chair. His eyes were blank, disconnected; it was just business to him. He was silent, staring past Mitchell, considering the collection of photographs crammed onto a nearby bureau.

Mitchell turned to see what he was looking at. There, frozen in time, sat his first wife, deceased, his current wife, Irene, and his five children.

Black stood up, and Mitchell's trance was broken. With his back to the senator, staring at a famous Monet, Black began to speak in his matter of fact tone. "You know why I'm here, Byron." He didn't consider anything he said an opinion. He wasn't interested in theory.

"Yes."

"When someone invests money and respect, he expects a return. I guess you misunderstood that. What you do understand are the who's and the why's. Answers are what my client expects now, and he expects me to get them from you. I feel he'd prefer them to be dragged out of you accompanied by as much pain as possible, and don't think that wouldn't get me off. It would. It would be like plucking a debutante's cherry for me. Believe me, I could make it last for days and days." Black was loosely circling Mitchell's chair as he spoke.

"I'll tell you anything you want to know," Mitchell said.

"You're the one who started all this wildness over on Capitol Hill, right?" Black turned to meet his prey's glare.

"Yes," Mitchell said. He sounded like a punctured tire; it was growing more difficult for him to get air into his lungs.

"Why?" Black said.

"Change. I suddenly found myself believing it was the right thing for America, and it suddenly became plausible to get paid far more for it. I didn't want to leave my legacy intact, let them find their own way for a change. That's the reason, for the sake of change."

"A resurgence of conscience," Black said, pausing only for a second to consider the similarity with himself. "That's not like you. As for the other thing, you know they'll go to any length necessary to close the book on it, don't you?"

"Yes, I can see that now," Mitchell wheezed.

"Now, back to that earlier advice I gave you. Easy or difficult? Tell me everything I want to know, and you have my word you'll die quick, painless," Black said with a snap in his voice.

"Quick would be best." Mitchell said. He had no choice.

2

"I hate paperwork!" Thomas Martin announced as he stretched his arms over his head, stood up, and moved around from behind his weathered six-drawer desk. He ran his hands through his groomed black crop and began to file loose sheets and bound stacks of paper into a tall gray cabinet. The days were getting shorter and shorter as autumn entrenched itself, and he was determined to escape his office before the use of fluorescent light was required.

Martin was forty, divorced, and Chief of Police in the rural town of Goshen, New York. He stood six-foot one and weighed a trim but athletic one-hundred and eighty pounds, and his dark eyes and the shallow lines running across his forehead gave him an almost regal presence.

Moving a short corridor away, he stood under the booking room's ceiling fan as it forced musty air toward the floor. "You read more than anyone I've ever met, Roberta," Martin said to the night dispatcher as he stuffed his arms into the sleeves of his gray fleece jacket.

"Can't help it. I have an intrigue deficiency," she said, turning her attention away from the novel she'd been reading all week. "You taking off?"

"So what's this one about?" he asked, leaning over to see who the author was.

"It's a psychological thriller, juicy stuff. This Kellerman can sure spin them."

"The Chris Parker Band is playing tonight over at The Inn, so I'll be there if anyone needs me," Martin said. The Inn was a jazz bar featuring live music five nights a week, and since four blocks distance from the police station was close enough to walk, he did.

"Needs you, that's a laugh. The last excitement we had was old man Donovan out in the middle of Golden Hill Avenue, nude, trying to coax his cat out of Mayor Oliver's tree. Besides, who are you trying to fool? You're going to that bar to see Paulina," Roberta chimed, returning to her novel.

He left her, shaking his head and smiling, closing the station's door tight behind him.

The Goshen Police Department occupied an old thin railway station heavily layered with red and white paint. Amber lights flooded brick sidewalks, while the American flag and the New York Excelsior whipped in the stiff breeze. Crossing the street separating his station from the post office, Martin strolled the two-block stretch along West Main Street toward the center of town. The local pharmacist, John, was helping a customer near the front plate-glass windows of Baxter's Pharmacy, and he shot Martin a wave as he passed. Across the street, he could see Sal inside Village Pizza, tossing pie dough into the air. He passed dark brick, stone, and painted buildings that housed the town's hardware store, coffee shop, and bicycle shop, and exemplified rural Hudson Valley towns.

The sidewalk was deserted, and the thin, pliant branches of young dogwoods brushing against each other provided the only sound, which soon yielded to the noise coming from the town's sole traffic light.

Fluorescent lamps were warming up as he covered the final two blocks to The Inn, and cement sidewalks gave way to blue-stone slabs where overpowering roots cracked and splintered corners, causing them to jut into the air.

As he passed the Methodist Church, he came within earshot of the heartening sound of a hi-hat and brush keeping time for the quick hand at the piano. There were a lot of drawbacks to living in a small town, a lot of things he could live without, but his jazz bar wasn't one of them. The Inn was a restored three-story brownstone nestled among a long series of connected row houses called Lawyers' Row, and shrouded by the explosive colors of autumn.

Martin grabbed the brass door handle and walked inside the small natural-wood foyer separating him from a packed main room where the light was faint and a thin cloud of tobacco smoke clung to the ceiling.

A Briggs grand piano was set off in the far corner serving as the stage for live performances. The Chris Parker Band, a local group and overall favorite, was well into a set when Martin slid onto a stool to wait for Robin to make his way down the bar.

The Inn was owned by Robin and Paulina Orange, first-generation Scottish immigrants who could run a hell of a bar and knew good jazz when they heard it. Robin was in charge of the bartending and music. His sister, Paulina, was in charge of everything else. They were a good team: The Inn had become trendy and successful, and the overcrowding had become perpetual. Martin liked the atmosphere, not to mention his obsession with Paulina.

Lining a custom piece of glossy oak were twenty-five rich leather stools occupied by local lawyers, clerks, secretaries, and county employees. Goshen was the county seat, and the government workers always made up a good bulk of the crowd. There were dark pinstripes next to casual clerks huddling around Helen Goodright, the administrative aide to the county executive. She was the latest goal for the young and dashing. She was in total control though, and worlds smarter than her single-minded pursuants. Being brunette and well-endowed made her an easy but underestimated target. Martin pitied the day her boyfriend, a U.S. Army Ranger, might just happen in to surprise her, and them. His fantasy was a scene right out of a Clint Eastwood movie.

At the far end of the bar were two local and three county justices, wagering their unwanted docket items on the football game playing on the television.

"So how's James Bond tonight?" Robin Orange asked, sliding a bottle of Murphy's Stout across to him. James Bond had been Martin's nickname ever since he'd returned from college. It was following his return, and a great deal of personal deliberation and pressure from his uncle, the former Chief of Police, that he'd accepted the position of head law-enforcement official in Goshen. He hadn't really regretted the decision in his fifteen years of service, mostly because he trusted his uncle and wanted to emulate him, but also because of the career's potential for action.

His uncle had raised him from the age of nine, after the death of Martin's parents. Michael Reeves was a barrel-chested moose of a man who gave his nephew everything he never had. Michael had never married, and when his sister and her husband died, Martin became his whole world.

"I wish you hadn't started calling me that, Robin" he said.

"Why? You do remind me of him. Hell of a compliment, I think."

"I never thought it would catch on."

"It did do that, didn't it," Robin said with a grin. "I see you made it back from D.C.?"

"Can't do anything in this town without everyone knowing."

"Privacy in this town?" Robin mocked. "You get to see the White House this time?"

"Next time."

"You said that last time, Tom. Quite a place the U.S. of A. Only country where you can wander around in the head man's digs."

"How's business tonight?" Martin asked, changing the subject.

"Another small fortune rolling in," Robin said. "How'd the policing go today?"

"Same as always. I stared at my air conditioner and sifted through paperwork, glorious paperwork," Martin said, taking a pull on his beer. Maybe it was his turning forty, or maybe it was the mindless tranquility of Goshen. Either way, questions about his future seemed to be rolling through his mind more and more often.

"You sound bored, chum."

"Yeah, the action bug's been biting me."

"I heard Murray retired."

"Yeah. We threw him a retirement shindig over at Oliver's," Martin said. "He's well on his way to the sunny, beach-bunny lifestyle in Fort Lauderdale by now."

"Get his replacement yet?"

"Starts tomorrow as a matter of fact, but he's going to meet me here tonight so we can get acquainted the way cops were meant to."

"Where's the lad from?"

"New York City."

"N.Y.P.D. Action central," Robin said.

"Oh yeah." Martin said, pausing to consider if his next question was worth the effort. "Your sister working tonight?"

"She's around."

"She still seeing the good doctor?"

"Jealousy is a waste of energy mate. Anyhow, I can't keep up, and try not to." Robin glanced at one of his signaling barmaids, preparing to go back to work. "You still got an eye for her?"

"Still."

"She talks about you now and again."

"I'm not that lucky."

"Another Stout?"

"I'll wait 'til I'm closer to the stage," Martin said.

Tonight the bar was busy, but there were still several empty tables near the stage. A trumpet exhaled an emotional solo as

Paulina Orange touched Martin on the shoulder.

"Hey, you," she said, smiling, and brushed her reddish hair away from her groomed eyebrows. She led him to a small table in a dark corner of the main room, and took up position opposite him. "So how's the town?" she asked.

Martin took his time looking her over. She had a precision that hypnotized him as easily as did her hazel eyes. Then there was that flawless, tanned physique, hiding underneath those cream slacks and cotton sweater. A sweater he had slipped off more than once.

"Are we safe tonight?" she teased.

"I personally locked the door and shut off the light," Martin said, disengaging from his trance.

Paulina hadn't seemed to notice, but had turned toward the door, watching a couple enter the bar. "I'll be right back," she said, pecking him on his cheek and heading over to the arriving customers, the county district attorney and his secretary. Both were married to other people, and Martin wasn't sure what to think of the situation. Rumor had it his wife was a part-time lesbian, and his secretary's husband was frigid and forgiving. They waved at him as they followed Paulina to one of the upper-level tables.

"Paulina Orange," Martin mumbled to himself with only half-hearted resignation, and slipped back into his trance.

He was watching her and wishing they were still lovers when Chris Parker announced that the band was taking five but would return for another set.

Martin had been nursing a few beers for two hours when his new officer, Matthew Light, entered. He was removing a black windbreaker and scanning the crowd when Paulina approached and pointed him in the right direction. A captivating piece of Cool Jazz was playing low as he made his way through the crowd. There was a confidence visible in his walk, and more than a passing resemblance to Martin's uncle. It was unnerving.

Martin rose to shake his hand. Sylvia, a barmaid, was on them immediately to take orders.

"How was the trip up?" Martin asked.

"You're not really all that far from the city. Never know it though, with all the cows and trees. Thought I'd strayed into Vermont."

"Seventy miles isn't that far, I guess."

He scanned the room and the band. "Nice place, good music," he said, running a hand over his crewed brown hair.

"You like jazz?"

"Not really. Rock is more my speed."

"I can listen to just about anything, except opera."

"I'll agree with you on the opera part of that one," Light said.

"In all the times we talked on the phone, I never managed to get the full skinny about why you wanted out of the city. Hell, it didn't matter, with a resume and a service record like yours." Sylvia had arrived with a Budweiser Select for Lightand another Murphy's Stout for Martin, studying Light briefly before leaving.

Martin tipped the bottle and addressed the glare as he looked at the band. "You'll be the topic of the town for a while. Until they get what they want, or they get bored with you. I'd count on the former."

"Why's that?"

"Small towns are notorious for a lot of things. Prying eyes and quick mouths are two of them, and in Goshen they award Olympic medals for both. Just warning you. You'll be the center of attention for a while."

"Well, I was just a number in the city, at least outside of my beat, so the change will be good."

"We'll see," Martin said. "So give me the full story this time, not the shrinked version I got from your psych-eval and background checks. Why did you leave, anyway?"

"A drug raid, routine stuff. We went in, and this guy just appears from the bedroom closet. A coke freak with an automatic. He killed three and wounded two others, including me. I guess he didn't like us that close to his blow. It was just time for me and the sleepless city to go our separate ways, if you know what I mean."

"Well, you won't have to worry about that in Goshen," Martin said.

"Not having to worry wouldn't be such a bad thing."

"There's plenty to keep you busy, though: DUIs, speeders, some domestic stuff, and the rare robbery, not to mention high school pranks. Last year, the shop students broke down a teacher's Mini Cooper and reassembled it inside his classroom. But mostly it's just patrolling, though, making the citizens feel safe, and that kind of crap."

"Good enough."

"The first time we talked, you said you were a Marine. You

share that with the former Chief of Police. What'd you do?"

"Recon," Light said, and Martin noticed his honesty and directness. He liked Light, even from their first telephone conversation nearly a month ago. Martin hoped this was going to work out. For a lot of reasons he needed it to. Light had been exactly what he'd been searching for, an equal, a successor.

"Well, I don't want to make you listen to the music or me any longer, so you can take off if you want. I have all of the benefit and quartermaster stuff at the office. If you want to come in early tomorrow, we can check it all out, see if we got it right. Then I'll show you the layout, get your feet wet."

"Sounds good to me. What time you want me in?"

"Let's say seven," Martin said. "Oh, listen, the bug has been biting me lately, so I won't mind if you bend my ear with a couple of juicy New York stories."

Light was standing and ready to leave. "No problem there, Chief, I've got a million of them." He shook Martin's outstretched hand, then disappeared through the crowded main floor.

3

It was still early on Monday evening when Black crossed R Street for the alleyway where he'd tucked away the Dodge. Carrying a heavy duffel bag, he eased into the bucket seat and dialed his client on Motorola's cellular version of their intelligence land-line. A deep and anxious voice answered.

"It's Dresden," Black said. "West Virginia is taken care of, but there's another problem."

"You waited long enough to get back to me," Scaffiotelli said. "What do you mean, another problem?"

"I think you know."

"I'm not very good at these games. What the hell are you talking about?"

"Seems the senator wasn't in on it alone," Black said. "The name Angela Wilme was mentioned. Does that mean anything to you?"

"A woman?" Scaffiotelli asked in disbelief. "Who is she?"

"That's not my problem, Mr. Scaffiotelli."

"No, of course not. It's just that this is very unexpected. I was certain it ended with Mitchell."

"I'll leave everything for you at the drop site you requested. This concludes things between us," Black said, allowing himself to be hypnotized by the swirling leaves in the street. The wind was carrying the crisp autumn smell he loved.

"No," Scaffiotelli said with desperation. "Let me call you back? At least let me sort this out." The man's anxiety made Black's head start to hurt.

"There is a procedure. You should know this by now—"

"Please."

"All right, but I'll call you. I'll give you five minutes only because this is unresolved and therefore incomplete." Black terminated the call, and heaved the bag into the backseat.

Staring at the estate, he thought about his completed task. He'd spent the better part of three hours overturning furniture, looking through bookshelves, under carpets, and in closets. The senator's wife wouldn't recognize her home when she got there. She would barely recognize her husband. Black had taken the things he thought his client would find of interest. Files, computer disks, printouts, the hard drive from an IBM personal computer, audiotapes, videotapes, a recording device from underneath a desk, mail, billing statements, and photographs.

He waited in the car, staring at his watch and waiting for those five minutes to slide away. He realized it was wrong to give the client this much room to maneuver. A patrol car could swing through at any minute, or someone from Capitol Hill. The longer he waited, the longer the list of variables became.

He hit redial. "It's Dresden. Your time is up."

"She lives at 118 E Street. Take care of it," Scaffiotelli said. An authority rumbled through the receiver, replacing his earlier anxiety.

"It doesn't work this way," Black told him.

"An additional five-hundred-thousand is being wired to your account as we speak," Scaffiotelli said.

Black was silent for a long while, a technique he used to unbalance people while gathering his thoughts.

"She's only a woman," the client interjected, breaking the silence.

This doesn't feel right, Black thought. But he was curious, and too intrigued to listen to the whispers of his long-silent conscience. Besides, Forest had checked, and like the man said, it was only a woman.

Half a million dollars versus one woman's life. There was no comparison.

"Providing everything is in order when I call Zurich, you'll be hearing from me before I leave Tuesday."

"She's in apartment 3A," Scaffiotelli said, and hung up.

———✦———

Negotiating the heavy traffic of Washington Circle, Black exited from Pennsylvania Avenue onto K Street. He made another turn at Mt. Vernon Place onto 7th Street and began looking for a convenient parking spot. He finally found one at The National Portrait Gallery. E Street was jammed in the direction leading toward The White House, but deserted in the opposite direction.

He pushed his way through the tourists and District employees, examining his surroundings. It was a fair section of a city known for its bad neighborhoods and was dominated by small businesses standing in the shadows of marble giants.

Angela Wilme lived in a four-story brick apartment building. The building's exterior was unspectacular. A solitary lamp flooded the recessed entrance where five cement steps rose to a set of double doors adorned with an autumn wreath. There was a small entry-card panel fixed next to the doors, and it looked too formidable to be quick.

"Damn," Black mumbled, cursing the obstacle.

Black moved into the alleyway and studied the wall of the building, and the fire escape extending just along the third floor and past an open window.

Lowering the staircase would make things easier but the inevitable noise would be a dead giveaway.

He moved into the small lot occupying the rear of the building. An extensive U-shaped carport ran the angles of the lot. Mercedes, Porsche, Corvette, BMW, Range Rover, and Volvo were some of the nameplates under the port.

"Convenient and expensive," Black said softly.

Large half-round windows looked down from each apartment. Three of them were brightly lit, but Angela's barely had light spilling from within. From the rear lot, he studied the alleyway again, and quickly planned his method of entry.

He'd use a section of thin olive cord, and climb to the third-floor platform. But he would have to wait. E Street was still heavy with pedestrians.

Black headed back to the car to wait.

He was uncomfortable knowing as little as he did about Angela Wilme, he thought, warming his hands in the rush of hot air pouring through the vents. It had been a long time since he'd gone into a situation blind like this. He'd grown accustomed to the extensive subject profiles, and he'd always attributed his success to an abundance of caution. That he had been doing this for twenty years without being apprehended was a testament to that.

"I hate the swell of a city," Black said, staring at the traffic flowing past his car. On the seat beside him was an open notebook computer. It was logged onto the Internet and he was waiting to see if the money had been deposited into his account in Switzerland. After a few seconds, his activity summary came onto the screen. The money was there. He logged off and closed the computer.

He knew nothing about this woman, her age, or what she did for a living, even whether she actually deserved her fate. He also knew nothing about his client, which was the way he liked it. He trusted Forest for the same reasons. He was cautious.

Patience and research were two requirements he demanded from his clients. Scaffiotelli had fallen short on both accounts.

Black tugged at the corner of his thick mustache and admitted, in a situation such as this, and especially in his profession, such requirements could hardly be constants.

It was pouring rain and cold at eleven o'clock, when John Cartwell paused at the entrance to Senator Mitchell's colonial. The worn wipers of his Chevy Caprice hissed as they pushed the water from the windshield. The headlights pressed through the heavy rain, illuminating a brick wall, an open gate, and shining blacktop. Two District of Columbia cruisers were at the top of the long, arcing driveway. He was amazed by the inactivity, and that he was the first plainclothes on the scene. He'd been sure there would be a swarm of people and media bullshit to contend with, but it was quiet, and that wasn't necessarily good, either.

He parked next to a detached garage, got out, and ran to the front porch. Officer Ed Dyroff was leaning against one of the front columns, smoking.

"Putting on a few pounds, ain't we, Ed?" Cartwell asked, shaking the rain from his trench coat.

Dyroff took a long drag on the Newport and exhaled before speaking. "Hey, John, how are ya?"

"Where's the main event?"

"Second-floor bedroom." He shook his head. "What a mess."

"How long you been here?" Cartwell asked.

"About ten minutes. Hoyt's inside. We both got here at the same time."

"Is it Senator Mitchell?"

"According to his wife."

"Is she the one who phoned in the call?"

"Guess so."

"Where's she at?"

"In the downstairs library. Hoyt's with her."

"Hoyt? I don't think I know him," Cartwell said. "Who is he?"

"Came over from another precinct last month. He's been around."

"Were you guys in the room at all?"

"Just to take a look, but we didn't go inside. Lieutenant Nagel said there was a plainclothes en route. He told us to wait, and that everything was being handled."

"Nagel called you personally?"

"He called both of us personally. Why?"

"No reason, that's good," Cartwell said, but he thought something else. It was odd that a reported homicide was being handled this way. Things were being kept quiet, which was good, but if it involved a government official it was usually the FBI doing the silencing. Lightning stabs were illuminating the property, and he could smell the ozone. "Do you have a radio on?" Cartwell asked.

"Yeah," Dyroff said, displaying his portable.

"I don't want this to turn into a circus, so call me before letting anyone else in here, and I mean anyone. I'll be set on channel two, okay?" Cartwell said.

"Sure."

Cartwell entered the house and closed the heavy door. Almost immediately a man rounded a corner and approached him.

"You Hoyt?" Cartwell asked.

"Yeah. You the detective?"

"Where is he?"

"I'll show you."

The polished black-and-white floors were littered with broken picture frames, torn photographs, and paintings. On the second floor, Hoyt led Cartwell down a wide hall that extended to the left and right of the stair's crest. A dark green Oriental carpet stretched its hardwood length. Hoyt stopped at the entrance of an open door.

Cartwell stood staring at the dead senator and then turned to address Hoyt. "I want you to go back down to Mrs. Mitchell and get a statement. Just stick to the basics. Where she was this evening, how did she get there, and home? What times did that involve? When did she get here, what time did she find the body and call us? Then get a little more specific. Who did she talk to at D.C.P.D., and why didn't she call the Feds? Then get her out of here. This place is going to be a circus, and she doesn't need to be the main attraction. Tell her it's for her own protection to remain with us. If she gets uptight about being downtown, find out where she would rather go and then take her there. You're her designated shadow if she wants to leave. But I want her out of here in ten minutes."

"Got it," Hoyt said, and retraced his steps while Cartwell moved to the threshold of the room.

Byron Mitchell was propped up among broken and scattered dresser drawers, picture frames, and indistinguishable items. Cartwell's stomach turned as he stared at the slumped and bloody man.

Turning away, he withdrew his transceiver and called the police dispatcher at his D.C. precinct.

"Has the Crime Unit, M.E., and E.S.U. been dispatched over here?" he asked.

"Yes, Detective, they're en route."

"We're going to need additional men. Patch me through to the watch commander."

"Hold for the commander, Detective."

There was a brief pause, and then a familiar voice spoke. "Lieutenant Roy Nagel."

"Roy, it's John."

"What's the story over there?"

"Mitchell's been beaten to death."

"Jesus," Nagel said, with what sounded like a full mouth.

The man was infamous for his twenty-four-hour-a-day diet of exotic sandwiches, and Cartwell assumed he'd caught him in the middle of one that sounded like it had too much sauce.

"The house is trashed, but nothing expensive seems to be missing. I'd say they were hunters. Whether they found it or whether this is a cover, I don't know."

"Listen, John, this is our ball of wax. I've dispatched a C.S.U. and an M.E. I'll have to contact the Commissioner and the Feds at some point, but Mrs. Mitchell called us." Nagel's voice was clearer now.

"What's going on?" Cartwell asked, knowing the answer was plain and simple politics. Acknowledging that this town, above all others, was drowning in it.

"If it's Mitchell, then it'll be out of our hands and into the Fed's. They'll be there as soon as I call them, but I'll hold off an hour to let you and your crew get started—"

"This should've been the Feds' headache from the get-go," Cartwell said. "Why should I bother getting hip deep in shit?"

"Most likely they won't exclude us if we're already hip deep in shit. It will at least keep us on the playing field," Nagel said, and hung up.

"Bullshit," Cartwell muttered, rising from the chair. He removed his trench coat, slipped on a pair of latex gloves, and moved slowly into the bedroom. He pushed his gold-rimmed glasses up the ridge of his nose with his forefinger as he bent over for a better look at Mitchell's body. His expansive chest heaved at the sight. No amount of exposure to this sort of sight would ever bring desensitization for him.

It was barely a minute when his transceiver announced that Dr. Myruski, the M.E., had arrived.

"Send him up," Cartwell said.

"The C.S.U. van is pulling up as well," Dyroff said.

"Let them through."

Doctor Larry Myruski was a short, round man, whose hairline was pulling away from his forehead.

"Hey, Doc," Cartwell said, moving down the hall toward him.

"And you are?" Myruski asked, responding with a typical question.

"Detective Cartwell, but John is fine."

"Anyone been inside yet?"

"Me briefly, but that's it."

"Amazing, I'll actually be the first for once. Usually I'm the hundredth to mull over a corpse," Myruski remarked. "You wouldn't lie to me, would you?"

"No."

Taking a pair of latex gloves out of his black leather bag and pulling them on with a snap, Myruski smiled his crooked smile and announced that he was ready.

They negotiated the scattered items and approached the body. Crouching down, Myruski grabbed the senator's chin with his left hand and felt for a pulse with his right.

"Want to make a little wager on the verdict?" he asked with a laugh. "Well, now he's officially dead."

"Thanks for the update, Doc." Cartwell moved toward the dark bathroom, shaking his head, as Myruski began speaking into a micro cassette recorder.

Inside the bathroom, Cartwell flipped a wall switch, and noticed a body lying in the deep claw-foot bathtub.

"There's another one in here when you're done there,"

Cartwell said, his voice echoing through the hollow tiled room.

———•·•———

It was late when Chief Thomas Martin closed the door to his small brick home. Four times a week, he spent an hour jogging a course through the town he'd grown up in, and was responsible for protecting. It was getting colder now, and he was wearing gray sweats, New Balance running shoes, and a New York Yankees cap.

Goshen was preternaturally quiet as Martin began his religious trek down Murray Avenue away from his home, and the impact of his feet on the pavement seemed to be the only sound in the world. Dim streetlamps battled large areas of darkness. Very few houses had lights ablaze at this hour.

He turned onto Lincoln Avenue, passing the middle school and its varsity fields, where he'd discovered his gift for football. Lincoln was lined with new sodium lamps, brick sidewalks, and a canopy of old maples. Turning left onto North Church Street and headlong into a bitter wind, he descended toward the center of town, past the lumberyard and firehouse.

Goshen's only traffic light, which during the day brought order to the five-pronged intersection, now blinked a cautionary yellow. There were no cars and no other pedestrians, and the feeling that he had the entire town to himself was what Martin liked most about running at this hour.

He loved Goshen, the quiet of it, even though he longed for action and excitement. He enjoyed the slow pace the town chartered for itself. He passed the Goshen Savings Bank, theater, Presbyterian Church, and moved into the Victorian section of town.

The homes and their property were bigger here, and the cars occupying their driveways cost more than he made in a year.

As he turned onto Parkway Avenue, the songs of insects and frogs joined the rhythm of his shoes. Paulina Orange lived on this street, and he became aware, as he did every time he approached her house, that he missed her desperately.

He was four houses away when he saw the silver 928 Porsche with physician plates idling next to her house, and he intentionally picked up his pace to a sprint. He was midway through his run now, and the acceleration made his chest pound. Martin left the road for the seclusion of a thick oak tree. He stopped to catch his breath and to watch. It was Dr. Strogg's car and they were inside saying their good nights.

Martin continued along his course, down Orange Avenue, putting them behind him, at least physically. He regretted having told her that he was in love. That confession had sealed their fate. He missed her body, everything about her. But he was no doctor, and Strogg was. On the other hand, he was single, and Strogg wasn't.

At the corner of County Route 207, Martin turned left again and saw the first pedestrian of his journey.

"Evening, Chief," Georgette Michaels said.

"Hello, Georgette," Martin answered.

Georgette owned The Farmer's Inn, a bed and breakfast which sat a block away in the opposite direction, and doubled as a boarding house for a few wealthy retirees. She was walking her Springer Spaniel, S'mores.

"Hello, S'mores," Martin said. The dog barked. "Pretty late for you two to be out."

"If she can't sleep, neither can I," Georgette said, as S'mores inspected Martin's shoes. "Out for your nightly inspection of the Orange residence?"

"You have to love a town like Goshen. Your granddaughter's been running her mouth again?" he asked.

"She's your dispatcher, Tom. Information is the name of her game," Georgette said, and tugged at the dog's leash.

He continued passed Lawyers' Row, a stretch of brick row homes that had been converted to offices years ago, the library, his favorite bar, the old county building, and eventually turned back onto North Church Street, and headed for home. He wished he hadn't seen Paulina. He didn't need the aggravation of a sleepless night. He had to talk to her. He couldn't go on without spending time with her, even if it was only to be intimate without commitment.

Thomas Martin needed Paulina Orange.

———◆◆◆———

Irene Mitchell was sitting on a high-backed red velvet sofa, staring into blank space, when Officer Walter Hoyt descended the tall curved staircase, crossed the foyer, and entered the Georgetown estate's library. The room was lined with books to its twelve-foot ceiling. The carpet was plush red, and directly in front of the sofa, a dulling fire glowed in the brick hearth.

Hoyt had been around long enough to know if someone was faking grief, and to his way of thinking, she was either in the clear or one hell of an actress.

"Mrs. Mitchell," Hoyt said, "I need to ask you a few questions. We can do it here, or we can go downtown if you'd like to get out of the house."

"I'll answer them here, I guess." She cleared her throat and wiped her eyes, smudging her makeup.

"Were you home all this evening, ma'am?" he asked as he sat down on the sofa next to her.

"No. I got home around ten-thirty," she said, somewhat angered. "You don't think I did this, do you?"

"It's routine, ma'am—"

"That's just absurd that you could think that. I loved Byron." She began to weep.

"Please, ma'am. I just have a few more questions. Okay?"

She nodded.

"Where were you this evening?" he asked.

"I was in Charleston, West Virginia. That's where Byron's campaign headquarters is. I was giving a dinner for contributors as a way of thanking them for their efforts in getting him re-elected this year."

"So you were on an airplane tonight?"

"Yes, from Charleston."

"And who picked you up at the airport?"

"A Senate limousine. Byron sent it for me."

"Do you remember the driver's name?"

"No, I don't. Is that important?"

"We can find that out, ma'am," Hoyt said. "Was there anyone in the house when you arrived?"

"The servant should have been here, but I didn't see him tonight."

"And his name is?"

"Leonard Evans. He lives here with us. He is full-time and stays in a room downstairs."

"Do you have any other staff members who work for you?"

"The gardener. His name is Philip Torroson, but he doesn't live here."

"Do you know where he lives?"

"No. Leonard usually dealt with him."

"That's all right. A few more questions, and that's it," Hoyt said.

"Okay," she said, wiping her eye with the back of her hand.

"What time did you find your husband?"

"About as soon as I got home."

"And when was that again?"

"Half-past ten. That's when I called the police."

"And who did you talk to there, do you remember?"

"Roy Nagel is an old friend, so I called him," Mrs. Mitchell said.

"That's great, ma'am. Thank you."

"Can you get me out of here now? Anywhere but here, please," she said.

He took her arm to help her to her feet. As Cartwell had prescribed, she was out of the house within ten minutes.

Standing in the doorway separating the bathroom and bedroom, Detective Cartwell was monitoring Dr. Myruski's preliminary examination of the senator. A ghost-white woman named Christine Straka, who was a technical advisor for the D.C. police department, called out to Cartwell.

"Chris, what a surprise," Cartwell said.

"Someone ripped through this house, huh?" she asked,

throwing her long flaxen braid over her shoulder.

"Oh, yeah."

"So, how have you been? It looks as though married life agrees with you," Straka said, without really making eye contact.

"Still as blunt as a cinder block to the face I see," Cartwell said. "Not my fault that you couldn't commit." Her freckled face made her look girlish, and her brown eyes could still cast a spell over him. He still loved her, he admitted to himself, and looked away to Myruski.

"Senator Mitchell, eh?" Straka asked.

"Yep, but I'll confirm that downtown," Myruski said.

"You both sound sure of yourselves," Cartwell said, and looked at the man's face again. It could have been anyone, as far as he was concerned.

"Some of us do watch CNN," Straka said.

"Really," Myruski agreed, and vanished into the bathroom.

"Oh yeah? He's been on there?"

"Where have you been? He's on every night over the abortion issue. Real controversial stuff," Straka said.

"I don't watch that shit," Cartwell said, thinking of at least two hundred other places he'd rather be and people he'd rather talk to.

She stepped out of the room and moved down the hallway, and began to give her seven-man team instructions. Three of the men stayed in the room while the others followed her to begin a sweep and search of the house.

"I requested additional black-and-whites for you guys," Cartwell yelled after her.

"Good. We'll need them," she responded, and disappeared.

The M.E. returned from the bathroom almost immediately. He was toting his black bag. "Cartwell, this guy's still alive. Get a Medico up here."

The Medico's from the E.S.U. moved the butler past Cartwell and Myruski, and toward an ambulance waiting in the driveway.

"Any other bodies?" Myruski teased.

"Straka will have her initial sweep done in about half an hour. Stick around until then. What's the verdict on these two?"

"My bet's on the butler, in the bedroom, with a candlestick."

"Very funny, Doc."

"I need more time with them to be sure."

"Well, based on what you know now, what do you think?"

"The guy in the tub is easy. There's a large bore puncture on his neck, probably from a tranquilizer dart. Toxicology will tell us what he's sleeping off. He was moved into the tub after. At least I can't see any reason for a fully dressed man to be in the shower."

"No, that figures right. What about the senator?"

"There's a wound on the right cheek from a blade. His hands and ankles have marks on them, as do the legs of the chair. He was fastened to it, with handcuffs, probably—"

"I didn't see any cuffs around." Cartwell said.

"No, neither did I," Myruski said. "Anyhow, his sternum and at least one rib are broken. There's localized bruising on the chest that appears to have come from someone's hand. His jaw's broken, too. Bottom line, someone beat the piss out of him. Whether or not it killed him, I won't know until I get downtown."

"Can you give me an estimate on time of death?"

"Mitchell is fresh, maybe four or five hours, based on body temperature."

"That puts it at about seven, eight o'clock. Thanks, Doc."

Myruski withdrew a Marlboro and lighter and seemed to be hypnotized by the C.S.U. who were busy sweeping, dusting, and bagging potential evidence.

Downstairs, Straka was assigning the newly arrived black-and-whites duties. "The rest of the house is clean, you can send the M.E. home," she said to Cartwell, then motioned for him to accompany her into the den. Inside, a C.S.U. officer was taking samples of cloth and carpet.

"Most of the house is just cluttered with displaced items," Straka said. "I'd bet that not a whole hell of a lot is actually missing. There's a digital entertainment system out in the living room that has to be worth ten grand, but they didn't take it. Doesn't make sense unless that wasn't what they were looking for."

"So it wasn't a burglary. What then?"

"Well, I'd say they were hunters. The hard drive to the PC is gone. Three disc files are empty, and those puppies hold about ten discs each. The filing cabinets are also cleaned out. Then there's the safe on the wall. They used explosives to open it, but here's where it gets strange: The grit from the burns around the safe are too smooth."

"Too smooth for what?" He reached out to wipe a small sample from the wall. He moved it between his finger and thumb: It felt like oily foot powder.

"I'm not sure, really, but it wasn't C-4. Just as powerful, though. Whatever it was, it's brand new, 'cause I've never seen it before. The Elemental will be able to tell us, once we analyze a sample downtown. Then there are the water marks and latex fragments on everything in a ten-foot radius. They must've used a balloon to deaden the blast. They were pros and looking for something real specific. They took everything related to information, probably took a hundred pounds of stuff.

He began to think of the possibilities. The senator had been killed because he had something important, and either Mitchell wouldn't tell them where it was, or died before he got the chance. In his gut he knew the senator's wife was out of it, but she was still a damn good source of information. He also knew that because of who she was, clearing her of Mitchell's death would be a priority. There would be digging to do. Then again, maybe the butler did do it.

"Thanks," Cartwell said finally.

"Detective," Dyroff said over Cartwell's transceiver.

"Yeah. What's up?"

"The FBI is here."

"Great," Cartwell mumbled, realizing how much he truly hated the egotism of an FBI agent.

"Now the real fun starts," Straka said, patting Cartwell on the shoulder and returning to her work.

"Just what I need, more fun," he said, and disappeared through the den's doorway.

4

By eleven o'clock everyone had abandoned 7th Street. Tourists had long since returned to their hotels from dinner, and local residents were home resting up for the next day of work. E Street's sidewalk was deserted, which for a city like Washington was odd, but fate often favored Black. He almost commanded it, and with it he made it back to the alley of Angela Wilme's building without being seen. He knelt next to the wall where pitched shadows made him invisible.

Rain began to fall as he opened his duffel and withdrew a compressed air gun and an auto-protracting grappling arrow with an attached length of cord. Black looped a section of cord near the arrow and fed it through a channel forged in the barrel of the gun. The arrow came into position as Black pulled the cord taut. He pushed the arrow tip into the ground and the gun made a hissing sound, signaling proper arming. The alloy arrow tip gleamed as he raised it above his head and fired a fastening shot into the grille work of the fire escape. The thin olive cord attached to the butt of the arrow dangled next to his ear.

Black disengaged the cord from the gun, threw it into the bag, shouldered it, and climbed to the second-floor platform. Once there, he moved up the stairs to the third-floor platform, and to the window of Angela's apartment. It was still open.

He removed a tan pair of mountaineering gloves, stuffed them into his windbreaker pocket and replaced his leathers. Black stepped through the window and onto a countertop. The kitchen was dark, but enough light spilled from the hallway for him to see a brick archway leading to the living room.

The hallway was painted bright apricot, and an Indian rug covered the hardwood floor. To the left, the sound of deep breathing and the smell of perfume gave away the location of his prey. He lifted his windbreaker and withdrew the 10mm from the small of his back. A quick, blind thumb released the safety, and he was ready.

He could hear faint exhalations. The open bedroom door created a thin triangle of light on the floor, beyond which shadows took control. He jabbed his head through the doorway and saw Angela.

She was sprawled on a queen-size bed, naked and flat on her back. An orange sheet partially draped her body so that her ankles, a breast, and her face were exposed. Wind and rain were pelting the tall bedroom windows facing E Street. Her red hair just covered her shoulders, and her face looked almost porcelain in the dim window light. She was thin but very ample and he was immediately attracted to her. His steps were slow and deliberate as he approached the bedside. It had been a week since he'd submitted to a woman of her physicality; it was the area of his life where he reveled in being controlled.

Black eased the cold muzzle to her flawless forehead. The silenced shot pierced her brain immediately. Black could feel his heart throbbing a slow beat, like the knocking of a cooling radiator. He slowly dropped the gun to his side. The body didn't move. She wasn't even aware she was dead. There had been a small lump fighting to choke him, and it caused him to clear his throat. It had been a long time since he'd felt anything. Emotion, any and all, terrorized him.

Now he was certain it was time to retire. Before his heart resurfaced and caused hesitation, which inevitably led to apprehension.

—————•≈•—————

It was a long while before Black exhaled and moved toward the living room to begin his search for any material threatening to his client. He threw his duffel on a soft leather sofa and unzipped it. Inside, were police-style evidence bags, a portable phone, two clips for his automatic pistol, surveillance devices, and the remainder of his equipment.

Lightning momentarily brightened the room, illuminating a large mural covering the entirety of the far wall. It was a scene he immediately recognized as Montana, complete with wild animals and monumental views. He was startled when thunder rocked the building.

He started with the entertainment unit surrounding the brick fireplace, and ejected a dated cassette from the tape player and threw it in a clear bag.

He opened the carrousel CD player and bagged the five discs. Stacked behind a glass door were about twenty discs; he bagged these, as well as a single drawer of video tapes. Throughout there were photographs, which he took, and figurines that he broke between his strong hands in order to reveal anything hidden within.

He pulled the cushions off the two sofas and then overturned them both. Lifting up his pant leg, he unclipped a buck knife and slid the blade into the cushions to find nothing. "One room down," he mumbled.

He searched the hall closet next, inspecting the pockets of the coats; he ripped open two drawers and found only gloves, scarves, and hats. He pitched clothing items over his shoulders and into the hallway, bagging a few rolls of 35mm film and two mini-discs from a digital camera.

The kitchen and bathroom were free of incriminating material.

The guest bedroom was locked, but a stiff foot tore the door and its moldings from their secured places. He found men's clothing, tax information, investment books, and a small fireproof box. He removed the hard drive from a Dell personal computer, bagged printouts, a shallow drawer full of files, framed diplomas and certificates from the wall, instruction manuals, magazine and newspaper clippings, and the box.

Except for some photographs and a bank statement, the master bedroom was material-free. Angela Wilme's mattress was soaking up blood. Staring at her now, Black felt nothing, and was glad his emotions had resubmerged.

He moved back into the kitchen, lugged the packed duffel out onto the fire escape, and then climbed through the window into the pouring rain. He was soaked instantly. Pausing, he stared back into the kitchen and smiled because his work was over, because this contract, his last, had been a success.

With the bag over his shoulder, he lumbered down the iron stairs. They were slippery, and he lost his footing once, but recovered in time to avoid a fall. Kneeling, he unfastened the rope and wound it around his free arm, and slipped it into the duffel as well. The rain was cold on his face and he was longing for the dry warmth of his home in Quebec.

His mind drifted to thoughts of his oversized hearth, his leather chair, and his wine cellar, as he pulled on the fire escape's wet handle, freeing the jammed staircase. The stairs fell with an eruption resembling the crashes of thunder erupting nearly every second. Even if it was heard, it was no longer important; he'd be gone very soon.

He strode from the alleyway and was almost to the corner of 7th and E streets when he saw them, exposed by a lightning pulse that illuminated the world for a blink of an eye. He stopped next to a lawyer's office on the corner of the intersection and backed into the shadows of a small recess marking the attorney's front door. Rain poured off his windbreaker's hood and streamed down his face. There was another stab of lightning.

Two dark figures were hiding in the shadows diagonally across the street from him.

They were waiting and they were watching.

In the quick light, their raincoats gleamed. Their hair was matted to their skulls, and in the back of his mind, Black sensed an unfamiliar feeling: fear. An old disheartening saying accompanied it: The first rule of assassination is to kill the assassin. Instinctively, he studied the windows across the street. It was too dark to tell if anyone was marking him.

Black moved slowly toward The National Portrait Gallery, feigning to his left as he approached the Dodge Charger Daytona. He went over a series of quick movements in his mind. Movements that would produce his 10mm so quickly, the two men would have no time to react.

Another lightning flash.

He jerked his head to confirm the two men had abandoned their hiding spot and were crossing the intersection. They were moving in behind him now, perhaps half a block away. Black couldn't believe it.

Inside the Dodge, he locked the door and tried to start the engine.

———◦•◦———

It was pushing one in the morning as Chief Martin waited for takeout from the Chinese Kitchen, the only Goshen restaurant open past midnight. Halloween was still a few days away, and it had been a week since Matt Light had started working for him. To Martin's way of thinking, a celebration was in order. Small towns weren't for everyone, after all.

Martin found Light checking radar on County Route 207, which intersected Goshen and turned into Main Street at the village limit. The cruiser was backed off the road, invisible, about a mile from the village line. Martin passed him and parked his Ford Bronco on a side street, then walked back to Light's hiding spot.

Light was standing outside the car watching him approach. "Don't you ever sleep?" he asked once Martin was within earshot.

"Overrated. Besides that, I was starving, and I hate to eat alone," Martin said, holding the Chinese Kitchen's brown bag in the air. "I hope you're hungry."

"Now, that will hit the spot," Light said as they got into his cruiser.

The heater in the car was on low, and Light had the back windows cracked open. The scanner was quiet except for an occasional squelch.

Martin divvied up the food. "How long you been out here?"

"About half an hour. Was about to take a cruise up by the high school and the Spring Glen development," Light answered.

"Any action?" Martin asked with a laugh.

"I've seen one car in thirty minutes, yours."

"So how does Goshen fit after a week?"

"You were right about it being quiet. That will take some getting used to. But I'll tell you, I can breathe a lot easier. Goshen has potential." Light smiled wryly around a mouthful of noodles.

"You met someone?"

"Maybe."

"I'm glad this is going to work out, Matt."

"Can I ask you a personal question, Chief?"

"Only if you start calling me Tom."

"How long have you been married? Only reason I ask is I've already met everyone else's wife or girlfriend. You never bring yours up."

Martin set his cup of soup on the dashboard and stared at his wedding band, and asked himself for the hundredth time why he still had the damn thing on. "You mean the ring? Ashley and I separated a good while back, and we got divorced last year. I could never take the damn thing off," Martin said, going to work on an egg roll. "So how about you, ever taken the long walk off the short plank?"

"Never even came close. It was the job, the city, the fact I lived in Queens, who knows. They all had a problem with the job, though, and they were all scared of what it was doing to me. It took a bullet for me to see what they were talking about."

"We're more alike than you know," Martin said.

"How's that?"

"Ashley had a problem with my pursuing the Chief's job. After I was appointed, it was only a matter of time before we were history. She thought I had so much more financial potential. Sometimes I agree with her, but it's too late for that."

"What's the deal with you and Paulina Orange?"

"I knew you'd fit in here the second I met you," Martin said, smiling. "Who flapped?"

"Our friendly neighborhood dispatcher."

"Figures. I should take away Roberta's reading privileges for a month."

"I'd forget about your ex. Paulina could be a model if she wanted," Light said, putting his empty containers into the brown bag.

"A true Goshenite after only a week, a new record," Martin said. "Get out of here and do your sweep, I'll bend your ear for a while."

Light pulled the cruiser back onto the road and began patrolling the areas around the high school.

"I signed the papers last year around this time, making mine and Ashley's end official. I never considered the separation iron-clad. We were apart for a lot of years, but I always thought it was just more of a rest, a pause. Back then I only knew Paulina as the co-owner of my favorite watering hole. But I found out she had an eye for me, and was willing to be sympathetic."

"She helped you through it," Light said.

"I still don't know why signing those papers hit me so hard. No more than why I still wear my wedding band. I never would've made it without Paulina."

"Love is one major pain in the ass."

"You're not kidding there."

"Did you ever tell Paulina?"

"Once."

"And?"

"It was one of those bridges I shouldn't have crossed," Martin said. "We got really, really close, up until two months ago. It seemed like the right time to take it a step further, so I told her. I was wrong."

"She backed you down?"

"She's younger than I am, not that age difference is any excuse. We both knew what I was getting at, but she didn't want anything serious."

During the trip back to Martin's Bronco, there was a long silence. Martin liked Light, but wasn't prone to opening up like this, and he was a little uncomfortable. The October air was especially cold to Martin as he opened the cruiser door.

"Plenty of good women out there won't make you wait. If you don't want to be alone, don't be. Paulina's hot, but doesn't sound worth the worry," Light said.

"She's got me hooked, and I'm stubborn."

"Like I said, one major pain in the ass."

"The Apple Festival is tomorrow. Lots and lots of people to watch, so get some rest," Martin said, and watched Light drive away.

Paulina would be at the festival, he mused, and who knew what tomorrow would bring.

———— ·•· ————

Dr. Robert Greene lived his life by what he referred to as two simple truths: Money equals success, and sex equals happiness. His long carved physique, groomed jet black crop, bronze skin tone, and boyish face belonged on a Levi's commercial instead of behind a white smock.

After graduating from Georgetown University Medical School, he'd returned to the Hudson Valley town where he'd grown up to establish his family practice. However, he often returned to Washington, D.C. to spend a horizontal weekend with a nurse he'd met in school. Angela Wilme wasn't his wife or his first mistress, but she was excellent at one half of his two simple truths.

During these visits, Greene made it a point to always spend some time walking around Chinatown, to reminisce about his college days, and shuffle underneath the Friendship Arch and down the sidewalks of H Street. It was after midnight when he entered Tony Cheng's Restaurant, the closest place to Angela's apartment, and for the first time he noticed he'd already been away from Angela's for over an hour. But Cheng's cooking was worth the extra wait.

It was raining heavier when he finally had the food and was

on his way, and the strong wind made using his umbrella with only one hand a real test of dexterity. It was a fifteen-minute walk to the apartment, down 5th Street and away from Chinatown. He liked the section of D.C. where Angela lived. His favorite type of food was a short walk away, and so were two pretty good museums. Angela was on the periphery of what was referred to as the Central District of Washington. She was close to everything.

A jet ascended into the sky as he climbed the front steps of 118 E Street. He stepped into a dark corridor, shutting out the steely rain, the noise from the occasional passing car, and far-off sirens. He climbed to the third floor and walked the length of blue-gray carpet to the end of the hallway.

He slipped a brass key into a lock and kicked open the door.

Flipping a hall switch with his elbow, he was shocked to find the place in chaos. He dropped the food and umbrella and ran for the bedroom, flipped another light switch, and saw the blood. He rushed to find a pulse, a sign of hope. There was nothing.

He knew she'd felt nothing at all; her soft expression confirmed it. He picked her limp torso off the sheets and held her against him. He cried uncontrollably, his shoulders bobbing with each gasp of air. He felt out of place, crying, and was distantly surprised that he still had it in him.

During his internship and residency at Washington General Hospital he'd experienced the loss of patients. Lives were resting in the palms of a doctor's hands. Invariably he'd lost some of them, the ones that came in from horrible accidents and were barely recognizable as human beings. Neither the victim nor the doctor had very much control over who died. Those were the ones that got to Dr. Greene. After several situations where he could do nothing but delay the inevitable, he'd made up his mind to devote himself to a cleaner portion of the medical field. He'd promised himself to keep his patients at a distance. He felt it was better for his soul that way, and he'd grown a bit cold.

But this time he couldn't keep it at a distance.

"God, no. Angela, no." He was speaking into her ear. He could still smell her perfume and the shampoo she'd used that morning, and could feel the lingering warmth in her body. He gently returned her to the bed, finally acknowledging that she'd been much more than a mistress.

His vision drifted back to consciousness, noticing the ransacked apartment again. He began to fear he wasn't alone. He picked up the receiver of the telephone on the nightstand. There was no dial tone.

The next thing to grip him was realization.

"I'll be next," he said aloud.

Reporting the incident to the police would alert those responsible to his presence. He ran out of the apartment and out of the building. He didn't know where he was going, but he had to find a safe place to make sense of what happened, a place with a phone that worked. Crossing E Street, he ran between two brownstones, toward the winding back alleys of Chinatown.

Once the car finally started, Black turned the leather-wrapped wheel and slammed his foot on the accelerator. The car struggled for a foothold on the wet pavement as he hammered down the deserted street. In his rearview mirror, he could see the red glow of his taillights illuminating the water's spray from the rear tires.

Confident that he was out of the line of sight, he tucked the car into a wide and sloping alleyway and sat looking over the seat back, out through the defroster cut-lines of the steamed rear window. In seconds the roar of a Cadillac engine propelled a DeVille past the alleyway at a pace well above the speed limit.

"All too easy," Black mumbled, and reached into the duffel for the phone.

"Hello?" the now familiar voice asked.

"Surprised to hear from me?" Black answered.

"Mr. Dresden?"

"I must commend you, Mr. Scaffiotelli. And also correct myself. Things aren't over between us."

"What are you talking about?" Scaffiotelli said.

"I don't like being fucked with."

"We were merely watching."

"Why? Half a million dollars carries a high amount of assurance."

"We're protecting our interests, Mr. Dresden. You couldn't fathom the extent of our problems or the thoroughness they demand. At no time did we doubt your ability to finish the job. Your reputation speaks for itself. We merely wanted to allow you to operate unmolested."

"Molested by whom?"

"If we knew everything, we wouldn't need to have you pack-ratting all that information for us. As I told you before, I expected this to end with Mitchell."

"I'm growing tired of talking to you. You're not being straightforward. E Street is taken care of, as you're already aware."

"Yes. But we would like you to remain in Washington, in our employ, for a while longer. Before you head back north."

"What?" Black asked. The northern reference sent a chill down his spine and he could feel goose-flesh cascade across his arms. It wasn't plausible for his client to know as much as he hinted; it had to be a bluff. "No, that's out of the question."

"We're not sure things are concluded, and we may need to enlist your services again."

"I have operated a certain way for a very long time, because it's never gotten me caught. Part of my protocol is to leave the contract site immediately. It's obvious you have the means to conduct this kind of work yourselves, which leaves me at a loss."

"It's Quebec, isn't it?" Scaffiotelli said, referring to one of Black's homes with as much bluntness as possible.

"Who the hell are you people?" Black said, his voice wavering between anger and awe.

"Just leave the information in the garage of the Hotel Washington. We'll take care of the car. All you have to do is hang out for a while. A room has been reserved at the J.W. Marriott on Pennsylvania. We'll be in touch, Mr. Dresden."

"I could disappear, you know, it's a gift. Quebec is just one of many. You'd never find me. I would find you."

"Are you really so naïve to believe that anyone, even someone with your careful reputation, can walk around in the information age without leaving footprints everywhere? You're quite popular within the Interpol and CIA mainframes, and I doubt you'd believe how easy it was to hack every cranny of your existence. We have photographs and you gave us your bank information. We're not in the habit of leaving things to chance,"

Scaffiotelli said with a confidence that lent credibility to what he said. It wasn't an opinion, it was fact. "Forget about trying to find me, and focus on how much wealthier I'm going to make you."

"I have no choice," Black said, because he had no time to think of another option, if one existed. He realized how much he sounded like Mitchell, and how much he regretted his answer.

"Not an entirely enviable position to be in, but it's so much better for everyone this way."

The phone went silent, and Black hung up.

Putting the car into reverse, he backed over the sidewalk and headed for the Hotel Washington.

5

After two days of digging, the FBI's top brass in Washington and the team investigating the death of Senator Byron Mitchell were crammed into a conference room, arguing across the long, cherry-wood table. A thin fog of cigarette smoke filled the non-smoking room and pressed against the windows looking out onto Pennsylvania Avenue. The only person missing was Director Kenneth Geehern, who was flying in from Chicago.

It was almost 4 PM when Geehern walked through the marble lobby of the Hoover Building.

He was a slim man with gray hair, and his easy air and slight tan brought to mind a golf pro more than the director of the FBI.

The lobby was bustling with tourists, and the final group of the day got the cheap thrill of seeing him. He raised an informal salute and flashed a wide smile when he heard the guide making reference to him, but continued toward the elevators.

He took the elevator to the fourth floor, which held a maze of cubicles, each with its own computer, telephone, filing cabinet, packed shelves, and one federal agent. Silence swept before him as he made his way to the two black doors labeled *4th Floor Conference*.

"Gentlemen and ladies," Geehern said as he entered the room, and took the seat at the head of the table. "The president's been bending my ear for the last two days, so what have we got?"

Twenty government employees turned to James Tobin.

"Not a whole lot, sir," Tobin said. "The bulk of the information we have is courtesy of the D.C. crime unit."

Tobin was creeping up on sixty, and together with Ben Williams, they'd taken charge of the on-sight investigation. Tobin was a Federal Agent of average ability who attributed his gradual but steady rise through the ranks of the FBI to diligence and thoroughness. His salt-and-pepper mop was devoid of style but short enough not to look out of place.

He'd been a corporate finance major at the University of North Carolina when a representative spoke with him at a career day in the mid-70s. In those days, the FBI was just beginning to look for people who had education beyond the undergraduate level, and Tobin had been considered one of the new breed. He'd spent a tour in Vietnam with the 1/83 Artillery Division before he'd started college and joined the FBI.

"D.C.P.D. is just trying to keep themselves in the ball game," Geehern said. "I hope they've been summarily kicked off the field." Moving to the edge of his seat and removing his blue pin-striped suit coat, he began to look over the thin report on the table in front of him. He'd seen an earlier draft of it last night, and very little had changed.

"They have," Tobin said.

"Go on."

"We sent for an additional five agents from one of our crime units to supervise their C.S.U. They're completely out of the loop."

Geehern got up and moved to the corner of the room where a small round table held eight-hour-old coffee and a leftover, unwanted pastry selection. "So who was at the autopsy?" he asked, returning to his seat. "Anybody know?"

Ben Williams answered with an affirmation.

"Well, let's have it." Geehern said.

"Mitchell died from a blow to the nose which caused cartilage fragments to puncture the soft sinus plate and enter the brain."

Williams, Tobin's partner now for a little over a year, was a stark contrast to Tobin. He was taller, thinner, younger, and brilliant. He wasn't even thirty, yet he possessed both a Master's and a Doctorate in Law and Criminology. He had risen to the headquarters office in three short years of federal service, and unlike Tobin, had no military experience. Williams was a fanatic about being meticulous and being right. His hair was slicked back from his face and hugged his large skull. His features were solid and defined. High cheek bones, thin lips, and shallow eyes made him look almost frightening, but his temperament was warm. He was the type of man to go more than the extra mile, and had gained a reputation as the most ideal person to have with you when the shit hit the fan.

"What did we find at the scene?" Geehern asked.

"A strand of medium-brown hair, a fiber strand from a pair of Levi's 501 denims, a footprint, and an odd burn mark around the senator's office safe," Tobin said. "Traces of Cheer detergent were found on the jeans. The lab boys chewed on the footprint and came up with a seventy-six-inch, two-hundred-and-thirty-five-pound suspect."

"What about this grit left around the safe?" Geehern asked Terry Rabinowitz, a forensic specialist who had been asked to sit in on the meeting in order to answer this very question.

"The compound is called Poly-10. It's very similar to C-4, sir, a bit more unstable, but nearly three times as powerful. The burn marks are what tipped us off to it."

"Where could someone get the stuff?"

"It's real big in the Middle East right now, but it hasn't really caught on over here. I learned about it from a Marine who was in a demolition unit in the Persian Gulf, but he never got any more than residual samples. As far as he knows, none of our guys has ever seen an unused portion."

"Interesting. What about Irene Mitchell, has she been eliminated?"

"In light of our interviews with her and the information obtained at the scene, along with Rabinowitz's additional findings, she's out of it," Williams said.

"I agree," Tobin said. "But, she knows Mitchell, and may still know something vital without even knowing she does."

"Okay, I know you've been debating all day, but I just want to hear what we know, not what we think, not yet," Geehern said. "What about the senator's gardener?"

"His name is Philip Torroson. He's been employed by them for three years, and he's missing," Rebecca Kerrigan, who was in charge of locating the missing man, answered. Kerrigan was tall and had hair so black it almost appeared to be blue. She also had the bragging rights of being the only Olympian within the Hoover Building. "He rents a room over in Adams Morgan from an elderly couple. They say they haven't seen him for a day or so, but I think they know something. We have someone there and at Mitchell's, but so far no luck."

"So, get some. Go over and sit on the house. He'll show up."

"Okay, now what do we think?" Geehern asked.

The group began to rifle through the chicken scratches they'd made on the legal pads in front of them, and fidget in their chairs, anything to avoid getting singled out. Knowing the director hated bickering discussions, none of them would make eye contact with him.

Tobin said, "Mitchell's on the news every night opposing the federal funding for abortion's proposal. So I can see one very big organization that would be pissed off at him: the Pro-Choicers. Maybe they exercised their choice."

The room filled with an uneasy laughter.

"He's also been in charge of the Appropriations Committee on the Hill for twelve of his forty," Williams added. "If you start digging there, you're bound to turn up suspects left and right. For the last twelve years, if you wanted money for anything, you had to go through Mitchell. Rumor is he ruled that committee with an iron fist. That much power means a lot of enemies."

A rustling swept across the room.

"He's also one of the few returning senators this year," a field agent named Douglas Grass said. "Just about everyone up there is a freshman. It's some kind of governmental record or something, the most inexperienced Congress ever. Even the president's new. Plus, Mitchell was a conservative, and a returning senator.

Most everyone associates people like him with the state of the country. That's why so much new blood was elected. I'd say there are a few liberals or just plain discouraged people who might see him as a threat to this new order. Whatever the hell that is. Still, he's a reminder of the old way."

"Okay," Geehern said. "Here's how we're going to proceed. I'm going to start with the gardener problem. Kerrigan, I want him found by Thursday evening. That gives you twenty-four hours. Williams, I want you to tackle the investigation into the Senate Appropriations Committee, and I expect shift reports. If this avenue pans out and we have to go to the mattresses, the Attorney General will scream his fat head off, so do it by the numbers. Tobin, I want you to dig around the Who Hated The Senator Club: liberals, other senators, the Pro-Choicers, who-ever. Grass, look into the wife and dig around in his personal life."

Geehern stood, signifying the end of the meeting.

"Remember, this has top priority. Everyone knows Byron and I had history, and it's why I'm going to be more involved in the day-to-day on this one much more than I normally would. So, the press will have a field day if we don't turn this thing inside out and come up with a bad guy ASAP, and I'm in no mood to listen to the media. If you need more agents or come up with something new while looking around, come and see me. If you have subordinates who are ready for more responsibility, now's the time to consign some of your other work. Oh, and I don't expect reports every eight hours from only Williams. Everybody except Kerrigan better have something on my desk tomorrow. And Kerrigan, have that gardener on my desk. Go to work, people."

6

A few blocks away, the Capitol Building rose above the wind-swept tree line in the same way it always had. Deep yellow light escaped from the long, slender windows of the two tiers supporting the white dome. Although lacking its crowning guardian because of renovations, it was still awe-inspiring and ominous. It represented both the ideal of what could be and the reality of what was.

To Dr. Robert Greene it symbolized the monumental situation in which he found himself. He'd hidden and run through the back alleys of Chinatown. An hour later, he was standing under a dark maple on the National Mall's John Marshall Plaza, his breath pluming into the autumn leaves still clinging to the branches above him. From his chosen spot he was invisible, just another shadow. The lush ivy beneath his feet was still wet and had soaked through his leather shoes. His feet were numb, and a slight tingle was setting in. Forty degrees had been the normal evening temperature in Washington for the last few days, but the breeze made it seem colder.

There were still cars everywhere. The true test for a city, Greene thought, was whether it went to sleep at night or stayed up. Washington, D.C. was a little drowsy but nonetheless awake. Pedestrians and drivers flowed along Constitution Avenue, including the ones that were undoubtedly looking for him. At least he believed they were looking for him. He couldn't think of any other explanation for why someone would want to kill Angela. The only logical answer was someone had found out about their professional relationship. He wasn't quite sure how. Who was an even graver question.

With his arms crossed over his chest and his shoulders hunched, he stared at an occupied telephone booth. He had to make a call. If they could find out about Angela and himself, then no one was safe. Everyone involved was being threatened, and Greene had to warn them.

He had to tell them, and he had to get advice from the only person who could give it to him.

The fear and blame swelling inside him had quickened his pulse and sharpened not only his awareness, but also his imagination.

The telephone booth cleared.

From the shadow-gripped safety, Greene crossed a herringbone brick sidewalk on his way to the phone. He looked around so self-consciously, and walked so slowly and cautiously, that he was drawing attention to himself.

He dialed a seven-digit number and listened hopefully to the pulsing rings.

A voice answered, and Greene sighed with relief.

Kori Svenson stepped off the elevator and into the lobby of the corporate headquarters building where she worked. She could hear the faint sounds of the Chicago traffic outside as she made her way down the narrow hallway stretching toward the security room. Her hard soled shoes ricocheted as she descended a set of six steps toward a portal fitted into a marble wall.

Kori punched a code into a small keypad and swung open the thick metal door labeled *Audio/Visual Storage*. She had always been impressed with the extent of the room's capabilities. The small room was elliptical except for a flattened portion where a thin black electronic panel was fixed into the wall. A desk sloped from the bottom of the panel, and an embedded keyboard served as the master control. Four rows of five-inch television screens displayed every corner of the building. Some of the scenes were produced by visible cameras, but others were clearly invisible to the viewer.

Privacy wasn't something Kori's employer was very concerned about or comfortable with. He wanted to know exactly what people were thinking, saying, and doing, and he'd spent a lot of money on a system that would give him that ability.

To the right of the screens was a series of audio speakers and other equipment, with thirty thin LEDs displaying either the words "Recording" or "Not Recording." She sat down on a leather chair and began studying the screens. Everything about the room screamed importance, including her own presence at the ungodly hour of 12 AM. She was the corporation's chief security officer, and for the last week she had been working twenty-hour days, which were beginning to take a toll. She was irritable and anxious. At 2:08 AM she monitored the phone call she had been instructed to listen for. She pecked a quick keyboard command that allowed the caller to be heard over a speaker.

The voice was clear and rich with a raspy southern accent. "Hello, you have reached Senator Byron Mitchell. Please leave a message."

The next voice was disappointed, breathless, and without accent, at least to Kori's ears. He wasn't from Chicago, but he could have been from Illinois.

Kori rose from her chair and approached the machine that had just recorded the call. She ejected the disc and replaced it with a new one, slipping the recording into her blazer pocket. She called her boss and arranged to meet him in his office in one hour.

It was 2:10 AM.

———⋯———

At 3:10 AM Kori climbed from her subterranean observatory to the fifteenth floor. She didn't have to wait long. He was punctual.

The office was enormous, elegant, and decorated in Edwardian style. It had always given her the impression she was in a mansion instead of downtown Chicago. The sharp tick of a grandfather clock broke the dead silence gripping the room, and for some reason, she felt time was slipping away too fast. Each swing of the gold pendulum brought something nearer, something she'd want to avoid.

Why was her boss interested enough in a United States senator to have the man's phone bugged? She had too many questions running through her mind. She hadn't been as well informed as she'd thought, and for the first time she realized that, within the company, she was inconsequential. Sure, she had observed, bugged, and even intimidated people as part of her job, but it was always local, and she had always assumed it was the extent of her employer's interests.

So why the sudden obsession with the Washington bigwigs?

But maybe it wasn't sudden at all. Maybe she just didn't know anything. She began to think she had no idea who her boss was or what he did. She had assumed a lot. For example, that he ran the organization. The word *Director* fastened to his office door didn't mean much to her now.

The clock seemed to be ticking louder.

John Scaffiotelli walked into the office wearing a pair of blue slacks, a striped leisure shirt, and loafers. His silvery-blond hair was wet and combed straight back. Although he wasn't attractive, he'd always looked meticulous. She'd never seen him stripped of his cool facade, and her uneasiness grew.

"Excuse the attire. I was asleep," he muttered. He was edgy.

Kori handed the disc to him. Opening a cabinet door rich with stain, he shoved the recording into a player and then sat down to listen to the message.

"Byron, it's Rob Greene. Listen, I have to talk to you. I'm being followed. Angela is dead. Murdered. I think they know who I am and are after me. We have to talk. I'm returning to New York tomorrow. Please phone me."

Kori watched Scaffiotelli's face. An open palm covered his mouth. His eyes searched the room and displayed failure and worry. His hand moved from his mouth and ran over his fore-head and scalp.

"That's all, Miss Svenson," he said.

Kori's expression of concern met his command.

"Please, Kori."

He seemed anxious to the point of instability, so she left.

———◆———

Scaffiotelli picked up a receiver and dialed a number from memory.

"Which idiot am I talking to?" he barked.

"Anthony, sir."

"Get that pasta out of your mouth and put Mark on the phone."

After a pause, Mark said hello.

"Where's Dresden?" Scaffiotelli asked.

"Upstairs in his room. Why?"

"You sure?"

"Yeah. We got it bugged. What's up?"

"There was someone else in Angela's apartment. Someone who called Mitchell's private line about her being murdered. You find out who this guy is, and do it tonight. He's still in D.C., but he said he was going home tomorrow. He's on the lam to-night, so you'll never find him. You find out where he lives in New York, what he knows, and take care of it. I want this bullshit to stop. We're running out of time. I don't want these people thinking they can just do this to us and walk away. I want them too scared to do anything but what we tell them. The last thing in the world we need is a witness."

"I'll make it real ugly. They won't be able to—"

"No. Wake up Dresden and tell him we're not finished with him yet. Call me when it's done."

"Sure, Mr. Scaffiotelli."

"Mark, don't fuck this up. It'd be a shame if this had to get any more personal for me."

7

Black found it difficult and painful to admit he'd been so careless. He'd been secure in the belief that he would never be apprehended. Slouching in a cheap vinyl chair next to a window, he basked in the moonlight angling into the hotel room, dimmed by moving clouds and barely visible, then bright white and illuminated. He was motionless, hypnotized by the straight, string-like light creeping from under the door leading out into the hallway, pondering his next move.

He couldn't help but think he was down a check, and regardless of any attempt to evade his opponent, it would lead to checkmate. He could just disappear, but Scaffiotelli's knowledge of his Quebec address and Zurich bank account made Black question that alternative.

He knew they were waiting, watching, and listening. He could feel them. They were close.

So careless, Black thought.

He was growing more and more paranoid by the second, and he could hear those seconds ticking away on his Rolex watch. Its movements were still precise, cold, and mechanical, as he'd once been.

The unanswerable questions began piling up. Who was the man he worked for? Who were the two men who had followed him to the killings? How had they found out so much about him?

He found the hand fate had chosen for the close of his career symbolic. His performance would seem to determine if he was entitled to retire after such a brutal life, whether he could just fade away and enjoy his accumulated wealth. A mixture of anger and vengeance swept over him, but he remained motionless and silent. He could feel his blood pounding through his carotid artery.

They could have picked him up at the hotel when he took the Dodge from the garage. They must have tailed him to Mitchell's house and then to Wilme's apartment. His bank code and the damn Internet had given them everything else.

But why didn't they intervene? He'd never had a client follow him or show any interest in being connected with him when he fulfilled a contract. It was easier and safer to enlist outside assistance. That way the client had no knowledge, no liability, and ample time to weave an airtight alibi. This time the client had been particularly interested in confirming the job had been completed.

The more the unanswered questions piled up, the more intrigued Black got.

Why hadn't they just popped the two people themselves? Probably because they didn't want to get their hands dirty.

Over the past twenty years, Black had killed men, women, children, business partners and competitors, CEOs, military and government officials, and even the leaders of countries. A senator and a woman had been of no particular interest or importance to him. He hadn't given them much thought.

Until now.

The client had to be visible, someone who might be suspected immediately. They also had to be powerful, wealthy, organized, and connected. After all, they'd found his home.

"Home," Black mumbled under his breath.

That would have to be remedied. He needed somewhere safe to retire to if he did pass fate's test. He would have to give up his Quebec retreat.

Negativity was a rare occurrence with Black, and his personality proved as resilient as usual. Confidence began to seep back in, washing over him like a wave, bringing with it a sense of purpose. He had reached a new plateau of enjoyment: A challenge existed again, mystery existed again. The game had taken a turn for the better, a turn he might not survive, but better all the same.

The phone rang and broke Black's meditation.

"Dresden?" the voice asked.

"Who is this?"

"That's hardly any concern—"

"My good man from earlier this evening, correct? You were a little too easy to lose," Black said.

"Sounds to me like I knew where to find you."

"Your boss is responsible for your grasp of my whereabouts. Mr. Scaffiotelli should really send professionals to do this sort of work."

"Well, the boss says to tell you that he isn't done with you yet."

"I figured as much."

"There's a man in New York, a physician. He was in the apartment with Angela and knows she was murdered. The boss wants you to take care of it. There's a red Mercury Grand Marquis parked directly across Pennsylvania Avenue for you. The keys and information packet are waiting for you downstairs at the front desk.

A witness? Impossible, Black thought. "You'll still be watching out for my safety, won't you?"

"Yes."

"I'll make sure to do the same thing for you."

"What?"

Black hung up, lifted his duffel off the bed, and headed for his new wheels.

───※───

Martin arrived at the village square early and parked near the Methodist Church. He stepped into the brisk air, amazed by the sprawl of this year's day-long Apple Festival. Tents seemed to canopy the entirety of Presbyterian Park. A small carnival complete with carousel was a new addition, and the 4-H arena was twice the size of last year's.

He cracked a wide grin when he saw *The Apple Dumpling Gang*, blazing on the theater marquee. Goshen's movie house had been closed for years, but it was a creative touch.

Martin crossed Main Street heading toward the lush lawn of the park, where the wind's snapping of tent vinyl was keeping time with the sound of stakes being driven into the ground. He could smell the warm caramel used to coat apples and could see

Officers Gold and Light winding their way through the maze of vendors, memorizing the layout.

By noon the center of town was mobbed with laughing parents and crying infants. A small stage was occupied by *Twist and Shout*, a Beatles cover band. They were singing a song about a small town, while antique and craft vendors haggled with shoppers, old ladies gossiped and sipped tea, and old men sat in lawn chairs telling lies to whomever would listen.

Martin was leaning against a thick oak, staring at the rows of classic cars lining Park Place. The car show was a good draw, and Martin was hoping his uncle's Packard would place this year.

"Step right up and don't be shy," cried a voice from the loudspeaker affixed to the tree above him. A few steps away, District Attorney Owens was bellowing into a microphone: "Support the Rotary and sink a politician." The surrounding crowd cheered at the sight of a local judge sitting in a glass booth, waiting for a talented arm to trigger his descent into five feet of October water.

Owens was all smiles, sporting his turn-of-the-century British hunting uniform, complete with cap. "Do I have any takers?" he barked.

"Tom will try," Paulina cried, appearing through the crowd and grabbing at Martin's wrist. The crowd cheered. "Sink him quick, we need to talk," she whispered in his ear.

"No fair, he's a ringer," protested the judge.

"Get ready to get those plaid trunks wet, Judge," someone called from the crowd.

"Sink the judge, Chief," called another, and it became a battle cry.

"Hold on, hold on," said Owens. "To make it fair, we'll double the distance."

Martin spun the ball in his hand and eyed the judge. The pitch caught the bull's-eye, and Paulina took his hand and led him away from the laughing crowd, toward the horse track, where the fire department was setting up for a bonfire.

"I've been thinking about you," Paulina said.

"Makes two of us."

"About what you told me that night. I liked hearing it."

Martin couldn't think of anything to say. He could only swallow hard and try to decipher where she was going with this.

"You caught me by surprise. I reacted all wrong," she said.

"I'm sorry for that," Martin said. "I had been wanting to say it for a long time. I needed to say it."

"I care for you, Tom. It's a hard word for me."

"What about your doctor friend?" Martin asked.

The question caught her off guard. "Robin's been flapping."

"Your brother didn't have to say anything. This is Goshen."

"In my heart, it's over between us. The whole time I was with him, all I could do was think of you," Paulina said, moving close so she could touch his cheek.

Martin didn't respond; he couldn't. He'd fantasized about this very conversation so often, but now he was mute.

"Do you still feel anything for me, Tom?"

"I never stopped."

"I need some time to break it to him, a few days," Paulina said. "It's complicated because of his wife. He's grown attached."

"Will he give you any trouble?"

"Not trouble like that. I have to do this my way. Wait for me a few more days, Tom."

"Losing you the first time was almost more than I could bear. Don't cross me again."

She kissed him, her eyes welling with tears. "You're all I want, Tom Martin."

Martin watched her as she crossed Main Street, heading for The Inn, and slowly became aware of the hooting and clapping firemen who'd seen the whole display.

It had turned out to be a good day.

———•———

Black was descending through a stretch of Pennsylvania mountains when he saw the sign welcoming him to New York State. The witness's hometown, a place called Goshen, was only thirty minutes away.

The last few weeks of October were the most vibrant times to view the change between summer and autumn. The trees seemed like endless waves of color, and the highway's only purpose was a means for spectators to enjoy them from the seclusion and protection of their temperature-controlled automobiles. Farms, with their dark green fields and dilapidated barns, were sprawled across the landscape. Dead, burnt leaves lined the ground and camouflaged the median separating the four-lane highway.

In his side-view mirror, Black could see the dynamic duo who'd followed him through Washington, trailing him by six lengths. He was going to enjoy killing them the most. He mulled it over, trying to determine the best possible way to illustrate to his client he'd bitten off more than he could hope to chew by getting too close to an assassin. Black honestly wanted to make his client vomit, and was even shocked himself by some of the vivid and perverse images filling his mind.

Goshen turned out to be rural and reminded Black of a skewed interpretation of Norman Rockwell, where the town's heyday of showplace and pride, at first glance, appeared to be long gone.

Some buildings were old and heavy with paint, like an old woman trying to hide her age by layering on makeup like joint compound. But upon closer inspection, there were new constructions and restorations, fresh cement sidewalks, and repaved roads.

Beyond the center of town Black moved among its outskirts, passing a long series of maintained row homes. There was plenty of green grass, colorful maples, oaks, and hawthorns. The outskirts held more charm than the center of town, and Black decided he may have passed judgment too soon. If the renovation effort was just making its way into the center of town, then there was hope for Goshen.

Small towns often fell prey to the larger ones. With the decreased interest and involvement of residents, they usually became victims of the same fate which had descended on Goshen some time ago, Black observed. Most people worked crazy, long hours, and the only thing they wanted from a town was it be quiet, far enough away from the bad elements of society, and that it be there for them every evening so they could sleep.

Goshen seemed to be making an attempt to stave off its fate, and Black identified with the philosophy, finding it fitting that he was there. It seemed the perfect place to complete his last contract, to seek revenge against his new guardians, then slip away. He became intrigued by the biblical context his journey now involved.

It was 11 AM when he pulled alongside The Farmer's Inn. The sight of a bed-and-breakfast caused him to double-check his information. It wasn't the type of hotel Black had expected, but then again, there seemed to be more and more turns for the unexpected.

Ten wide-planked stairs climbed to the wraparound porch. Inside, the lobby was large and loaded with antiques. A short, pudgy woman greeted him. "You must be Mr. Dresden."

"Yes, ma'am."

"Well, we have your room ready for you. You missed breakfast, but there are several places in town that serve it all day. I can recommend one."

"No, I've eaten."

"Well, then I'll show you up to your room." She led the way up the stairs. At the end of a dim hall she opened the door to his bedroom. "Here you are. Lunch is at one. Shall we set a place for you?"

"Yes, that would be fine."

"Good, we'll see you then," she said, and left him.

It had been a long time since he'd stayed at this kind of establishment. At the beginning of his career he'd killed a little girl in a small Virginia town. That client had set him up in a rural bed-and-breakfast very similar to this one. The target's father had been an intelligence officer for the CIA, and was more profitable alive than dead, but was posing certain loyalty problems. Black had taken the lives of children many times since then, but the first had been the hardest. He hadn't been scared by it, or by any of the killings, for that matter. One either had the capacity to be an assassin or one didn't. There was no gray area.

He sat on the bed and took off his loafers, socks, jacket, and shirt. A small-paned window overlooked a stretch of grass and a line of colorful maples. Two children bundled in sweaters that only a mother could force them to wear were running across the grass. They were chasing a red and white soccer ball, catching it, kicking it, and then chasing it farther. The road running next to The Farmer's Inn veered off into the woods, where glimpses of homes could be seen through the trees. The kids were screaming at each other and laughing as a golden retriever leaped from the woods and chased them out onto the road.

The B & B's parking lot had only three cars in it, including his, and Black wondered how many of those belonged to the proprietors. He wasn't in a question-and-answer mood and he was hoping lunch would be very boring.

Black began his search for listening devices. There were none. The client must not have found out about the physician until early that morning.

As he stretched across the firm mattress, he was keenly aware of his surroundings, and began daydreaming of delicious and horrible ways to murder the two men who worked for his client. Black was growing more and more certain his future would have purpose and meaning.

Black made his way to the dining room at one and sat down at a crowded table, finding he'd been deceived by the inn's parking lot. There were twelve wooden chairs set around a long walnut table. The room was comfortable and smelled of country cooking. Only two of the chairs were empty when he arrived, and

Black sat next to a young couple. The remainder of the guests were elderly patrons who were most likely permanent residents and too old to be driving.

That explains the empty parking lot, Black thought.

They were all able enough, though, and intent on finding out every little tidbit about the tall, dark stranger with the noticeable accent.

Black picked up a pitcher of ice water from the center of the table and poured himself a small glass.

"You're French, aren't you?" a man asked while taking a bite off a roll.

"Yes, I am," Black said. He had nothing to hide and would be only a memory in a day or two.

"I was over there in the forties, you know. Good men. Real good," the man said. "Good cows too, good cheese."

"Yes," Black said, sipping his water, completely unaware where the old fool was going with things.

"Can't eat it these days, though. Lost a foot of intestine this year to that quack doctor of mine. Now I can't have cheese. Still have all your parts, right?"

"Yes, thankfully." Black was fighting back a smile.

"Keep it that way, m'boy. They asked me if I wanted to keep the damn thing. Now does that make any sense to you?"

"That's quite enough from the colon brigade, honestly," the innkeeper said, coming out of the kitchen with two plates of food, setting them in front of the young couple. It was an ample serving of roast beef and mashed potatoes smothered in gravy, with a generous helping of snow peas on the side. The innkeeper made five trips to the kitchen, the final plate set in front of Black.

Black was the only single person at the table, and most of the couples became engrossed in private conversations. He was asked the occasional question, which he answered with the proper degree of truth and a sincere and convincing smile. There were times when he enjoyed spinning an intricate lie just for the hell of it.

After lunch, he took his plate to the kitchen first. The elderly woman was busy scrubbing dishes and humming a tune he couldn't quite place.

"There was a man here while you were in your room sleeping," she said, not looking up from her scouring.

"Sleeping?"

"Well, I knocked on your door, and there was no answer."

"Yes, I was asleep," he said, allowing himself to relax. The old bird was harmless.

"He left an envelope. It's lying on the front desk, if you want to grab it."

"Thank you, ma'am."

"Oh please. It's Georgette."

"Thank you again, Georgette."

Ducking through the short doorway separating the dining room from the main reception area, he leaned over the front desk and grabbed the large manila envelope.

In his bedroom he opened the envelope and dumped the contents onto the bedspread. There was a copy of a New York State driver's license for one Robert E. Greene, M.D. The license told him where the man lived, that he was six-foot-three, had blue eyes, and had been born on April 18.

There was also a fresh photograph of the local row house

which held his medical practice and a photo of his home, also located in town.

The first typed page described what his client had found out about the physician. It wasn't a lot. It was obvious they were pressed for time and desperate to stop something.

Dr. Greene's practice was a few short blocks away, but his residence was too far to walk.

The next article in the envelope was a copy of a faxed document from the United Bank of Switzerland. It confirmed that one and a half million dollars had been deposited into a numbered account. Black was surprised to see the deposit included the fee for killing Dr. Greene.

Black didn't quite know what to make of the situation now, but he had been insulted and it demanded he wield retribution. His plan was to lose his new wardens, and after they had searched for him high and low, called their boss and admitted their incompetence, he would kill them.

They'd never see him coming. Then he would disappear.

In a private room directly above the Senate Chamber of the United States Capitol Building, a nervous man stood staring out one of the northwest windows onto Constitution Avenue. He tugged at the thick curtain to allow more daylight into the room. The weather had been noncommittal all afternoon and the sky couldn't decide whether to clear up or rain, justifying the weatherman's forecast of a partially cloudy day.

He moved toward the long mahogany table occupying the center of the room and joined twelve of his colleagues, who had at last been graced by the arrival of the fourteenth and final member of their group. The senators had gathered to discuss the death of their committee chairman, Senator Byron Mitchell.

The group was old, conservatively Republican, and had formerly comprised the majority of the Senate Appropriations Committee. Mitchell's death had brought the committee's overall membership down to twenty-eight, sixteen Republicans and twelve Democrats. There were only fourteen present because two of their fellow party members had the reputation of floating when it came to votes. They voted their conscience or were influenced by forces outside their party, so they were always excluded from these meetings.

Before Mitchell's death, the floaters had been of no concern to the assembled group because they still held the deciding vote no matter what, but that comfort margin no longer existed. If both the floaters chose to side with the Democrats, the Republicans would find themselves in foreign territory.

Earnest Bennette, a senator from Louisiana, and the man who had been staring out into the steel gray daylight of Washington, D.C., finally spoke. "There are going to be a lot of people snooping around over this. A friend told me the president is all over the Bureau. It won't take long for their investigation to lead them up here."

"We've got more important problems than the FBI finding out Byron was a little corrupt," Senator Keith Grotto said. He was the youngest member of the group.

"A little corrupt? If half the involvements he was wrapped up in get out into the open, we'll all come under the microscope. None of us can afford that, not even you," Peter Feathers said.

"All I'm saying is there are three major votes being argued in the Senate now. Our interests mandate the Appropriations Committee approve two of them, and most importantly that we bury one in particular," Grotto said.

"He's right. The Democratic members of the committee could easily persuade Finkstein and Sauder to vote in the interests of liberalism," Frank Bapto added, referring to the Republican floaters.

"But why was Byron killed? If it did have something to do with the Hill or what he was involved with up here, who's to say any of us are safe. It could be argued that his death was a warning," New York Senator Susan Braun said. She was the only woman of the group.

"A warning from whom, and for what purpose?" Feathers asked. "No one knows about this conservative pact we've formed here. Are you trying to say through a mere agent of association, that we're all in danger—targets?"

"This pact, as you call it, was put together by Byron and it stands for and supports a select group of interests," Thomas Yorkshire said. "Now, we all subscribed to that philosophy when we signed on with this membership. Personally, I don't know half of what Byron was up to. But, I do know he was always changing the sides he represented, the sides we represented. We left that up to him because he had a nose for finding the money, and finding it in places that wouldn't require us to sacrifice our conservatism whatsoever. If he pushed the right person far enough with one of his little switches, then we could all be in danger. If that particular person, organization, group, or whatever it is identifies all of us as to blame, then I'd say we're deep in our own territory."

Yorkshire was powerful, elegant, and since the death of Mitchell, the oldest member of the group, and he struck a chord. They had comprised the most powerful voting block within the United States Senate. They were in charge of approving everything that took place in the government. Everything needed money, everything had a budget, and they either approved it or shot it down. They had wielded that power throughout four presidencies and had forgotten what it felt like to be out of control. For the first time in years, the group felt uncertain about its future.

Senator Braun was still on Capitol Hill as late afternoon came upon Washington, and in the darkness of her personal office, she sat motionless. At one end of the room, behind her large desk, stood a massive bookcase dominated by academic texts. At the other were her framed diplomas: A Bachelor's in History from the University of Chicago and a J.D. from Harvard.

Braun had spent five years working in the Manhattan District Attorney's office before running for and winning a vacated New York seat in the United States Senate. She'd been here ever since.

Thomas Yorkshire had made a lot of sense, Braun thought, and she agreed that as a member of the pact, she was the only female member of a doomed group of men.

She had only one regret with respect to her chosen course of action, and it was coming to Washington. Nothing was worth dying over, and she couldn't help but think death was gunning for her. Mitchell had dealt the hand and sealed their fate.

Rising from the chair and grabbing her notebook computer, she left her office and the Capitol Building, got into her Mercedes, and began to think of someplace safe to hide as she drove throughout Washington. Someplace where she could figure out what to do, whom she could trust, and who was behind Mitchell's death.

There were several probable candidates, and she'd have to eliminate all but one. Then she would have to figure out what to do about that one.

8

An amber sun was falling behind a distant tree line as Black plunged down the front steps of The Farmer's Inn with a choreographed speed, as though keeping time for a song with a quick tempo. He noticed it right away, the absence of his red Mercury from the parking lot tucked next to the inn. His chaperones had stolen it in broad daylight, but Scaffiotelli's attempt to control his every move would be thrown back in the man's face soon enough.

Black's attention then fell to the government building across the road. It could only be described as a nightmare of architecture, and it caused him to laugh out of amazement. His thick mustache rose and elongated with the smile. The wet grass was almost blue as he crossed for the slate sidewalks dogging the town's main artery, County Road 207, heading for Dr. Greene's office.

Black journeyed beneath heavy trees and was enjoying the peace of early evening in Goshen, focused on the fallen, crisp, autumn leaves as he walked through them. To his left, a red clapboard house was the last standalone structure before a series of brick row houses began. Each house bore a carved wooden sign with an address and the words, *Lawyers' Row*. A small alleyway separated one series of row homes from the next series.

Dr. Robert Greene's was the last in the first set of row homes. Black turned into the thin alleyway separating the doctor from his neighbor. As he moved away from the drone of traffic, he could hear a vacuum cleaner running somewhere on the downstairs floor. A long stable provided Lawyers' Row a parking barrier and separated Black from a thoroughbred track. He could hear horses settling into their stalls for the night as he climbed toward Greene's back door, which he found unlocked. The vacuum cleaner was louder as he stepped into a small kitchen; its fluctuating hum poured over him.

Black made the decision to return when it was darker and hopefully void of people. He'd planned only to survey the place, anyway.

By the time he returned to the Farmer's Inn, the leather of his shoes had gotten cold, and so had his feet. His nose was running, and the stiff air made it feel frozen. At the front door, he glanced over his shoulder and focused on the road separating him from a neighboring vacant lot. He could see exhaust pluming from an almost invisible car, and he instinctively knew that his chaperones from Washington were in that car, his car.

━━━━◦━━━━

Within an hour, Black was asleep on the cool quilt of his bed. It wasn't until nine-thirty that he opened his eyes and found the room dark and hot. He sat up on the edge of the bed and reached down to slide his long duffel bag from underneath. Rubbing his eyes, he stood up and arced his back. It popped. He tilted his head from side to side, and his neck did the same. He disrobed and stood naked in the room, lit by a dim, amber streetlamp.

His sinuous muscularity was evident as he heaved the bag onto the bed and unpacked a clean forest-green sweatshirt, jeans, insulated socks, running shoes, leather gloves, and a ski mask. He donned everything, but shoved the mask and gloves into a hip pocket. He threw a folded sack over his shoulder and went to the window.

Drawing one side of the curtain away from the glass, he saw the panes of the window were wet along their edges, and a hint of October's cold air rushed through their broken seals, hitting him in the face. Despite the mist, he saw the sedan clearly. It was parked under the streetlamp with the engine running.

There was only one person in the car and he was looking up at the bedroom window. Black searched the rear lawn for the other one.

An orange cigarette tip appeared from the wood line bordering the property. The figure of the older and much larger chaperone became visible as he left the shadows of the trees and crossed the grassy backyard.

Black went downstairs, negotiating the dark house, heading for the front door. The floors creaked and moaned so loudly that he was sure either a guest or the men in the car would hear him, so he walked as near to the walls as possible. The house fell silent.

The front door was unlocked but sang as it swung into the night. Black closed it, crouched along the front wall of the inn, and vaulted the porch railing, landing on wet grass. This side of the house was dark, and he sprinted the twenty yards to the woods. He looked over his shoulder at the county road. It was deserted.

The government building's parking lot was illuminated, but none of the light seemed to make it across the county road. The only real light came from the street lamps poised along the curving gravel road. Dead, wet leaves blanketed the ground and the soft soles of Black's shoes disguised his movements.

He moved through the shadows, keeping his eye on the two men watching his bedroom window. At the rear corner of the property, he ran out of the trees and across the grass of the adjoining lots. Within seconds he was out of sight.

He crossed the gravel road and stood next to a large oak, pausing long enough to pull at his collar and flush a draft of cold air onto his chest. Crossing another street, he ran behind a bank, hurdled a picket fence, and crouched up against it.

Beyond the bank's picketed lawn, Black could see the line of stables dividing the main building of a horse museum from the racetrack. He hurtled the rear section of fence and jogged along the back wall of the stables. He continued along the wall until he recognized the rear porch of Dr. Greene's row house.

The rear parking lot was empty, and he assumed the building was as well. As he approached the staircase, the sky began to mist, and by the time he'd reached the door it had become full-fledged drops.

The door and window were locked, and the vigilance of the cleaning person irritated him. Black swung the sack from his shoulder and withdrew a thin vinyl pouch. Unfolded, it revealed eighteen specialized tools.

He went to work on the door and was stepping into Greene's office before he was even wet.

Black searched the office and found nothing of interest until he spotted an old IBM Selectric typewriter buried at the bottom of a closet, with a single piece of blank letterhead resting in the spool.

Black yanked on the sheet and moved toward the windows. A flood lamp mounted on the corner of the horse stable illuminated the room, but in order to see it well enough to read he had to move right next to the window.

The letterhead listed three addresses for Dr. Robert E. Greene: 36 Main Street, Goshen, New York 5th Professional Building, Office 4, Arden Hospital, Goshen, New York 115 Greenwich Avenue, Goshen, New York.

The first was the office he was standing in. The other two were not on the description sheet his client had given him. He didn't feel at all comfortable with the situation and its apparent lack of preparation. The home address his client had given him wasn't on the letterhead at all.

"Unacceptable," Black muttered. Scaffiotelli was overextended and Black knew he'd been dumped in the same barrel.

He knew in his heart that Scaffiotelli had brought him into the game too late. Too many holes were appearing. He would have to call the two chaperones for assistance. There was no way he could risk stealing a car and then driving it all over town. Someone would see him. Besides, his plan necessitated keeping his chaperones close.

Black continued his Holmes activities but when he began to slip the letterhead into what he intended on turning over to his client, he hesitated. It was a bargaining chip, an advantage, and for reasons he really couldn't understand, he slid the letterhead into his hip pocket instead and then reached for his cell phone.

"It's Dresden. I'm not inside that window, so stop staring at it and pick me up in front of Greene's Main Street office."

———•••———

Outside the professional building where Greene had his principal practice, the two escorts from Washington sat in a secluded corner of a parking lot next to what appeared to be a deserted Buick Electra.

Black had circled the long rectangular, single floored building, but the only way in seemed to be through the domineering front door. Its lock was of the card entry system type, and he wasn't equipped to attempt it without an alarm going off. That meant the roof held the only possible remaining option. He summoned the men from their secluded corner, and as they moved their car tight against the building, Black surveyed the portion of Arden Hospital he could see.

It was a large cube standing in front of the five professional buildings like a sentry. The quarter of the hospital facing him was dark. There were three loading platforms, one with a tractor trailer backed against an open garage door, but there didn't seem to be anyone around the truck or the loading docks. For the time being fate was on Black's side. It began to drizzle again and his attitude sank deeper still. The rain and the United States were wearing his patience thin. He was closer to the interstate here and could hear the roar of tractor-trailers and could smell their monoxide.

From the roof of the sedan, Black could just reach the roof-line. As he pulled himself up, the car returned to the most inconspicuous spot for it, next to another car.

Black swung his leg up to the roof and used it for leverage to help him the rest of the way. He felt fatigued and his disheartedness was tremendous. When he was twenty he could have negotiated the building like a gymnast, and without the use of a car. Twenty suddenly seemed like a long time ago.

The roof was flat and the selvage had been tarred and stoned for protection. A single hatch rose off the stones and Black sighed with relief. The hatch had a bubbled piece of plexy-glass attached to a hinged metal frame. He grabbed the exterior handle and pulled, but it jammed against an inside lock. The bubble was faded yellow and had a rotting rubber gasket beading around its metal frame. He withdrew a needle-nosed screwdriver from his tool pouch and began to punch holes along the gasket where it met the metal, and within five minutes it finally showed signs of loosening.

His concentration shifted from the task at hand when he heard the engine of his sedan shut off and saw headlights moving across the tree line at the far side of the hospital. Another car was coming up the hill leading to the professional lots. He heard two car doors open and slam shut, the sounds of heavy feet on asphalt, and then on wet leaves.

Someone was coming.

The world closed in around Black as he crawled on his stomach to the edge facing the other buildings. He could hear the sound of the rain landing on the stone rooftop next to his face, the bursting sighs from large hospital vents, and the friction of slow tires on wet pavement. It was a police cruiser, a navy Chevy Caprice with a large light bar fastened to the roof and a Goshen Police Department emblem painted on each of the doors. Its trek was slow and deliberate as it headed for the two cars parked next to each other.

One of the cruisers' searchlights came to rest on the D.C. license tag.

"Oh, shit," he mumbled. Black knew the officer was running the plate.

The searchlight then darted between the parking lot and the professional building where Black was lying on the roof. In a few moments, the light went off, and he heard the car door open.

Black looked back over the edge, his 10mm drawn.

The officer stood between the sedans, shining a flashlight into each interior.

Both were locked, and the officer neglected to feel the hoods for heat. Heavy drops were tap-dancing on the thin metal of the cars, and the officer at last turned for the protection of his cruiser. Black watched the cop leave and the two men reappear from the dark wood line, and then went back to work on the hatch.

Once the bubble was free of its track, he stepped inside the hole and descended an iron ladder fastened to the wall, passed the two shining Master locks which had held the hatch in place. As he stepped onto the cement floor below, he noticed the electrical panel warning him that opening the master breaker would disable the security system as well as the building's power. He kissed the palm of his left hand and slapped the panel while considering how often luck favored him.

He threw the breaker.

Black stepped out of the closet into a large room filled with vinyl chairs and wooden end tables stacked with magazines. His flashlight made things bright enough for him to make out

Greene's nameplate on one of the five doors exiting from the large common room.

Black searched the office and found nothing, and retraced his steps back to the car.

"You two are quite the dynamic duo. Top-notch work eluding the cop," he said, removing his mask and gloves while settling into the backseat of the chaperone's car. "I'm going to have to start calling you Fatman and Robin or something. Take me to Greene's house."

"How 'bout I throw some of this fat behind one of my fists and turn your face inside out?" the heavy man said.

"Funny, but I'm not looking for a date," Black answered. "That cop is going to be suspicious as hell if he spots this car again, driving around this late, in this one-horse excuse for civilization. So while I'm inside Greene's house, find a New York tag and slap it on this car. You two are way too fucking sloppy."

"You think he's going to be at home?" the younger man asked.

"Inquisitive, aren't we? Master Scaffiotelli must have called."

"He's not a patient man, and he requires updates."

"He's in his hometown, and it's quite far from Washington, D.C. Hopefully he thinks he's safe and we'll get lucky. I can beat the necessary information out of him for your boss, and then get the hell off this job. If he's not home but his wife is, then I'll beat some information out of her."

<hr />

Martin pulled his Bronco off Murray Avenue and into his gravel driveway. His small brick house was shaded by autumn foliage, and Martin bent down to pick up the local paper from the porch.

He opened the unlocked front door while he flipped open the paper. "Distinguished West Virginia Senator, Byron Mitchell, Brutally Murdered," read the headline, and was accompanied by a recent photo.

Martin stood in the doorway and turned to the page covering the story. Mitchell had been killed in his Georgetown home late Monday evening. Also found at the scene was a houseman whose name was undisclosed. The FBI had no substantial leads but were confident they would apprehend those responsible quickly.

He closed the paper and the door behind him, noticing his house had a faint musty odor. Maybe I shouldn't have skipped Spring cleaning after all, he thought, walking to the kitchen.

He switched on the radio and began rooting through the refrigerator for something resembling a meal.

He selected a loaf of pumpernickel, a bottle of mustard, a red onion, tomato, ham, and bologna. Martin moved into the living room with two thick sandwich halves and a Stout, to watch CNN. The president had addressed the nation and those who killed Mitchell, saying that his administration wouldn't rest until those responsible were found, and punished.

Martin had heard of Mitchell, but really had no opinion of the man. He didn't deserve to die the way CNN was describing —beaten to death. He turned the television off and decided against going down to The Inn for a drink.

Martin nodded off, but was startled awake by the tapping of air in his heating system. He was surprised by how the brutal death enthralling the country had buzzed him. He searched a few minutes for the keys to his Bronco, threw on a sweat suit, and stepped out into the silent night, locking his front door behind him.

Goshen was quiet as he made a slow street by street check of town. There was so much violence out there, and he was somewhat regretful of his longing for it. Most of the houses were dark as nine o'clock rolled around, and the streets were empty. The "No Parking/Plow Season Law," didn't go into effect until November first, but Goshen was already adhering.

Martin spent a little over an hour cruising the streets, twice passing the officer on duty. Nothing was happening and he was relieved, satisfied. It was late when he pulled back into his driveway and called it a day.

———•———

Greene's home was a mile from the hospital in a section of town gripped with nineteenth-century colonials, Victorians, and Georgian-style homes. Greene's colonial was set farther off the road than most of its neighbors. It was also darker than most.

The sedan pulled into the driveway which graded downwards, wrapping around the house and underneath a carport. Black got out of the car and the two men waited until he was inside before going off to pilfer a New York license plate.

The back door was locked. Black was losing patience with the town and this contract. The sooner he found Greene and ascertained his involvement, the sooner he could put his plans into motion and disappear. He broke the narrow frosted window of the door and reached for the lock. There were three.

The house was huge and would take hours to search. Everything would be so much easier if Greene or his wife were home, but it felt deserted. There was no heat on, and a stale smell hung in the air. After twenty minutes, Black found the doctor's empty bedroom closet. Greene was so scared he'd already gotten his family to safety.

After all, he was college educated and most likely had the ability to reason quite effectively. His adrenaline was probably on overload which would make him paranoid and alert. Sloppy but alert.

Black finished his search and made his way back outside to the sedan's backseat, which was nearly filled to capacity.

"We're heading to Greenwich Avenue next," Black said, informing his chaperones of their final destination only after he returned to the car.

"What's on Greenwich?" the younger man said.

"Yeah, where are you getting this from?" Fatman said. "If you've got information, you need to tell us."

"I found something inside. Now let's go." Black said.

After the two men studied a small map, they made their way to the Greenwich Avenue office. The trip was very short. The office was small and set back on the top of a hill where a single flood lamp blinded a small parking lot and one complete side of the house. The car came to rest bathed in light, but was invisible from the street.

The house at 115 Greenwich Avenue was dark and silent inside except for the wind pelting the siding. The front door was unlocked, however, and it whined as the wind helped Black push it open. He could smell the scent of sweat in the air. He withdrew his silenced Colt from the small of his back, and his senses sharpened. He opted to leave his flashlight extinguished; he didn't want to tip off the owner of the body odor. A tall flight of stairs rose to the second floor, but instinct told him to remain on the ground floor.

He passed the staircase and walked through an archway into a shadow-laden room, his eyes struggling to adjust to the blackness. The scent was growing more potent. He moved into another room and stumbled across a piece of small furniture. There was an open window on the far wall and a sheer curtain was flapping. Black ran to the window, withdrew his small night-vision scope, and stared into the darkness behind the house.

There was no movement, no sound.

Black knew Greene had been here, right here. He gripped his pistol tighter and cursed his poor timing. He closed and locked the window and made his way to the second floor. The upstairs consisted of three rooms: two possessing nothing of interest, and one screaming importance.

The room of significance was dominated by a long polished table and four leather high-backed chairs. Black moved toward four cubicles. Each held the kind of state-of-the-art machinery sorely missing from Greene's other offices, as well as a brass name-plate with a physician's name—Edward Delaney, M.D., Peter M. Dunnelo, M.D., Robert E. Greene, M.D., Eric X. Strogg, M.D., and all the desks and cabinets were locked except one, Dr. Greene's.

Greene's cubicle had been a casualty of a hasty exit, and the desk was strewn with literature published by an organization called Physicians for Social Responsibility. Black gleaned that the four doctors were cofounders of the organization and 115 Greenwich Avenue was clearly their headquarters. But the knowledge made him none the wiser, and all he could do was begin to bag all the evidence he deemed pertinent.

Black had to wedge himself into the backseat before he could brief his client on the situation and his belief the good doctor was in hiding.

"Listen, Mr. Dresden," Scaffiotelli said on the phone, "I want you to kill these three doctors. The ones in this organization with Greene."

"That's awfully messy for a small town like this. There will be a lot of heat. I've been here too long already."

"I want you to change hotels and I want you to take care of this situation."

"You want an awful lot for a man in no position to make demands. Why don't you just have one of these two orangutangs do it? They seem perfectly able to pull a trigger."

"I wouldn't have any degree of certainty with those two men, and as you pointed out, it's messy. At times my men do take care of small and insignificant problems, but this is too big and too public. That's why I hired you."

"This is very reckless and ill advised. I'm having difficulty fathoming your trouble if you're willing to kill anyone that may or may not be remotely connected to what you have yourself wrapped up in."

"Killing Greene's fellow members, his friends, will force his hand. Force him into the open. He's still in Goshen," Scaffiotelli said confidently. "He'll know that he won't be safe anywhere then. We found him in Washington and in Goshen, and he'll know it. He won't run, though. I'd bet on it. If anything, he probably thinks he has the advantage, being in his own town and all. But you'll prove otherwise, Mr. Dresden. From what you've told me, he obviously cares for his friends and it might force him into contacting the police or becoming sloppy. You're probably right that he's hiding out, but I'd also say he's watching. I would be if I were in his shoes. He'll have to trust someone. Tell those two idiots to put the police under surveillance and put together an extensive brief on each of the doctors for you to look at."

"If this plan of yours doesn't work, I'm out of here very soon after the third body hits the floor," Black said. "If it does work, then I'll pop Greene for you. But no more information gathering, and I'm not wasting any time extracting information from Greene. The only thing holding me in this town is my ego. I've never had an incomplete contract and I'm not about to conclude my career with one. But it's going to cost you one million."

"One?" Scaffiotelli said, sounding surprised.

"A quarter a bullet is the price for that profession; after all they're doctors not senators," Black said, pulling his automatic and pressing the barrel into the seatback in front of him. It was soothing for him to have a life in his hands like this, to be totally in control of something. He was staring at the small earpiece in the driver's ear, knowing full well that Scaffiotelli or someone else was feeding him instructions. If either of his chaperones made a move, he was planning to blow holes in them right here in the car.

"Fair enough. I hope this is the last time we have to speak, Mr. Dresden."

Both phones went silent. Black briefed the two men, and they returned to The Farmer's Inn for his things. Then they headed for the town's only other lodging, The Comfort Inn.

9

When Black was younger, the long hours that accompanied his chosen profession had little impact, but now that he'd passed the forty-mile mark, each extra hour beyond the point he customarily remained awake was a physical test. He'd demanded unwavering excellence from his body and had put himself through physical hell without regard. It was coming back to haunt him.

He sat, rolling his fingers across the tabletop dividing him from the younger D.C. warden perched in front of a whirling heater. They were awaiting the return of the elder D.C. from his information quest.

There were two light knocks on the hotel room door, followed by the sound of lock tumblers, and the heavy man entered and pitched a light folder onto the table in front of Black.

"I know you wanted a more in-depth analysis of the subjects, but there ain't a whole lot I can dig up at this hour. If you want to wait, I'm sure I could get more during the day," the man said, walking past the table and into the bathroom.

Black opened the manila folder and fanned out four documents. The first three were double-spaced typed pages on each of the doctors. It was an ample amount of information, more than he'd gotten on Greene.

The fourth document was a fax confirming that the money had been transferred to his account in Zurich. He slid the papers back into the folder and tapped it on the table to align the contents.

"I need to get a couple hours of sleep before I finish this off. Shut-eye will make me sharper. Plus, it'll allow all three of these men to get home and be sound asleep," Black said, and moved toward the dark adjoining room. The younger man stood and negotiated the tightness of the table.

Without warning and with a fluidity that shot a jolt of pride through him, Black produced his Oplus-XT from a shoulder holster and fired a tranquilizer dart at the younger man's neck. The drug concoction hit the lightweight so hard, that his legs turned to Jell-O, and his face caught the edge of the table as he collapsed. The collision upended the table, which in turn landed on the base of the man's neck.

The next thing Black heard was the lock disengaging on the bathroom door. He negotiated the double bed, coming to a crouch alongside the wall separating him from bathroom. The older man rushed into the chaos of Black's arms, his .38 Smith & Wesson drawn and cocked.

Black leveraged him into an end-over-end flip, and the gun came loose into Black's hand. He uncocked the revolver and, with practiced precision, emptied the unspent rounds and tossed the weapon onto the bed behind him. The man had enough composure to grope for his backup in an ankle holster, but Black was quicker and pumped a dart into his neck. What he really wanted to do was just snap both their necks and be on his way. He wanted to put his plans of disappearing into motion and begin his crusade to Scaffiotelli's doorstep.

A concoction of rage and adrenaline was surging through him, but he had to admit, Scaffiotelli's continued payments had softened Black's resolve. He didn't kill for free, and he had a nagging feeling that the two chaperones may be able to serve some purpose. So he spent a few minutes dragging them into the bathroom and securing them to the toilet.

Black bent over, picked up the file from the floor, and strolled from the hotel room. He was looking forward to the release his upcoming triathlon would bring.

The room had been reserved for a week with implicit instructions that it not be disturbed or even cleaned. If there was a nosy or anxious maid, the bodies would be found before then, but if the room was left alone, Black reasoned, he had enough time to earn his money while they took their siesta. With any luck, he'd have two or three days to watch for Greene after he killed the man's associates. It was a safe bet that when the doctor heard, he'd trip up somehow. The man wasn't a professional at the game, and Black had a feeling Greene would show himself again.

Black's feelings were rarely wrong, and he was counting on that.

Black opened the file again and scanned the information on the three physicians. He committed it all to memory, then laid the folder on the sedan's bench seat.

Next to the folder was a map with Orange County, New York, on one side and Goshen on the other. He scanned the legend for Fletcher Street, where Dr. Peter M. Dunnelo lived.

Dunnelo lived in the newer section of an apartment complex called Carriage Hills. Black turned down a thin one-way road leading into a dark parking lot. The new buildings ran along the main complex road and then turned in a parallel direction with Fletcher Street on one side and the local stretch of interstate on the other. Apartment 105 was in the farthest building next to the highway.

Because of the season and the recent weather, the building's large front-facing picture windows and doorways were visible between skeletal trees. A single glass lamp lit the cement walkway winding around trees and shrubs, leading to each building's main door. It was pouring rain, and the leaf-blanketed ground amplified the heavy drops.

The rain felt like the shards bare feet always seem to find on unfamiliar back roads, as it pricked the skin of Black's face and ears. He kept his head tilted down, his eyes focused forward, and his hands stuffed deep into the pockets of his wool fleece.

The building was unlocked, and Black stepped inside. A single staircase rose along the right side of the vestibule. The carpeting was worn and smelled of mold. Repaired holes in the sheetrock were evident. Black wondered why in hell a physician was living in such a place, but he felt sure once Dunnelo came into his own, he would find himself a huge, beautiful home, a Mercedes, and an expensive lifestyle, the way every other physician seemed to.

"Too bad that's all going to end in less than five minutes," Black mumbled.

Black climbed the staircase, which moaned with each of his heavy steps. He slipped the lock and pushed the door shut behind him. His gloved hand held his 10mm against his leg. The apartment was essentially a large loft with a living room and bedroom sharing the majority of the expanse. There was also a bathroom, a closet, a small kitchen, and a sliding glass door overlooking the interstate. A ceiling fan was pushing around the smell of sex and waffles.

Dunnelo was prone, snoring and naked among a mountain of corduroy pillows.

Black lifted the gun and aimed for the back of Dunnelo's head, but then hesitated. Too easy, he thought.

He grabbed Dunnelo's ankle and turned him over, waking him from a heavy slumber. Dunnelo jolted to a sitting position. The barrel of Black's gun came to rest against the man's cheekbone.

The curtain covering the sliding glass door was pulled open and the deck's lamp was blazing, pouring enough light into the room for Dunnelo to see the face of the man holding the gun.

Their eyes stayed fixed for almost a minute. Black said nothing. Dunnelo said a lot.

The Big Three questions: *What, why*, and *who* were repeated over and over again as the doctor began to sweat. When Black was convinced that Dunnelo was fully aware of the finality of his situation, he moved the gun away from the man's cheek and in front of his left orbital. The description sheet had said Dunnelo was an Ophthalmologist. The choice seemed poetic.

A single shot punctured the eyeball and the thin bone backing of the cavity. The bullet flew into the brain and whipped the doctor's head back onto the mattress.

Dunnelo's body flinched as blood ran out of his punctured eyeball, down his face, filling his gaping mouth and overflowing onto the yellow bed sheets. Black returned the gun to the small of his back and pulled his fleece coat over it. He pilfered a gallon of orange juice from the doctor's kitchen before he left the apartment and the building.

———

Across town, Dr. Eric X. Strogg was taking advantage of his freedom while his wife visited her relatives in New York City.

The words *Spring Glen*, were etched on a wooden sign at the entrance to Strogg's development. The road rose, fell, and wound between the main stretch of dark homes and occasional cul-de-sacs arcing off into seclusion.

Some of the lawns were green and maintained, while others were still blanketed by a season's worth of dead, wet leaves. Strogg's home stood on the main artery called Gregory Drive, and Black passed it, surprised to see dim light pouring from the windows.

Strogg's Tudor-style house perched on a groomed and green lawn. A blacktop driveway climbed to the left of the house and wrapped around the rear to a concealed garage. Black headed farther down the street, turned around, and made another pass. From this direction he could just see the outline of a light colored car sitting next to the house.

The street lamps stretched out like long metal tentacles from every other telephone pole, casting large circles of bright light onto the street between hourglass-shaped patches of darkness.

Black parked in one of the patches, two houses down.

At the back of the house incandescent light pressed through the glass of two rear windows, beyond which a religious choir piece by Mozart could be heard as an accompaniment to the passionate breathing of a female wrapped in orgasm.

Black moved underneath the windows, passed a Porsche, and climbed the staircase of a large deck separating the house from a detached indoor swimming pool building. He picked the lock on a sliding glass door and stepped into a house decorated in a style Black hated. Polished onyx and silver bordered glass at every turn. Exact angles and positioning of leather-wrapped chairs, tables, and furniture mocked the seeming disarray with which the rooms were arranged.

He weaved his way through the rooms until he reached a hallway and heard the love nest's noise again.

The door was cracked and Black couldn't believe his continued luck. With an easy push he would be in the room, silently and deadly.

He fixed it in his mind that this killing would be cleaner and quicker than the last one. An overflow of the rage caused by his decision not to kill the chaperones had gripped him earlier, and he couldn't afford random emotion. After all, it was Scaffiotelli he was at odds with, not these physicians.

Black feather-touched the door, and it creaked but then fell silent as it swung open. Black thought the sound was almost deafening, but they didn't hear a thing. A thin, tan woman was perched on top of Dr. Strogg. Clad in sweat, rising and falling in rhythm—the scene was hypnotic.

Strogg gripped her waist, his fingers kneading her firm ass, his head tilted back into a lazy pillow. His eyes were closed and his facial expression met her every thrust. She was beautiful, calculating, and absorbed in her own satisfaction.

Not more than eighteen inches from them was a picture of a clean, polished, controlled man and woman, leaning against a thick oak tree. The man was Strogg and the woman was probably his wife, but she wasn't the woman in the bed. Strogg's wife was poised, but unable to hide what Black saw as maturity. The woman in the bed was younger by a few years, but by no means lovelier in Black's estimation.

He was glad Strogg's wife wasn't in the bed with him. It would be a shame to kill such a woman. The kind of woman he loved to submit to, an intellectual equal. To Black, murder was a job, and that was all. Infidelity, for someone who'd taken the vow, was contemptible. He didn't think it odd how his mind worked, what he considered sickening and not particularly bothersome.

He tapped the barrel of the gun on the door. The lovers broke stride, looking at him, horrified.

Black lowered the gun and squeezed off a round, catching the headboard of the bed. "Your wife sent me, Doctor," Black said, without a hint of emotion. He fired another round, catching the mistress in the temple, throwing her wildly back against a bedpost, snapping it off.

"Jesus Christ, help me," Strogg managed as he watched blood spill onto his bed. His eyes darted around the room, as though he actually expected an occurrence of divine intervention.

"I'm afraid He's unavailable. But if you leave your life with me, He'll be sure to get your soul," Black said, grinning.

Two shots pierced Strogg's neck. The final one caught him

in the nose. Strogg fell limply onto the side of the bed and then rolled onto the floor. Black was gone, once again unable to allow his victims to escape life without seeing their assailant.

———

Dr. Edward Delaney lived four blocks from the center of town, in that all too familiar section of restored Victorians, and not that far from Dr. Greene. Their domestic proximity wasn't the only similarity; Delaney wasn't home either.

Black was outside in his car, wondering if he'd spread himself too thin by sedating the chaperones too soon. If Delaney proved to be in hiding also, then Black had been too hasty. Those two fools could have sat outside this house while Black searched for Greene, or the other way around. He was uneasy about the prospect of having to risk staying in the town looking for two physicians.

There were a certain number of prerequisites for his success.

First: He had to kill all three of the physicians before sunrise. Second: The two stooges couldn't be found for at least forty-eight hours, plenty of time for the news of the physicians' deaths to reach the police, the newspapers, and Greene. Third: He would watch the police and thus find Greene, assuming his client was correct. It was the logical move for Greene to make.

The only real problem was, what if Greene and Delaney were in contact with each other? They might be able to come up with a solution he couldn't anticipate. Greene would stay in town because he would feel safe here. That is, until he read about the deaths of his Physicians for Social Responsibility group. Then he'd feel threatened.

Then Greene would seek protection, probably with the local police. Black was counting on Greene's reluctance to trust federal or even state authorities because a United States senator was mixed up in the situation.

Greene had been on the run for a while, and Black was also counting on a heightened level of paranoia, hoping it would inflate the suspicion that all large government agencies in the U.S. were to some extent corrupt. Black was hoping that would scare him off. Watching the local cops would be a safe bet.

But if Greene and Delaney were together, there was a lot less he could predict.

Black suddenly envied their knowledge. They might know a lot about Senator Mitchell and why Black had been hired to kill him. Greene obviously knew a lot about Angela Wilme, and how she fit into the puzzle. He and Delaney understood the workings of the PSR Organization and how it fit into the scheme.

Black didn't know anything, least of all about his client, why he was killing everyone from recent medical school graduates to senators and young, sexually vibrant women. He toyed with the notion of torturing the final two physicians. It was puzzling to him that he was concerned about the nuts and bolts of an assignment. *Why* was of absolutely no consequence in his line of work; only *who, where,* and *when*. It was the client's very odd monitoring of his operations causing the bubbling questions where there had never been any. People died all the time, and whether they deserved it or not had always been irrelevant to Black. But this assignment was different in every way. Different because it made him wonder, made him question why. He wanted to find out, and there were ways.

This time when he tortured the men, he wouldn't have a set list of questions, and he wouldn't stop until everything was clear. He knew the client would be interested in knowing what the hell was going on, and so was Black. It could be a powerful leverage tool to lure his client into the open, into the crosshairs.

It was the first time he'd considered operating for himself. He never took it personally and considered that an important aspect behind why he'd never been apprehended. He was a professional. He didn't care about the client or the victim.

He was weighing the pros and cons of personal illumination when a BMW pulled into Delaney's driveway and triggered the motion sensor floodlights.

The grounds were overgrown and in dire need of Greene's caring landscaper. Thick and patchy evergreens, dead leaves, splotchy sections of grass that looked more like cancer than a lawn, untrimmed hedges, and wild bushes seemed to grow uncontrollably wherever nature had placed them.

The car stopped under a carport, and Delaney got out, stretching his arms over his head and arching his back. A cardiologist on staff at three local hospitals, he most likely had been saving a life. Black could see the doctor well from the invisible seclusion of the overgrown hedge hanging over the hood of his car. Black watched him arm the car and fumble for his housekeys.

The lights inside the house came on and one of the exterior security lights went off. He decided to rush the property before they all went out. That way neither Delaney, nor his neighbors, would think anything of the lights. The driveway arced in front of the house, slipped beneath a carport, then returned to the street. It was a gravel semi-circle, but Black's steps were silenced by wet leaves. The rain had stopped and was replaced by a stiff wind blowing mist from branches. He crouched beside an open window not far from the BMW. The first-floor light went off, then a second-floor light blazed.

When the last of the downstairs lights were extinguished, Black slid his switchblade through the screen creating enough of a hole to slink into the house.

He hurried up the staircase to the second floor, and was reminded of Senator Mitchell's house when he reached the top and was confronted by a long hallway stretching in both directions.

He could hear Delaney in what he assumed to be the master bedroom. The sound of running water flooded through the open door as he recounted the number of times he'd fired the 10mm, deciding he had enough rounds to suffice.

Through the wide door of the bedroom, Black could just see the channel running along the hinged side of a bathroom door. It provided little visibility and he wasn't even sure the man was in there.

He stretched out his arm so the pistol was parallel to the floor of the bedroom. He stepped into the room with caution, each movement deliberate but confident, past a chair and into the threshold of the bathroom. No one was there.

Water was roaring into the porcelain sink, and the shower stall door was open and empty.

He swung around, half expecting Delaney to be standing behind him.

There was no one.

Black stepped away from the bathroom. On a small writing table, a lawyer's lamp was lit. Across the room a king-size bed was turned down, and one of the two nightstands lamps was on. Past a high-backed velvet chair were two tall closet doors with light pouring from behind them. It had to be where Delaney was.

Black maneuvered around the bed and the chair, and knelt low beside the closet, remembering an old saying from his years in the military: An amateur always shoots from shoulder level, and a professional never gets shot.

He pushed the doors open and a blast of sound came from inside. A flash of light and a spray of wood left a round hole in the middle of the door. Much lower than the average shot, but Delaney had aimed at the wrong door. Black leapt into the walk-in closet, rolling to his right and onto his stomach, getting a brief glimpse of his opponent before another shot passed his head and landed in the wall behind him. It was a pump-action Remington pistol-grip shotgun, and it was firing industrials.

Black fired a round into the man's shoulder and another into his hand, expending the final rounds. Using the shotgun was now impossible for Delaney, and he dropped it on the floor. The 10mm was as useless, but Black held onto it.

Delaney fell to the floor. It was obvious he was in pain, but he remained silent. He was gripping his hand and gritting his teeth, his back hunched, favoring his shoulder wound. But when Black stood, Delaney's foot extended suddenly and quickly into Black's groin.

Delaney's second flail of foot dislodged the 10mm from Black's hand and launched it out of his immediate reach.

The look of shock and wonder filling Black's eyes gave confidence to Delaney. Bleeding profusely, Delaney stood up and lunged at Black with his foot. Black dodged it, caught it in mid air and yanked the man onto his back. Delaney extended his other foot into Black's jaw, splitting his lip and snapping his head backwards as though he'd been hit in the face with a sledgehammer.

Delaney was back on his feet and preparing to stomp Black to death, which put Black past the point of preserving him for questioning.

Black's breath suddenly returned, and he recovered enough from the groin shot to maneuver again. He swept the physician's legs from under him and swooped over him, grabbing the man's chin and forehead. With a violent turn of the skull, he snapped the doctor's neck. The world seemed to grow as still and silent as a church on an empty early morning.

Delaney wasn't particularly big, but Black had misjudged him. He was a skilled shot who possessed and fired illegal rounds; he had been trained in hand-to-hand combat and could take pain. Black stood looking down at the physician, slumped against the wall of a closet. He looked out of place among power ties and Italian suits, leather loafers, coordinated suspenders, silk socks, and patterned underwear.

Back in the bedroom on the small writing table Black found a wallet and a set of car keys. Black wondered if he'd been warned by Greene or if he'd just been good.

Downstairs, Delaney's combination office and library provided the answer. An impressive wall of accomplishments, including an Honorable Discharge Certificate from the United

States Marine Corps, a Purple Heart and Citation, a Bronze Star and Citation, and a letter of gratitude from President Reagan.

There were also photographs of Delaney's Marine Corps Basic Training Class, Infantry Class, Special Combat Reconnaissance Class, a diploma from Harvard University Medical School, and citations for academic and medical excellence.

Black stared at the wall a long time, soaking up the weight the man had both nationally and therefore locally. Black had been very lucky Delaney was so far removed from his military career. At his peak, he might have caused more problems. He had been an adversary, a word Black rarely used. Most people were victims.

Black wasn't sorry he had killed the man. It was his job. He was sorry he hadn't had the opportunity to squeeze anything out of him. Not that men like him talked.

Senator Mitchell had been a Marine in Korea. He had cracked, but he was old. Black doubted a man so young would spill his guts. He might have, but Black doubted it.

Outside, it was raining again and Black felt chilled. He stared at the sedan across the street as he moved toward it. It was just about invisible, but not quite.

He pulled away from the curb, scratching the car on the bush it had been parked under. He raised his left hand to his lip, and with the aid of the dash light, saw his finger tips were covered with blood. Upon closer inspection he noticed the incision made by his teeth, three of which were loose.

Black was finished for the night.

In the morning he would wait for the news to hit the local police. Underneath the ashtray of the sedan a scanner and telephone had been bolted to the bottom of the dash. Black turned on the scanner and a dull green analog display ran through the available channels that could be monitored. Every once and a while it stopped scanning and let him listen to a conversation, then it would continue to look for another occupied band. Black soon learned the band the local police used and set the scanner to that position.

He drove around debating his next move. He felt fatigued, his lip was bothering him, and his balls were numb. Rest was the next order of business, though where to get it was a problem.

10

Chief of Police Martin eased onto a couch in the dark sanctuary of his small living room and dozed off. Frank Sinatra's voice reverberated against the windows that looked out onto a deserted Murray Avenue. Sinatra had been his uncle's favorite.

The house had been willed to him by his uncle, Michael Reeves, along with twenty thousand dollars, which he'd invested. Martin considered himself lucky to have been loved so dearly.

Reeves was employed as the Chief of Police of Goshen and had no fears of being removed from his appointed office. The small town knew him and respected the job he did. He had never been married. Not that he was unpopular with the ladies, but he went to work early in the morning and returned late at night. His chosen profession seemed to gridlock him into loneliness.

Reeves hadn't fully understood how alone he'd been until he'd taken in his fourth-grade nephew. Thomas Martin became everything in the world to Reeves, and the boy grew up to be a man he was very proud of.

Martin had spent most of his life in the house. He'd made out with his first girlfriend in the backseat of his uncle's restored

Packard sitting covered in the garage. From the roof of that garage, Martin and his uncle had watched many a high school football game on the field lying just to the other side of the fence dividing his property from the school districts. When Martin began playing, Reeves would pull his police cruiser in somewhere just behind the end zone to watch, irregardless of it being home or away. What had started as catch between the two evolved into rigorous coaching and had turned Martin into one hell of a receiver. Football had afforded him the luxury of college, and his uncle's generosity picked up where his athletic scholarship left off.

Martin had met his wife in college, who as fate would have it, grew up in Warwick, a town only a few miles from Goshen. Her full name was Ashley Scout and she was tall. It was what had first attracted Martin to her. She stood just shy of six feet and had piercing ice-blue eyes, blond hair that fell below her slim waist, and ample curves. She was the proto-typical campus phenomenon, the girl everyone considered beyond reach or already spoken for, but in reality, she was extremely lonely. Ashley had jumped at Martin when he showed the slightest interest in her.

After their marriage and Martin's refusal to accept an influential favor from her father which would have placed him at Harvard Law School, their relationship grew sour. Her disapproval became a constant battle, sealed by Martin's appointment as Chief of Police. He'd been Chief only a few years when Ashley left him.

He still missed holding her at night, feeling her heartbeat, her warmth, next to him. He missed the smell of her hair and the almost satin touch of her hands. He missed having someone to come home to, someone's hand to hold. But most of all, he missed the Ashley he'd known in college, and those endless sessions of passion that filled his years at the State University of New York at New Paltz.

He could have made a different decision, one not so obstinate, but he'd chosen to go his own way. For as long as he could remember, all he'd wanted to do was be a cop. It had a certain lure he couldn't dismiss. At times he wondered how anyone could live with himself if he wasn't doing something he enjoyed. That wasn't the norm, Martin realized. Most people barely tolerated what they did for money. He felt lucky to love his job, still, he couldn't help wondering what kind of a man would let Ashley go.

It wasn't six months after their separation that Martin lost his uncle, and the combination made his losses almost unbearable. Paulina Orange proved to be his redeemer, in that she possessed everything he needed to be brought back from the brink. It made his heart race to think that their relationship was back on the front burner. He was certain that everything would work out this time.

Having been entranced by the past, Martin dozily lumbered from the living room couch and slipped into bed. He was unaware he'd surrendered to seven hours worth of dreams about his ex-wife, his uncle, and Paulina, until his old, discolored Western Electric telephone began ringing. His Sunbeam clock displayed the ungodly hour of 5 AM as he rolled over for the phone. It was Wednesday morning, October 28, and one of his officers was describing a situation that convinced Martin he was still dreaming.

"Chief, it's Charles," Officer Gold began. Charles Gold had seniority among the Goshen P. D.'s officers, even over Martin.

"This better be good," Martin said. His voice sounded like a two-pack-a-day frog.

"Someone killed Dr. Strogg at his house. Gunshot wounds."

"What the hell are you talking about?" Martin asked. He sat up, wide awake. Goshen had never had a homicide. In fact, Martin was hard pressed to remember the last accidental death. "Is anyone else there, or just him?" Martin asked, fully aware that Paulina had been ending things with Strogg.

"His wife phoned it in. She's here."

Martin sighed. "Sit tight, I'm on my way." He hung up, got dressed, then called Matthew Light.

"Remember when I told you this was a sleepy little community, and if you wanted to get away from the hectics of N.Y.C. that this was the place to be? It looks like I was full of shit."

"Why, what's up?"

"We've got ourselves a homicide, I guess. I'm going to need your expertise on this. I'll be going by the book, but if at any point your experience tells you the book and I don't know what we're doing, pull me aside. I want you to get over to Dr. Strogg's house on Gregory Drive. Gold's there already, so just look for his cruiser. Block off the place and set up a scene log. We'll have to get the State Police to send a Crime I.D. Unit for the nuts and bolts. Got all of that?"

"Yeah, Chief, and listen, I was getting bored anyway, just like you said I would, so you weren't completely full of shit."

Senator Braun locked the front door of her row house on 35th Street in Georgetown, then made her way back to her Mercedes. She'd parked down the street from her red-and-white three-story in the only spot she could find.

She lifted her small wheeled suitcase into the backseat and got in behind the wheel. Withdrawing a cellular from her overcoat, she remembered a set of hearings early last year, where she'd learned how easy it was for someone with a notebook computer, and some communications knowledge, to pull a cellular call right out of the air. She scanned the cars parked across the street from her, acknowledging someone was probably watching as well as listening.

"You're being paranoid, Susan," she said to herself, dialing her administrative aide at home. "And now you're talking to yourself."

"Hello," the aide answered.

"Gill, this is Susan."

"Yes, Senator?"

"I had a disturbing call this afternoon from New York City. I am going to have to fly up there and take care of a constituent issue."

"Will you need me along, ma'am?" Gill asked.

"No, it's sensitive, I'll have more luck solo," Braun said. "I should be back in a day or two at the most."

"I'll take care of everything here."

As she pulled away from the curb and made her way toward Key Bridge, she noticed the gray sedan pull in behind her.

She wondered if it was the FBI, which was ignoring her refusal for protection, or if it was someone with a more direct hand in Mitchell's fate.

Very paranoid, she thought, accelerating into the southbound traffic of the George Washington Memorial Parkway.

Braun parked in the daily lot of National Airport and wheeled her suitcase into the domestic terminal. She could see the reflection of a man leaving the gray sedan in the glass of the automatic doors; he was moving in behind her.

She made her way to the American Eagle ticket counter and purchased a round-trip ticket to JFK in New York, going through the identification and questionnaire protocol implicit with air travel in the U.S. She used her credit card and the discount available to members of Congress, so that all the proper red flags would be tripped as a result of her flight.

The man from the car was more than a few people back on line.

This will be my only chance to loose him, she thought, after she'd made it through the security check blessedly quickly.

The first bend in the terminal cut her off from the man's line of sight, and she ducked into the ladies' room that wasn't visible from the security line.

She found an empty stall and went to work. She tucked her shoulder-length blond hair under a brown wig, removed her makeup with cleansing wipes, and changed out of her suit. She reemerged wearing jeans, a turtleneck sweater, and a camel-colored jacket. She had to admit this was her first bit of fun in days. She'd been a brunette in college, and the sight of her former self made her crack a toothy smile.

Her next stops were an ATM for cash, and a Sprint store to buy and activate a new cell phone.

Then she made her way back out of the terminal and found

a cab. "Budget rentals, please," she said once she'd hailed one.

———◦———

The late October sky was heavy and medium gray, and Gregory Drive was empty and silent. The occasional early commuter was leaving for work, but passing cars were a rare sight; to a great extent the development was a bedroom community still asleep.

Orange County District Attorney Owens was already on the scene when Martin pulled to the top of the driveway and parked next to Strogg's Porsche. Bright yellow tape had been stretched across the garage doors at the rear of the house and was blocking the base of a rear stairway. Matt Light was standing guard at the front door.

Owens and Martin signed the scene log and stepped into the foyer just as Officer Gold appeared atop the staircase. He stared down at them, empty-faced. Something was wrong, something beyond the horror of a small-town resident being killed.

"You alright, Charlie?" Owens asked as they climbed the staircase toward him.

Martin stared at Gold for a long time, soaking up what the man's eyes were saying. His stomach knotted and his pulse rose to a breakneck pace. "Charlie?" Martin asked.

Officer Gold nodded to Martin's unspoken question, then turned away and walked down a hallway with Owens, disappearing into the bedroom.

Martin's journey down the hallway seemed to be happening in slow motion. He could feel the blood coursing through his neck with each step. When he reached the threshold of the bedroom, fear stopped Martin in his tracks; his legs had turned to lead. He knew what he was going to see, but he had to muster all of his strength to even inch toward it.

Paulina's body was slumped against the headboard, and Strogg's was on the floor. Blood stained the wall and the headboard; it had sprayed a Tiffany lamp and soaked through the bed sheets and carpeting.

"I'm sorry, Tom," Owens said.

Martin stood in the doorway, staring at Paulina's naked body. Tears rolled down his cheeks as he moved to her side. His hands were shaking.

I love you, he thought, and slumped against the wall next to her, his eyes glazing over as though he'd been drugged.

"Who found the body?" Owens asked Gold.

"His wife. I took a statement already, but she's downstairs if you want to talk to her," Gold answered.

"I'll get right on this, Tom. We'll get who did this one quick, I guarantee it," Owens said, motioning for Gold to help him walk Martin back outside. "I'll take care of calling the State Police and the coroner."

Martin stepped off the porch and took several deep breaths, filling his lungs with cold October air. He felt as though a part of his soul had been ripped away. A numbness had set so deep into his body that he could almost hear it in his ears, like the faint hum of a transformer. Everything seemed distant and unfocused, and he was only dazedly listening to Gold's description of his earlier conversation with Diane Strogg. The man's instinct was that she had nothing to do with the death of her husband. Gold knew crimes of passion were usually textbook jealousy cases. He had to admit she had a strong motive. He'd been found in bed with a beautiful woman, and if finding out about the involvement pushed her over the edge, then she was guilty. But from Gold's point of view, she wasn't conveying very much emotion, either hysteria or deadening shock. Something about her had convinced him of incapability. According to Gold, she was a flake.

"Tell her to pick a friend to stay with, then take her there," Owens instructed Gold. "She's not to leave Goshen, though, no debates."

"You want me to baby-sit?"

"Tom, all this sound right to you?" Owens asked, but he got no response.

Martin had turned away and was staring at the breath pluming from his mouth. Their voices sounded like distant echoes.

"Jesus, Tom!" Owens said, redirecting his attention on Gold. "A trooper will relieve you, so just get back here."

"I'll go get her," Gold said, and went back into the house.

"Tom, you still with us?" Owens asked, staring into Martin's face. It was blank, as though his thoughts were a million miles away, but his eyes were somehow different, harder, frightening. "Tom?"

———

Detective David McElroy, an investigator for the New York State Police Bureau of Criminal Investigation, arrived in a late-model Ford, with a C.S.U. conversion van following close behind.

McElroy forced his mammoth frame out of the Ford and followed four men dressed in jeans and State Police windbreakers into the house.

On the far side of the driveway a white Buick station wagon with the seal of Orange County, New York, on the door, and the word "Coroner" printed above, sat waiting. A large man was sitting behind the cracked driver's window, smoking.

By the time Gold returned, Martin was only somewhat more composed. He was outside with Light, nodding his affirmation to wild conjectures while a C.S.U. member was giving the coroner the green light to remove the bodies. The overweight coroner and his assistant carried two stretchers inside and Martin opened the door for them twice as they left the house for the rear of the station wagon.

Martin stared toward the bottom of the driveway at the growing group of curious onlookers, watching what they had seen depicted before only in movies. There was something very different about the reality of death, he thought. The primary difference was that it was real. It wasn't happening to the other guy, it was happening to them, their friends, their neighbors. One mile away, one street away, one house away from their home.

He watched the coroner pull away and felt the same sense of loss as when he signed his divorce papers and buried his uncle. But this time, loss was giving way to rage. In his mind he'd won Paulina back. It wasn't meant to end this way.

Matthew Light completely understood the look sweeping over Martin's face. He could still remember the exact moment he'd had his innocence stripped from him.

It was like being raped, a criminal psychologist had told Light once. You could never go back to the way you were before it happened. Something was different, the way you saw things, the feelings you carried from then on. You could never be clean again, and any reservations or naïveté you once had became faint, childish memories. What Light couldn't understand was how the Chief of Police had sustained that innocence for so long. The town and the people he protected were an oxymoron within the violence of law enforcement. Nothing had ever touched the town or Thomas Martin, at least nothing serious. Maybe it had come close a few times, but it seemed almost phobic; unwilling or unable to cross into the Chief's territory.

One of the reasons Light had joined the department was reputation. Goshen had the lowest crime rate in New York and ranked very well in the country. The town stood in contrast to violence, and though he'd wanted to run away from that kind of crap, it had chased him. In a small quiet town, the beast had found him. He couldn't help but think he'd brought it with him, and the beast liked virgin territory. There was so much to taint and corrupt, and before it left Goshen, it would turn everything black.

Martin lifted the transceiver off the dashboard of his Bronco and asked his dispatcher to connect him with Dr. Benjamin Tafton, the county examiner. Tafton was a huge, heavy man, and a close friend of Martin's uncle.

"I'm sending you two bodies, Ben," Martin began. "I need you to do the autopsies."

"Bodies, what are you talking about Tommy?" Tafton asked. Tafton was the only one, aside from Tom's uncle, who had ever called him that.

"A doctor by the name of Strogg."

"Eric Strogg?"

"You know him?" Martin asked.

"Arden is a small hospital, I know everyone. You said bodies?"

"The other is Paulina Orange." Martin could hardly force the words out of his mouth.

"Oh, Jesus, no," Tafton said. "Tommy, no."

Martin didn't say anything, he merely bit down on his lip so hard that he began to taste blood.

"I'll take care of everything, don't worry. Send Gold with the coroner. It's important someone is here."

"Ben, about the funeral, Robin's Catholic. He'll want it open."

"I'll take care of her, Tommy. You just catch the son-of-a-bitch. You set him straight."

Martin replaced the transceiver and backed his Bronco out onto Gregory Drive. He was on his way to tell Robin Orange that his sister was dead.

Pulling away from the house and the full-fledged crowd at the bottom of the driveway, he choked down the lump in his throat and pushed back another tear. He should have made a move on Paulina a long time ago. Maybe she wouldn't have been here in the first place. Maybe she would have rejected him and been here anyway.

———•◦•———

Martin sat in the darkness of his kitchen, his head resting on an open palm, his mind flashing photographs of Paulina's bloody body and her brother's subsequent breakdown. It had begun as an angry attack on his bar and had ended with him clutching Martin, sobbing.

He stood up and moved out the back door and across his lawn toward the garage. The side door was unlocked and once inside he negotiated the tightness around his uncle's Packard. A small-paned window provided the only natural light, which was shining on an old boxer's bag hanging in the back corner, weathered by his uncle's fists and bandaged with duct tape. Martin slipped out of his uniform jacket and threw it on the covered hood of his Camaro.

The smell of oil, wax, and rotting wood melded as he began to strike the bag. Softly at first, and then with more violence as the photographs started to come again. The taste of her lips and the sweet sound of her voice.

His eyes were streaming tears, and his fists had become weapons on the bag. The overhead chain protested in a rusty chorus, and Martin's knuckles were growing bright red. His breathing became heavier and heavier, and after almost five minutes, he fell into the bag, clutching it for support. He felt as if he were spiraling down into hell.

"Please God, no," he pleaded. "Not Paulina."

Special Agents Williams and Tobin had responded to the initial D.C.P.D. report that Senator Byron Mitchell had been killed, and although they had separate duties, they found their paths criss-crossing. Assigned the individual tasks of digging around the Senate Appropriations Committee and establishing a list of probable and able suspects who hated the senator seemed to Williams and Tobin to be one and the same thing, so they combined their efforts.

With the combined strength of more than enough federal agents, Williams and Tobin began to unearth anything and everything about Senator Mitchell.

Since the meeting with Director Geehern had ended after five, traipsing around Capitol Hill in search of information would have been a waste of time. So, for the better part of Wednesday night, the agents sat at their computers producing pages and pages of material from the IRS, the accessible files on the Hill, and across the country. By ten they had a pretty good idea the senator was in the red up to his eyelids.

For the last five years he'd been audited due to concerns about income discrepancies and deductions, but the audits had never materialized. It was safe to assume Mitchell had somehow buried them. One of the agents assigned to the new-founded Williams-Tobin team was a whiz-kid tax attorney who had, in five short hours, broken down Mitchell's financial life: Mitchell's assets didn't equate with what he earned as a senator, and his tax-exempt foundation and campaign fund were huge. The fund was of particular interest, because the election organization Mitchell had founded happened to have a balance rivaling the amounts some presidents used to get into the Oval Office.

The agents then focused on devising a list of Mitchell's enemies. It was obvious he'd gotten rich off of somebody; and though it wasn't the primary objective of the group, they were nonetheless interested, and decided to find an answer.

They knew Mitchell chaired the Senate Appropriations Committee, and that he'd been in the news for the last several weeks because of his staunch opposition to the plans to get the federal government to fund abortions. The group standing to lose the

most if Mitchell got his way would be the conglomerate of interest groups comprising what was known as the Pro-Choicers. In
fact, both sides of the abortion issue had a history of threats and
violence, and that fact alone garnered them the number-one spot
on the agent's suspect list.

By the time midnight rolled around the group had exhausted
all of the computer and conjectured leads they could come up
with during evening hours. Everyone had an understanding of
what they'd dug up so far, and everyone had a specific task to
take care of as soon as Capitol Hill opened for business Thursday morning.

Martin pulled back onto Gregory Drive and into the midst of a
media onslaught. He was shocked to see Channel 7 and Cable 6
news vans, along with newspaper reporters, twenty busybodies,
and two additional State Police cruisers. He was exhausted, his
head was pounding, and his hands were on fire. All he wanted to
do was crawl into bed for a month.

The men from the crime unit were either loading up their
van or standing around smoking. Detective David McElroy was
taking long drags on a thick cigar, nearly invisible through the
thick smoke lingering around him. As he exhaled, he motioned
for Martin. Reporters were screaming after Martin as he walked
toward McElroy. Five or six reporters waved at him as if they
actually expected him to rush down the driveway and brief them
on a situation he himself didn't understand.

"Let's have a talk," McElroy said, directing Martin into his
Ford sedan by slapping its roof with his open palm.

"Why in here?" Martin questioned as his friend wedged himself behind the wheel.

"Just get in!" he commanded, and shut his driver's door.

Martin did.

"News-hounds," he barked with distaste. "Video cameras with zoom lenses aid those little lip-reading pricks."

"How the hell did they find out? And why are they here in the first place?" Martin asked.

"News-hounds," McElroy repeated. "We're all finished with the identification here," he said, getting on with his intended conversation.

"So what have you got for me?" Martin asked desperately.

"The man used a 10mm, assuming it's a guy. The angles seem to point to someone fairly tall. He was close too, right at the foot of the bed." McElroy paused a moment before continuing.

"The guy was a pro, Tom. There were no casings anywhere, which meant he took the time to collect them from the floor once he was done."

"A professional? Here?" Martin asked.

"We'll be able to perform the preliminary for you, but I have to warn you our ability to follow up on this is going to be restricted. We're up to our armpits with Grason."

Grason was an apprehended multiple murderer, Martin recalled. He'd killed, dismembered, and buried twelve young women, and the case had been receiving national attention, as well as occupying all of the State Police's time and resources. It explained Channel 7's presence. The conclusion they would draw and impart to their evening viewers was anyone's guess, but Martin could think of more than a few doozies.

"That explains your news-hounds," Martin said. "So I'm on my own, eh?"

McElroy nodded. "I could maybe swing you some time with a couple of men, but I can't guarantee anything. I'm already catching shit for authorizing too much overtime."

Martin knew the husky detective wanted to help. The pain of what he was saying showed in his face. The interdependent relation among time sheets, budgets, and justice held a special place in McElroy's heart, ranking high on his list, along with news-hounds.

"One thing I'm definitely going to do is get Dr. Varbero involved," McElroy continued. "He's lower New York's best criminal shrink. He helped us bag Grason. He's got too much gray matter for his own good, and he takes a lot of getting used to, but he'll help you pin the wife or clear her, regardless of whether she passes the gunshot residue test. He'll also be able to paint a pretty good picture of who you should be looking for if she ends up being cleared. Either way, it will help you in the long run."

"Whatever help you can swing would be appreciated," Martin said.

"If we're lucky we'll find the pistol when we canvas the adjoining properties, and it'll have prints all over it. Then Owens can take over for you."

McElroy looked away from Martin for a moment as though something outside the car had caught his attention.

"What?" Martin asked after an uncomfortable pause.

"I'm sorry about the woman, Tom."

A member of the crime unit interrupted to tell Martin that he had a call from one of his two dispatchers. It was Debra Chen, the village's part-time meter-maid, crossing-guard, and dispatcher who seemed to know everything about everyone in town; and this time she had bad news.

"Chief, you know Connie Robuck?" the dispatcher said when he picked up the transceiver in his Bronco.

"Yeah, she works over at the lumber yard. Why?"

"Well, she was supposed to meet her boyfriend for an early lunch, and when he didn't show up, she went over to his house. She found him dead in his closet."

"Who's the boyfriend?"

"Dr. William Delaney." She paused. "What's going on with these doctors?"

"I don't know. Give me Delaney's address."

Martin called and woke the final member of the Goshen Police Department, Officer Myers, a few hours before his shift was supposed to start, and began to tell him a tale he thought was some kind of prank.

When Martin briefed McElroy and the crime unit, they packed up and headed for Delaney's address, following Chief Martin. Everyone agreed that he might have something on his hands. McElroy's earlier attitude had evaporated. The fact that they were both doctors made Martin's mind race. He was never more sorry he had wished for something and gotten it.

——— ❖ ———

Special Agent Kerrigan sat in a cold Chevrolet Corsica thinking about her fiancé and his strong hands. He would be unhappy she'd missed dinner for the second night in a row. How unhappy was one of the questions on her mind, seeing as how tonight was date night. The other question was where Philip Torroson, Senator Mitchell's gardener, had disappeared to.

Philip Torroson lived with an elderly couple in a suburb of Washington called Adams Morgan, and Kerrigan was parked three car lengths and a street's width away from the trio's thin row house. Beneath a front porch, a set of steps descended to Torroson's apartment door, and two rectangular windows provided her with proof of whether or not her prey was home.

Staring out the driver's side window Kerrigan saw an orange sun falling below a skeletal tree line. Thick patches of fog clung to the small section of Rock Creek Park separating her from the bare trees.

Geehern had given her two days to produce the gardener, and as Thursday evening threatened to turn into Friday morning, time was running out. She'd been assigned two additional agents to help her wait and watch, one of whom was shadowing the gardener's landlords around the city.

The other was finishing up a box of fried chicken in the backseat of the Corsica. Every once and a while he'd pick up a pair of binoculars and scan the house, but it was only an involuntary reaction to procedure.

Kerrigan knew it was a bad detail, but if she was lucky, the guy would just show up and that would be the end of it. She'd dump the man downtown and go home and make love to her fiancé, if he'd have anything to do with her.

Early on Saturday morning, October 31, Chief Thomas Martin
sat on a worn and faded diner stool in a small corner restaurant
called Elsie's. The long chipped Formica counter was crammed
with hard-roll and pastry cases, plates of pancakes, eggs, bacon,
and cups of hot coffee. Elsie's sat wedged between the police
station and the main artery of town.

Martin picked at his omelet, trying to pinpoint the precise
moment his life had gone to hell. To the left of his plate lay a
copy of the local paper. "Goshen's Double Murder" was printed
across the top, with photos of Dr. Delaney and Dr. Strogg underneath the headline. He was having difficulty eating with the
caption staring him in the face: "Chief of Police Thomas Martin, with the aid of State Police investigators, has turned up no
leads in the mysterious deaths of two Goshen physicians."

The statement wasn't altogether incorrect. Wednesday afternoon and evening Martin had torn through Delaney's home with
the State Police and then gone to the morgue to bear witness to
the worst detail for a cop, at least according to Tom Martin.

He had watched two autopsies that turned up only times of
death and the fact that the men had been killed within an hour
of each other, very early Wednesday morning, and with the same
weapon. Whoever killed the men had too long of a jump, and
Martin knew it.

Martin had spent most of Thursday canvassing the areas
surrounding the Delaney and Strogg scenes, cursing the unco-
operative weather, and screaming at Owens about search warrants. He'd enlisted all ten men from the Goshen Department of
Public Works, and together with his officers and a few from the
State Police, they went through storm drains, garbage bins, mail-

boxes, woods, and neighboring properties up to a three-block radius. They'd found nothing.

The cook, moved away from the grill to answer a ringing telephone and then reappeared to tell Martin the call was for him.

A third body had been found, another physician. He wasn't surprised by the call but didn't relish what problems it brought with it. The press, the morgue, the State Police, his officers, and his town would all be involved in another horror.

Martin had had his fill of big city problems. As he hung up the phone, he had never felt so out of control. He stood near the back door of the small restaurant for a while, staring at the back of the police station and the people streaming past the post office. He could almost see Paulina again, climbing the stairs to get her mail, and the numbness began filling his senses again.

———————

Black sat reading the daily paper in the corner farthest from the restaurant's counter. He was enjoying the adrenaline boost coming from being in the same room as Tom Martin. Everything about the man screamed failure; his demeanor, his appetite, but most of all his face. Black could see the blood drain out of it when the man cooking, answered a ringing telephone and then pushed it toward the cop.

As was the case so often in life, the thing or answer a person sought was invariably right under your nose.

11

Dr. Robert Greene tucked a copy of the local newspaper under his arm and juggled two cans of soda as he fished through his pockets for the keycard to his hotel room. There was a bitter wind whistling across the deserted rear angles of the hotel, but it was when it took hold of Greene's door and elicited a prolonged cry from the un-oiled hinges that the peculiar noises coming from his neighbor's room abruptly stopped.

Greene's senses heightened as Goshen seemed to grow unnaturally still, and for reasons he couldn't explain, he felt even more uneasy. He pushed the door back into place and the hinges seemed twice as loud. The deadbolt anchoring itself sounded like a gunshot. He could feel his heart pounding and sweat beading up on his forehead.

His thoughts drifted to the man who'd been staring out the window of his Greenwich Avenue office as he stood motionless in the dark woods, listening and waiting.

He was looking right at me, Greene thought. But he just let me go. Why?

It had to be the man from Washington. Greene considered it

blind luck that he'd lasted this long. But he also began to consider that Mr. Washington might be in the room right next door.

It had been his too-hasty phone call to Senator Mitchell that enabled the killer to find him with such ease. The thought of someone having access to what Mitchell had described as a personal line only he and God knew about, baffled the mind.

He felt as though fate had dealt him a second chance, and he had to use it to his advantage. The only thing he knew for certain was he was in over his head. All of the friends he considered trustworthy, including Senator Mitchell, were dead.

The District of Columbia Police Department and the FBI had experienced no more success than the Goshen Police Department with figuring out what was going on, at least according to the newspaper. Of course, the FBI and the local police didn't know the events in Washington and Goshen were connected. The Feds, however, had a preliminary description of the suspect: Six-foot-five and about two-hundred and forty pounds. Two ominous figures that further terrorized Greene.

He was jarred from his revelations by the twisting of his door handle, which escalated to a forceful rattling of door against deadbolt. This time blind luck was nowhere to be seen.

———

After Senator Braun had pulled off her disappearing act, finding a hotel that accepted cash without question was trickier. She was finally forced to pull into the Holiday Inn and hope the staff she knew would be working.

She sighed when she caught sight of the front desk and the familiar faces.

"Hello, Senator," the man said, glancing at her identification. "It's so good to see you again."

"I think you have me confused with someone else," she began, withdrawing a folded wad of bills from her jeans pocket. Her grandfather had always said, Susan, if you're carrying more than fifty, carry it in a front pocket. "The name is Gill, and I'll need a room for the week."

"Of course, Miss Gill," the man said around a wry smile while taking her cash, and sent her on her way.

Inside the room, she hung her coat over a chair and stretched out onto the bed. She pulled on the pins and slid the brown wig off her head, dropping it beside her, and began massaging her scalp.

It had to be, as her fellow members of the pact had surmised, one of the bills they were reviewing, that was to blame for Mitchell's murder. But there were more than ten subcommittees and God only knew how many bills being reviewed. It seemed like an insurmountable puzzle.

Reaching over to the nightstand for a pad and a pen, she began to rule out ideas. When she was at Harvard Law, her advising professor, Dr. Lee, had drilled her about the benefits of working in reverse, and arguing the other side of the case like it meant your life. The philosophy had made her a good prosecutor and a good anticipator, so she began to create a list of things to be ruled out.

She was on the Commerce, Justice, State, and the Judiciary Subcommittees and was able to rule them out immediately. The Agriculture, District of Columbia, Legislative, and VA/HUD subcommittees had been relegated to the penniless category, thanks to the current Administration, so she eliminated them as well.

The balance consisted of several potentials, including those that were lovingly referred to in Congress as "The Three Monsters:" Defense; Homeland Security; and the subcommittee for Labor, Health and Human Services, and Education. Mitchell had sat on all three and was chairman of the last, so it was here that Braun planned to start digging.

But it was after midnight and her brain was sending her urgent rest messages. She would head for the Library of Congress tomorrow and curl up with one of the computers in the main room. She hoped it would be bustling; she needed a crowd to ease her paranoia about going out into a public that knew her face.

When the rattling stopped and the noise next door resumed, Greene stretched out on the bed, turned on a small lamp, and unfolded the Halloween edition of *The Times Herald-Record*, the local newspaper serving Goshen and the surrounding areas of the county.

As with every paper for the last few days, there was a wild headline speculating that a serial killer with an appetite for doctors had arrived in Goshen.

Second Goshen Physician Murdered by Apparent Serial Killer

Another physician's body was discovered yesterday in Goshen, as questions abound concerning Chief of Police Thomas Martin's abilities to handle a case of this type.

Dr. William Delaney, a cardiac specialist and surgeon, became the second victim of the apparent serial killer. Chief of Police Martin has been relying heavily on the State Police's Bureau of Criminal Investigation (BCI) unit for assistance. That assistance has been greatly limited because of the Nathaniel Grason case. Grason, a multiple murderer who was captured nearly two months ago, came to dominate the BCI's resources statewide, and continues to do so.

As of press time, no suspects or significant leads were reported by the Martin/BCI collaboration. Meanwhile, the residents of Goshen, in particular its physicians, have to be content with the hope that they will not be the next victim...

"The only word you have wrong is serial, he's a professional," Greene muttered to himself, throwing the paper aside.

The noise stopped again.

It was the sound of furniture being righted, Greene decided, although he was desperately holding onto the naïve hope that a hulking maid was over there cleaning. But somehow, he knew the person had been up to something far more sinister. If his new neighbor was someone connected to the killer, or Mr. Washington himself, Greene couldn't leave the hotel until he did. And once Greene left, he knew he couldn't chance coming back.

He'd wanted to buy a copy of *The New York Times* or *The Washington Post* to see if there was any news about Angela Wilme, but he didn't dare risk being seen in town, so he had to be content with stealing the local paper from a nearby driveway each morning. He hadn't been to his house except to get some clothes and supplies, because they would surely be waiting there.

In his heart, he knew Angela was still lying in a pool of blood. His stomach knotted as a flash of Angela's face passed through his mind. Her death had been so pointless, her involvement so minimal. He had to find a way of doing something, but he had to be smart about it.

And then there was his wife. With all the commotion during the past week, she hadn't crept into his mind once until now. He didn't love her, at least that was what he told himself, but he'd remitted the same lie about Angela time and again.

He always tried to stay clear of emotion, a symptom he considered too expensive for his well-being. Passion and sexuality were as close to love as Greene liked to get. He was the product of an early domestic war which resulted in an eleven-year-old boy being dragged into court to watch lawyers put his family through the personal ringer, with the lofty and fallacious purpose of proving which parent was the right, and best parent for him. He'd emerged from that situation numb, hurt, and sure of only two things: The court system was the vilest and most self-serving entity in the universe, and what his parents had said about each other shattered all his illusions about relationships. In time, the philosophy extended to all things and people. He'd gotten into medicine for financial reasons and because science and math came remarkably easy for him, not because he wanted to help his fellow man. Greene believed that as long as he had what he wanted, everything else could go to hell.

But now he would have to pay for what he had done. He needed help, and he didn't trust anything connected with Washington. He was also leery of an organization as large as the New York State Police, and that left only the local Chief of Police, which was no great comfort. How would a local cop protect him from an assassin? How would Martin be able to clean up the mess and make it all right again?

The Chief of Police wouldn't be able to, but he was the only hope.

According to the *Times Herald-Record*, Chief of Police Thomas Martin was too incompetent to lead an investigation of this level, and wouldn't be doing so if the State Police weren't tied up with one of the biggest multiple murders to come down the pathological pike.

It would be natural for Martin to suspect him, so he'd be arrested if he just showed up at the village station and told the police his story. He'd have to do it over the phone. He'd have to convince him, and he'd have to find out about Angela and his wife. He had to do things different this time. He had to make it right.

12

Chief Martin left Elsie's restaurant and stepped into a windy Halloween day. He stared down the stretch of West Main Street toward the center of town as he pulled his fleece coat tighter around his neck. An abundance of crisp leaves swirled along the stretch of buildings. Everything was feeling more and more random to him.

Once inside his Bronco, he began his trek through the streets of the small town. En route, he left another message with the State Police about another body, and he requested the use of their Crime Unit, again.

A crowd was gathering around Officer Light's cruiser outside the apartment complex of Dr. Peter Dunnelo. The car's emergency lights projected onto the buildings, bouncing off the windows and back at the sullen crowd.

Martin angled his Bronco so it blocked the stairway leading to Dunnelo's building. The building's foyer had a single flight of stairs leading to the second-floor apartments, where a small Hispanic woman was leaning against Dunnelo's door frame.

Martin approached Light and asked, "Who's the woman?"

"The cleaner," Officer Light answered, and followed his boss into the second-floor apartment.

A tall, skinny man was lying face-up on the bed, a gaping hole where his left eye had been.

"This guy was a physician?" Martin said, gazing around the apartment. It was austere to say the least.

Martin turned to Officer Light. "Listen, get a statement from the cleaning lady. She's the one that found him, right?"

"Yeah," Light said, and they moved back into the vestibule.

"Then I want you to get a complete list of everyone who lives in this building from the super, make it everyone in this section of the complex. Talk to all of them and make sure if someone else was with them the last couple of nights, that you find out who they were and how we can get in contact with them."

"What about the crowd?" Light asked. "If they get curious, I mean?"

"I'm going to have to call everyone back in on this one again, so I'll sit here until Myers comes to relieve me."

"Where are you heading after that?" Light asked as they stood next to the small woman.

"I'm going to start expanding the canvass area around the other two scenes and see if anybody knows anything or heard anything. Then I want to talk to Strogg's wife and Delaney's girl-friend again. A few days usually clears up the mind a little. I'll get the DPW again, get them to help you go over the complex's property with a fine-tooth comb. But I want you to get on this immediately, so go on." Martin said, giving a gesture-push on the back of Officer Light's shoulder as he descended the staircase with the cleaning lady.

Martin followed behind them once he'd fixed a strip of yellow police tape across the apartment door. Outside, he opened the door to the Bronco and depressed a switch that opened the tailgate window. Dropping the gate, he grabbed two tall plastic cones and set them up ten feet into the parking lot and away from his truck. Stretching a long strip of police tape between them, he created a barrier for the crowd to move up to.

A few of them knew Martin and he knew them, but he ignored their questions, even if they were just remarks of communal concern. He returned to close the tailgate and then walked around to the transceiver bolted to the truck dashboard.

"Deb?" He said, calling the village dispatcher, Debra Chen.

"Yeah, Chief?"

"We've got another one, alright. Call Ben Tafton at the Medical Examiner's office. Also, wake up Officer Myers and get him down here to relieve me. I'm in Carriage Hill Apartments."

"Which section?"

"Just tell them to look for the circus overlooking the Interstate."

"You got it," She said.

Martin leaned into the truck to replace the microphone into its cradle, deciding to hop in and wait for someone else to arrive. It was a long wait, during which he'd gotten out twice to check on the crowd and the apartment. He devised a list on a small steno pad of the people he wanted to question, and questions he wanted to ask. He also composed a list of things-to-do that took up three pages alone.

Officer Myers pulled into the lower lot and made his way toward the Bronco. It was drizzling, and most of the crowd had given up. Martin was thankful for the arrival of bad weather.

Martin grabbed an orange and navy-blue raincoat from the hinge behind the driver's seat, got out, and approached Myers as he was putting his cruiser into park. Myers already had his coat on and a clear protective bag over his hat.

"Another one?" Myers asked in disbelief.

"I don't know what to make of it, except for the obvious of course," Martin said, looking at Myers, who stood head and shoulders above him with his renowned boyish face. He looked fresh and unaffected by the grim news, but he always gave the impression he was happy-go-lucky, even if he wasn't.

"Meaning someone has it out for our physicians?"

"Yep. All of them male, around thirty years old, and fresh out of medical school; except Delaney, he was older. I'm getting tired of waiting for the State Police to send me their evaluation. Not that it'll help any."

"Did you know Delaney was my doc? Feels weirder when you know them really well."

Martin didn't know what to say.

"Did you send for everyone?"

"Yeah, I want you to sit on the place while they do their stuff. I'll send Gold to the morgue this time, so just sit on the apartment until you're relieved," Martin said. The stress of a third unexplained dead body was showing on his face and in his posture. He wished he could give the impression of being happy-go-lucky, even though he wasn't.

"Sure thing, Tom," Myers said, and walked toward the apartment.

Mrs. Strogg was staying with a friend on an adjacent street from her home and Martin pulled his Bronco into the driveway, parking behind a gray Lexus sedan. He gave an acknowledging nod to the state trooper parked in the street, who'd been assigned to watch the widow.

He climbed to the wide cement porch and knocked on the front door. An attractive woman greeted him with a smile, stared briefly at the name tag on his fleece coat, then motioned him in. Her name was Wendy Roginson, wife of Harold, the New York City attorney. She was rich and she was tan.

Martin was dressed in duty uniform, and although he wasn't in the habit of wearing his uniform cap, he intentionally wore it for certain encounters, like this one.

He removed the cap as he entered the house. "I'm here to see Mrs. Strogg."

"Well of course you are," she said.

"Diane, there's someone here to see you honey," Wendy called out, and turned back to meet Martin's gaze. "She'll be right out. We can wait in the living room." She led him into a large room painted blue and white. "You know you're a very attractive man, Chief Martin," Wendy continued, easing into a mahogany chair. "Not at all like they're making you out to be in the papers."

"Will Mrs. Strogg be long?" he asked, avoiding the remark.

"Are you always so serious?"

He didn't answer.

"Pay no attention to her, Chief," Mrs. Strogg said as she came in. "She's a flirt through and through. Her husband works too many hours, and she's left alone in this house too long."

"Oh, be quiet," Wendy said, then left the room.

"Sorry about that," Mrs. Strogg said. "She's just like a kid."

"You seem to be getting on all right, Mrs. Strogg." The woman showed no real signs of grief, and her carefree tone unsettled Martin.

"Diane, please, and yes, I'm doing fine. Wendy and Harold have been very nice to me over the last couple of days."

"You seem to have put your husband's murder behind you very quickly, I must say," he said.

"My, we're very direct," she said. "My husband was a whore, Chief. He cheated a lot. We had a marriage of convenience where, for me, the benefits far outweighed his indiscretions."

"Benefits?"

"I'm a very comfortable woman. Accustomed to a certain lifestyle, and Eric was very good at providing for me. It was nice not having to crawl back to my mother for money all the time. In some ways I'll miss him tremendously."

"Such as?"

"A man who could do the things he could in bed can be forgiven for just about anything." She was grinning.

"Where did you meet your husband?" Martin said, feeling it was time to cut to the chase, and see if she was prone to jealousy and violence as easily as she was prone to a sense of entitlement.

"He pumped my stomach years ago. He was fresh out of medical school then."

"And when did you marry him?"

Nostalgia swept over her face. "I started dating him right after, and we got married a few months later."

"Did you know of any problems he was having? Anybody threatening him or calling the house all the time?" Martin asked.

"Eric was promiscuous, but he never hung onto them, although I'm sure they wanted to hang onto him. As far as the other stuff goes, I don't know. I was at my mother's all of last week, right up to the night he was killed. We hadn't seen a whole lot of each other lately."

How convenient, Martin thought. "Was infidelity a one-way or a two-way street in your house?"

"You can't be this conventional, Chief. I mean, I'm nothing like my husband was, but I did have other lovers besides my husband. Everyone does. Don't you?"

Martin didn't answer the question but was aware of his wedding band. Her flippancy about universal infidelity began to boil his blood. "Do the names William Delaney or Peter Dunnelo mean anything to you, Mrs. Strogg?"

"Peter went to Harvard with Eric. Why?" Her air of stupid unconcern dissipated.

"We found his body this morning. How about William Delaney?" Martin asked.

"No, I don't know Dr. Delaney. I'm not a suspect, am I, Chief?" She appeared sobered now.

"But you know he was a physician."

"It was in the paper, right?"

"Could you tell me where you were up until this past Wednesday morning?" he asked, ignoring her comment about *The Times Herald-Record* headline. He wasn't certain if there was anything north of the neck besides nips and tucks, never mind if the ditz could even read.

"I already told you, I was at my mother's house in New York City." Diane hesitated. "I was there for a week."

"Did you drive yourself there?"

"Yes, of course I drove."

"And what time did you leave to come back to Goshen?"

"Around midnight on Tuesday."

"What time did you arrive at your home?"

"I went through this already with one of your officers, and with the State Police Wednesday morning," she said.

"I just want to refresh my memory."

"About 2 AM."

"Was it crowded at that time? The traffic, I mean. Do you remember?"

"It wasn't bad."

"And what time did you call the police?"

She paused. "It wasn't until after 4 AM."

"Where does your mother live in New York City?"

"On the Lower East Side."

"And can anyone verify that you left at midnight?"

"I understand what you're trying to do, but I didn't do this. Sure, I waited an awfully long time to call you guys, but I didn't know what to do. Christ, I just found my husband in bed with the town whore."

"Was your husband dead when you found him?"

"What?" she asked. "Yes, of course he was."

"How did you arrive at that conclusion?"

"He was shot!"

"Not always a definitive means to an end, Mrs. Strogg," Martin said.

"What the hell does that mean?"

"What I mean is, did he have a pulse, did you check for one?" Martin stood up and glared down at her. Her referral to Paulina had stoked the fire inside him and he could feel his pulse throbbing in his neck.

"I'm not a doctor, Chief!"

"But you were married to one, and now you want me to believe you have no idea how to tell if someone is alive or dead?"

"Am I under arrest?" she asked, completing the metamorphosis from lackadaisical to near-hysterical. "Do you honestly think that I killed Eric?"

"You've told me you had almost no feelings for your husband when he was alive, and you've demonstrated you have no feelings for him now that he's dead. You and your friend act like my presence here is some kind of social call." He paused. "Do you have anything you want to tell me, Mrs. Strogg?" He unfastened the leather security guard on his gun belt. It would be improbable he'd need the weapon, but her friend Wendy was, after all, out of his immediate sight. "Or do you really want me to believe that you may have been the last person to see your husband alive? Because your hesitance in calling, plus your attitude today, sure makes a strong argument for that."

"You played along with me just now, didn't you?" she asked. "While you tricked me into telling you what you wanted to hear. This is one hell of a set-up. Did that shrink you had talk to me coach you on how to set me up? What tiny little pricks you men are." The volume of her voice brought her friend back into the room.

"I didn't have to trick it out of you. I'll ask you one last time.

Is there anything you would like to tell me?"

"You son of a bitch, I would have played the grieving little brokenhearted bitch if I'd known that's what you wanted to see. I didn't kill my husband. I'm not telling you another damn thing." Her screaming had also carried through the room's open windows, and out into the street, to where the state trooper was sitting in his cruiser.

"Chief Martin?" the trooper called from the other side of the front door.

"Get in here," Martin beckoned and the trooper entered.

"Get the hell out of my house," Wendy barked, and began flailing at the trooper while Diane continued to swear at Martin.

"Diane Strogg, I'm placing you in protective custody until I can get a handle on what's going on here," Martin said.

"You're arresting me?" Diane bellowed in disbelief.

"I'm bringing you in for questioning and for your own protection. This isn't an arrest."

"Why don't you fuck off! My own protection, horseshit. This is harassment," Diane screamed.

"You don't have probable cause, and you know it. She's not going anywhere with you. I'll have your fucking badge," Wendy called out.

"We can do this with or without handcuffs, but make no mistake, you're going," Martin said to Diane, ignoring Wendy.

"Please calm down, ma'am," the trooper advised Wendy.

"I'm not talking to you, scumbag. I want to call my lawyer. Wendy, call Harold," Diane said.

"Mrs. Roginson can't call your attorney, because she's coming along for the ride," Martin said, motioning for the trooper to move Wendy to his cruiser.

Both women were screaming at Martin, but a small portion of his helplessness was evaporating. He wasn't sure if they'd been involved in the killings or not, but he was suspicious, and that was all he had to be. He would call District Attorney Owens and let him take it from there. At the very least, the press would get off his butt for not doing anything. A suspect, whether it turned out to be correct or not, was a positive sign in the eyes of the press, and getting the vultures off his back turned out to be a bigger priority than he could have ever imagined.

Following the trooper downtown, Martin took the two women inside and locked them into one of the station's small rooms. He told his dispatcher to keep an eye on them, sent the trooper to the Dunnelo site, and headed for Dr. Delaney's residence.

———

The ride between the police station and Delaney's house was blessedly short and didn't give Martin a chance to think about what he'd just done. He was hoping there was no one in the house except for Connie Robuck. Martin was no longer in the mood to deal with anyone but those directly involved.

Rain was falling in lazy sheets, and he could see Connie waiting for him at the side door.

"Heard you pulling up," she said, holding an old screen door open for him. She was dressed in loose blue jeans and a blouse that matched the red in her hair. She led him through the side foyer and into a bright green and white kitchen where a natural wood table and six chairs were sitting in the corner of the large eat-in room.

"Nice house," Martin remarked, looking away from her bloodshot eyes and staring at the high tin ceiling.

"Thanks. It took me almost two years to get it right."

"You did it?"

"That surprises you?"

"Well, I guess so."

"I work at the lumber yard, you know, and my father was a carpenter."

"Well, then, it doesn't surprise me."

"So what can I help you with, Chief?"

"I just wanted to ask you some more questions. I realize you've probably been asked most of them before, but if you could indulge me, I'd appreciate it."

"Of course. Can I get you some coffee?"

"No, I'm just fine," he said. "You found the body?"

A runaway tear fell over her cheek and onto her lips. She nodded. It was both saddening and heartening to see someone with normal feelings on such a matter.

"I'm very sorry," he offered, dialing himself down a notch. She nodded. "I'm all right."

"You were supposed to meet him Wednesday for lunch?" Martin asked.

"Yes, we had reservations at Catherine's downtown. I sat there for an hour before I left to see what was the matter."

"And what time was that?"

"Twelve-thirty."

"How long had you two been dating?"

"A little over a year. He asked me out after he'd hired me to do some work on the house."

"Did you have any plans to get married?"

"I moved in with him last month, so I guess it was getting serious, but we hadn't really talked about it."

"Do you know of anyone who would've wanted to hurt him?"

"No, of course not. He was a kitten. Even with what he did in the service, he was always a kitten."

"He served in the military?" Martin asked.

"The Marines. That's how he paid his way through school."

"Was he getting any weird mail or telephone calls. Pranks?"

"Not that I know of, but he had office lines as well as the ones here at home. Whether someone was bothering him at work or not, I don't know. He never mentioned it to me. I can't believe this happened to him. He was so trained, you know. A kitten, but a kitten with claws."

Martin decided to get off the topic for a moment, changing the discussion to something less painful. "I'd love to see the house if I could, to get an idea of what kind of work you do."

"I'd like that. It came out so nice, and William rarely showed it off," She said. "The living room is my favorite. How about we start there?"

"Great," Martin said, following her into the large room dominated by wood and striking paint.

"The paint was William's idea, bold isn't it?" she said, acknowledging his wide eyes. "I milled the Wainscoting and crown myself. The floor is actually old panels from a Warwick barn; the original floor was totally infested."

"What's over there?" Martin asked, noticing a gap in the paneling along the far wall.

"Ah, that's William's study," Connie said, and opened the

tall mahogany door leading into Delaney's personal study. "The door is pressure latched, so that it's hidden when the door's closed. He loved mystery novels, so I built him a secret room like the ones in his books."

Martin's jaw dropped. He'd missed this room during his initial visit with the state police. The study walls were packed with photographs, citations, diplomas, medals, and letters. It was decorated to inspire rather than portray a self-centered man. He'd been a well decorated veteran. There were pictures of Delaney with a past President, and three letters from two different presidents, Christmas cards from senators and Marine Corp officers. There were also academic citations from Harvard University Medical School. It was the kind of room Martin could spend a day in, just looking around.

An impressive mahogany desk dominated the center. One wall was a display of Civil War pistols and swords. Another was packed to the breaking point with texts and novels, and there were photographs everywhere. One brass-framed picture in particular caught Martin's eye. It was of four men standing outside a house Martin recognized, but could not immediately place.

"What's this picture of?" he asked.

"Oh, that's William's little social organization. Those are the founding members. They have an office over on Greenwich Avenue. You know, across the street from the old hospital."

"Oh yeah, right. Now I recognize it. What do you mean by his social organization?"

"It's some kind of social get-together thing, but you have to be a doctor to join. I guess everyone needs a club, right? I don't know any of the men in it. I never really thought to ask, and

William never really thought to tell."

"Would you mind if I took this photo?" Martin said, and acknowledged he'd just found a big piece of the puzzle.

"No, go ahead, as long as I get it back."

"Sure, sure. Listen, you've been a real help, and if you plan on going anywhere will you promise to take advantage of the protection outside?"

"I will," she said, sounding her young age for the first time.

Martin followed her back through the house to the side door and left. The screen door and inner door closed and bolted behind him. The rain was now being pushed by a stiff breeze and the sky was growing darker and darker.

November, Martin thought, as he lowered his head away from the sky and climbed into his truck. Why does it insist on raining for a month straight every year at this time?

District Attorney Owens was seated at a long table in a small room at the Goshen Police Station. He was questioning the two women Martin had brought into custody. They seemed calmer when Martin entered and motioned for Owens.

Standing outside the room with the door ajar, Martin pulled the photograph from his coat and showed it to Owens.

"Why'd you bring these two in?" Owens said, taking the photo but ignoring it.

"Never mind that now. I just came from Delaney's. This got overlooked Wednesday."

"Why do you hate me, Tom?" Owens demanded. "You must. Do you know how much trouble you brought down on us, bringing in those two fools?"

Martin took the photo back and pointed to each man. "That's Delaney, that's Dunnelo, and that's Strogg. They all belonged to some social organization over on Greenwich Avenue across from the old hospital."

"So who's the fourth guy?" Owens asked.

"Don't know."

"Who'd you get the photo from?"

"Delaney's girlfriend, but she claims not to know who any of them are."

"You believe her?"

"Yeah."

Owens stared at Martin for a moment. "Have you found a fourth body?"

"Nope."

"And if you don't?"

"Then I say Mr. Mystery is our number-one suspect. Maybe he's killing all of the organization members. If we find him dead, then someone else is killing them. But this photo is the key, I'm sure of it."

"That doesn't sound too far off base. I don't mind telling you, Tom, I was worried about how you'd handle Paulina and this mess. But you seem to have your feet back under you again."

"It's an illusion I'm afraid. I'm just trying like hell to block it out, you know?"

"I guess you'll be wanting to snoop around over there?" Owens asked, changing gears.

"Good grasp of the obvious, Owens," Martin said.

"I'll try and get a warrant for you tonight, but no promises. In the meantime what do you want me to do with Tweedle-dumb and Tweedle-dumber."

"They're a real pair, ain't they?"

"But they probably had nothing in the world to do with this. In fact, they don't care enough one way or the other," Owens said, pulling the door to the room closed.

"Is there any way we can hold onto them for more than the usual amount of time?" Martin asked.

"Without a formal charge? You know the law as well as I do."

"They're going to sue me anyhow, so let's keep them for now. By tomorrow we should know one way or another. The other three bodies have turned up pretty quick. No reason to think the fourth won't. They're safer with us, anyhow. Besides, the media knows about them and shutting up that group of piranhas has become monumentally important."

"Okay, but Tom, give those two what they want. If you don't, Roginson's husband will crawl so far up your ass you'll be screaming for a proctologist. He's a big-time lawyer, you know?"

"You're a lawyer, Owens."

"Little *L*, as opposed to big *L*, Tom. There's a difference."

13

When Martin returned to his station later that Saturday afternoon, he was met by the familiar mob of reporters.

Grinning, as though he'd gotten the upper hand in some secret game they were playing, Martin gave them enough of his news to whet their appetite. "A short time ago we discovered a connection among the deaths in the physician case. We've identified three potential suspects; we haven't made any arrests, but we do have two residents in protective custody due to concerns for their safety. Thank you," Martin said, and disappeared through the station's front door amid a flurry of new questions.

Martin moved behind his decrepit desk and dispatched Officer Gold to the morgue. His next call was to Officer Myers.

"Go ahead, Chief?" Myers finally answered.

"How are things going inside Dunnelo's apartment?"

"A mass of people are running around trying to uncover what's going on. One of the tenants from Dunnelo's building got herself cornered by the press as she was leaving for work," Myers said.

"So everyone knows Dunnelo is the third?"

"It's a safe bet, Chief."

"Stay put, someone will relieve you eventually," Martin said, knowing full well that eventually was a vague term at best.

Then he tried Officer Light, who was having no luck producing promising leads.

He stood up and walked outside into the dispatcher's office toward the copy machine. The dispatcher was on the phone trying to reassure a Goshen resident her husband wasn't in any danger of being hurt, and that they would send someone over to check on them from time to time. When she pressed the keypad disconnecting that particular call, she depressed another key and began talking to someone else concerned about safety.

Martin made two copies of the Delaney photograph, one for himself and another for the file he was building on the case. Then he made three enlargements of the unknown man; one for himself, one for the file, and another for the state police.

Back in his office, he pulled out a long and packed filing cabinet drawer and slipped the copies into a file labeled "October Homicide," and then returned to his desk.

Paperwork, he had decided years ago, was something he could do without. No matter how distasteful a job was, if there were no trees involved, it was a good thing. He no longer believed in that philosophy.

Swinging in his swivel chair, Martin coasted across the chipping tile floor to his fax machine. He placed the copied photograph into the track of the fax, dialed a seven-digit number, and sent the photo.

He turned back to the desk and called David McElroy of the state police.

"I've sent you a fax," he told McElroy. "It's a picture of a guy that's somehow connected to the killings down here."

"You should have taken it over to Dunnelo's apartment building. The Crime Unit has a system hookup in their van. They could have patched into the computers here and found out who it is."

"Well, I won't bother you with it, then. Just keep it for your file." Martin felt embarrassed that he didn't know anything about a Crime Unit's range of equipment.

"Listen, that preliminary evaluation is almost done from what I hear," McElroy said. "Keep an eye out for a big son-of-a-bitch. With the aid of this wonderful autumn, Hudson Valley soak-fest, the boys found a nice indentation on the rug inside the sliding glass door at Strogg's. It definitely doesn't belong to the Stroggs."

"How big?" Martin asked, excited by the news.

"At least as tall as me, a bit lighter, but he'd stick out."

"Thanks," Martin said.

He was anxious to find out who the mystery man was, so he grabbed his coat and the photo from the fax machine tray. As he was slipping his arms through the sleeves, his office phone beeped. It was Debra Chen, the dispatcher.

"There's a guy on the line I think you should talk to. He sounds like he's full of shit, but you better make sure."

"Full of shit, huh? What's he want?"

"Sorry, Tom. He says he has information about these deaths, but we've gotten a couple of those. You know, just nuts who want attention. I mean, I took down their names and everything but I didn't take them seriously."

"But you're taking this guy seriously?"

"Yes."

"Did the electrician from the phone company come and fix the Hewlett yet?" Martin asked, referring to the station's communication system.

"Nope."

"So we still can't trace any of these lunatics?"

"You want to talk to him?"

"Put him through," Martin said as he eased back into his chair. He slid open the center drawer of his desk and withdrew a small pad of paper and a pen.

The man on the phone had a deep, wavering voice. "Is this Chief of Police Martin?" he asked.

"Yes, who is this?"

"That's not important. What I know is very important."

"And what is it that you know?"

"I'll run this conversation, if you don't mind. I don't have to talk to you."

Martin was silent.

"So I see you found Dunnelo?" the man asked.

"Thanks to the media, everyone knows." Martin was cold.

"True. Those reporters are such a pain in the ass. Always have their noses where they don't belong."

"Are you going to tell me something? Because I'm an awfully busy man."

"Busy," the man said with devoted mockery. "You have no idea what's going on, do you? What did Connie Robuck tell you? It must have been something interesting. From the look on your face when you left Delaney's house, you'd think you solved all the world's problems."

"You were at the house?" The man had Martin's full attention now.

"I've been following you around for a while. So what did she tell you? That all of the victims knew each other? No, that couldn't be it, because they never met her, not once."

"I can't divulge that kind of information," Martin said, staring at the photograph and focusing on the fourth man in the picture, the mystery man.

"You're not at liberty, right? Buddy, you don't know jack about what you're involved in. Now, what the fuck did she tell you?"

"She gave me a photograph of four men, four members of an organization. Three were brutally killed, and one is talking to me on the phone, planning on feeding me some line of bullshit in an attempt to implicate someone else. How warm am I getting?"

The man tried to speak, but Martin continued. "Now, listen to me, Doc. I know a lot more than you think, and what I think is you killed all of these men. I don't know why you did it, but that's only a matter of time. Why not turn yourself in and stop all this clowning around?"

The man found the question humorous. "Chief of Police Tom Martin, both parents killed in a boating accident when he was in grade school, raised by his uncle whose strong-armed tactics and personal assurances to the village trustees got a completely inexperienced man appointed Chief of Police. Holds both a Bachelor's and Master's degree. Is divorced from his wife and lives on Murray Avenue, in Goshen, New York. You don't know me, and you couldn't catch me. Hell, I've had a professional killer on my ass for a week, and I'm still alive. You don't even know my name.

That picture you have, that's me, all right, but it makes you none the wiser. I didn't kill my friends, but I could help you crack this wide open if you'd take your head out of your ass long enough to listen to me. I could make your damn career. All you have to do is trust me and check something out. Then you'll have at least an idea of how big this thing is."

Martin bit his lip. Not that he had nothing to say, he just felt it was better to let the man go on. He'd been too abrupt so far, seeing as this was the first real pay dirt he'd hit in this case.

"There's a woman who lives in Washington, D.C. She has a loft at 118 E Street, Apartment 302. Her name is Angela Wilme, and she was killed by the same man who killed my three friends here in Goshen."

"You've got to be kidding me. Where did you come up with a story like this?" Martin was unconvinced.

"You have to believe me. The man who is doing this is still here in Goshen, looking for me. I'm the only one left who knows why this is happening."

"Why don't you tell me what you think is happening?"

"Why don't you prove to me I can trust you by following up on this for me? Then we'll talk."

"What makes you think there will be any trust? If there's a dead woman at this address, I'll just think you killed her, too," Martin said.

"That's not really important at the moment. What you think of me, I mean. What you'll learn should convince you of what's true. I'm not guilty, and if you check this out, you'll see that."

"Why didn't you report this to the Washington police?" Martin asked.

"Trust an organization of that size to help, that's a joke. The only reason I'm talking to you is you're small-time. You're out of the loop, out of the game. If there's one pure cop in the country, you would have to be him. If I'd called D.C., they'd have traced and bagged me already. You're barely in the twentieth century," he said and hung up.

Martin stared at the phone and then at the scribble he'd made on the pad. He stood, slipped the pad back in the drawer, and headed for Dunnelo's apartment.

———————

Only after Martin had stood in the pouring rain next to the open door of the state police's Crime Unit van for ten minutes did an investigator finally get up from the small terminal bolted to the inner wall, bend over, and tear a piece of paper from a secured printer before handing it to Martin.

"Photo identification makes things so easy," the investigator said, and patted Martin on the back as he hopped out of the van, closed the rear door, and went back into Dr. Dunnelo's apartment.

Martin ducked his head to avoid the lenses of the media as he walked toward his truck. It was warm inside, and he sat studying the sheet. The man's name was Dr. Robert E. Greene. If he wasn't lying about the professional killer, he was a perfect target. He was a young doctor who lived in town, and a member of the local organization. Then again, he could fit the profile of the killer just as well.

He wanted to check out the Greenwich Avenue address, and waiting for a warrant was pissing him off. They never waited for warrants in the movies. The justice system was instant-pudding-and-microwave-fast in that other reality. Cops just barged in to find the bad guy sitting around with his thumb up his ass, waiting to get caught.

Martin began to consider calling Washington just for the sake of being able to tell Greene, the next time he called, that he'd followed his instructions. That Greene had known so much about his private life bothered him. In fact, every element of the case was beginning to annoy him, and as he pulled back into the station, he was relieved to find that the press had vacated for a bigger and juicier story. He fleetingly wondered what it was.

Director Kenneth Geehern pulled up to one of the perimeter guard booths, flashed his identification badge, and drove onto the White House property. The light-colored pavement was wet in spots from the overnight storm, and the tires of his Crown Victoria made sloshing sounds as he drove to the top of the driveway. He had barely entered the side door when the president and two Secret Service agents came down the long hall toward him. President Hanland was commencing his daily chaperoned walk across the South Lawn.

The president was an outdoors man; he was clad in jeans and a Polo sweater. He signaled for the two agents to give him a little more privacy. They separated to flanking positions but were never so far enough they couldn't provide a human shield in a matter of seconds.

"So where are you with Mitchell?" the president asked, not looking at Geehern. He was a serious and poised man, very educated and well read. He had an uncanny ability to see through things, and though he was new to his current job, he was a veteran of the political game.

"He was dirty as hell," Geehern said. "About a half million dollars a year for the past five. Turns out the IRS had him under investigation, but either couldn't make anything of it or were told to stop pursuing. Whichever, he got away with it. It's going to scream of campaign finance reform in the media."

"Just great," Hanland said. "Do we know who killed him?"

"No, sir. We have suspects, but nothing concrete as of yet."

"Who do we suspect?"

"There are a few groups on the pro-choice side of things. They're the ones with the most recent grudge against him. They have the financial means to pull something like this off, and both sides have the history for it."

The president glanced at him. "I don't buy the abortion option. Who else?"

"The three others have to do with previous involvements between Mitchell and the Senate Appropriations Committee. The first is an energy company that was up for a hundred-million-dollar contract two years ago. Mitchell buried their bid in favor of another company. The second was a piece of labor legislation he killed, putting a stranglehold on two unions. The third is a defense contract he turned down, and it cost four companies billions," Geehern said.

"So how long until we nail one of them down?"

"We're still investigating, trying to sift through suspects. The man had a lot of history on the Hill, a lot of it was bad. It's not going to be an overnight success, but we're closing in on it."

"I need this situation taken care of. I have both personal and national concerns I would much rather have everyone focusing their attention on. His death has superceded everything. Frankly, Congress breaks for the holidays shortly and their attention has also been diverted toward fears about their safety, as I'm sure your office has heard. I need them concentrating on work, concentrating on the cogs of government. Find me a culprit. Allay the fears of the legislature and the media, and do it quick. Am I making myself clear, Director Geehern?" The President stopped walking and placed a dominating hand on Geehern's shoulder. The move made his skin crawl.

"Yes, sir," Geehern said. He had wanted to comment but held his tongue.

"Good. I'll expect to hear from you shortly. This way we all come out looking capable instead of expendable," he said, and moved across the lawn with the agents away from the director. He really hadn't wanted a response.

"The cogs of government," Geehern mumbled as he walked the short distance back across the lawn toward his car. Even with the sun beating down on the manicured green lawn, it was chilly. "Where do these guys come from?"

Geehern hadn't been the director of the FBI for long. His predecessor, Carl Major, had been dismissed due to an inter-agency communication problem and an incompetence issue within the FBI. Congress and the previous president had appointed Geehern as Director and placed on his shoulders the responsibility of cleaning up an extensive mess and bringing the FBI into the twenty-first century.

For the last eighteen months, he'd done his best to identify the problems and eliminate them. He'd done a lot of firing and promoting and spending, the results of which were an FBI with an experienced upper level and a greatly inexperienced lower level, along with next-generation equipment that very few could operate or implement effectively.

Since his arrival from the Chicago field office, he had acquired a near-psychic knack for seeing through the political smokescreen covering Washington. What the current president had just asked him to do was find a scapegoat for the Mitchell killing, or part with his job. He wasn't ready to part with the power he had, or listen to the president's unlawful request.

Geehern was serious about several things in his life: his golf game, his wife, and his power position within the United States government. Very often it was a balancing act among the three, but he wasn't about to let someone else dictate his personal path or his professional one, least of all a man who, with any luck, wouldn't be around to bother him in three years.

14

The long cement walkway stretching along the rear section of the hotel was deserted when Black stepped into the cold air to investigate what he'd thought had been someone lingering outside his room.

"I know I heard someone," he muttered, staring at his neighbor's room.

He reached out for the handle and rattled the door in its frame. It was locked, and looking over the portion of Goshen he could see, he saw that everything appeared quiet and locked up for the night.

He returned to his room and continued to repair the damage done by his subduing of the two Washington chaperones, who were still propped against the bathroom toilet, sleeping off their syringe cocktail. Black realigned the displaced mattress, turned the heavy wood table upright again, and pushed the chairs into the imprinted marks they had created over the years in the carpeting. The room was finally back to normal, but there was still one thing left to do.

With one of the men thrown over his shoulder, Black glanced down the empty rear stretch, and left the room, heading for the sedan parked just on the other side of the walkway. The trunk was open and he dumped the man into the deep compartment. The man's head landed square on the lip of the rear quarter panel with a blunt thud. Black pushed him sideways and forced him in.

Leaning over, he rolled him toward the back wall. The second body required some judicious footwork, but after it was secure, he broke the key off in the lock and disabled the keyless entry, so the compartment couldn't be opened without some trouble.

A loud pulsing tone drew his attention back toward the room. It was coming from underneath the bed.

The chaperone's leather briefcase was ringing. Pulling it from under the bed, Black flipped two brass latches and opened the case, exposing an expensive piece of custom hardware. Fastened to the lid was a flat screen and a small pouch containing various supplies. The floor section of the case possessed a micro-terminal and a telephone similar to his Motorola. Black picked up the phone.

"You two idiots let the damn phone ring long enough." The client's voice was harsh.

"Well, I'll have to be more prompt next time." Black was calm.

"Mr. Dresden?"

"Your two idiots are thinking about their loyalties. You could say they're sleeping on it."

"What?"

"So what is it you wanted to talk about? Maybe I can help."

"What happened to them, Mr. Dresden?"

"They foolishly believed they had something uncontrollable under control," Black said cryptically. "You underestimated me."

"It seems I may have done just that. I'm surprised you're still there to answer my call."

"You've made many mistakes where I'm concerned. I'm a professional, and I've never left a job incomplete. You should have relied on my reputation. You could have spared your men the amount of damage drugs like the ones I used cause."

"Inconsequential. It was far more important for me to be a hundred percent certain the contracts were complete. I couldn't participate myself for obvious reasons, so I sent them. They had two sets of eyes and drivers' licenses, so they fit the bill. I've lost nothing."

"Why are you calling?" Black asked. The man's voice was beginning to sound like a vindictive teacher's fingernails on the blackboard.

"To find out the status of our operation. Now I'll have to rely on your interpretation."

"The three physicians connected to Greene are dead," Black said.

"Did you find Greene?"

"No. But I will."

"So what of this Physicians for Social Responsibility Organization."

"That information is in the car, as is the material I gathered from Greene's offices."

"Where are you? Still at the same hotel?"

"I'm not going to answer that one, and I'm not staying in this town forever. If Greene doesn't show soon, I'm leaving. I've already got my neck stuck out too far."

"Greene's bound to crack, and when he does he'll have to trust someone. He'll go to the cops. Keep the briefcase with you so I'll be able to keep in contact. Did you get the confirmation of the deposit?"

"Yes, but I don't understand why you paid me when you had me somewhat under the gun. You might have been able to press me."

"At no time did I consider not paying you. And when you finish this job, you can go back to Quebec. We aren't going to interrupt your retirement."

Black replaced the receiver and closed and latched the leather case. He removed the silencer from his 10mm and replaced it with a new one. The baffles were worn after the Delaney kill, and it was barely quieter with than without.

The local justice, Earl Calc, lived just outside the village of Goshen, in one of the more rural sections of town. When District Attorney Owens came knocking on a weekend night to get a warrant, there was no argument. Familial commitment was one of the benefits of the small-town criminal justice system.

Calc was standing under the fluorescent lamps of his open garage, arranging tools into a red Craftsman tool chest, when he looked up to see Owens stamping the mud from his shoes. "So what brings our friendly neighborhood DA all the way out here at this hour?"

"When are you going to pave your driveway?" Owens said.

"In the spring, now that the house is restored," Calc said.

"Tom thinks he's got a lead on the murders," Owens said, stopping Calc from his busy work.

"I knew that boy would crack it."

"There's a business over on Greenwich across from the old hospital, and all three of the victims were members. Tom found a photo in Delaney's house, a picture of the four founding members."

"Four?"

"I know, we haven't found a fourth. Tom thinks, and I agree, we will, or this unknown man is involved."

"You boys need a warrant," Calc said, motioning for Owens to follow him into his house.

A short hallway led from the garage to a large family room dominated by a Brunswick pool table. A Wurlitzer was off in the corner playing an old big-band song Owens recognized but didn't know the name of.

"This came out really nice. Really nice," Owens said as he looked around the room.

"Benny Goodman," Calc barked, answering the attorney's unspoken question. He entered a small den off the hallway to get the paperwork. "Yes, it turned out nice. My wife would hate it, but she's not here to bitch about it."

Owens walked around the paneled walls, staring at bookshelves covered with diplomas, discharge papers, and photographs of children, grandchildren, cars, and endless rows of novels. Dartboards and an impressive collection of Budweiser beer lights hung on the walls alongside posters satirizing New York City and college life. A horseshoe bar separated the Brunswick from a couch, coffee table, and wide-screen Sony television. It was a young person's room, not one you'd expect to see in an elderly man's home.

"How's he doing anyway?" Calc said, and handed over the warrant.

"I honestly don't know. He's not the kind to show what he's feeling, but I get the sense he's near the edge," Owens said, and looked over the paperwork and stuffed it into his coat pocket. "Thanks for this. Tom's probably pulling his hair out waiting for the thing."

"Damn shame about Paulina, sweet young girl," Calc said. "Keep me up on the investigation, will you? I got an unsettling call from a doctor friend of mine who is concerned. The man is medication-happy, but his chemistry has kept me alive longer than I've deserved to be. So keep me abreast, eh?" Calc said, following Owens back into the garage.

———————

Martin usually spent autumn Sundays attending church, helping there with some sort of function, and then going home to watch football. But since Owens had come through with the warrant, he planned on searching the PSR property.

Before that though, he wanted to call the D.C. Police Department before his new friend Dr. Greene called again. Martin wasn't sure it was a sound move, and he was positive he'd look like a fool if Greene turned out to be feeding him a line of bull, but he called them anyway.

It was a little after ten in the morning, and a stiff, hot beam of sunlight was slicing through the slits in his office blinds. His door was standing wide open, and the hallway was dark. In the station's outer room, the ceiling fan was making enough noise that Martin would have wagered a week's salary it would die or fall off the ceiling. The two choices had been a running wager in the department for years. However, it would probably remain fastened and running until long after he'd retired.

A Washington dispatcher answered after seven rings and, after a five-minute wait, connected him to a shift commander.

"Lieutenant Dougherty. Can I help you?" The woman's voice was low and strong.

"This is Chief of Police Martin with the Goshen Police Department in New York. I'd like to report a homicide tip given to me by a suspect we have up here in a triple murder investigation," Martin said.

"What's the name of the suspect, Chief?"

"His name is Dr. Robert Greene."

"And the name of the victim."

"Angela Wilme. She lives at 118 E Street, in Apartment 302," Martin said.

"You've got the wrong precinct, first of all, but I can take care of that. Do you have anything else you can give me?"

"Nope, that's all he told me, and now I've told you. I'd appreciate a call if you could one way or the other. Greene is supposed to be calling me back."

"You don't have him in custody?"

"Not yet," Martin said, knowing how bad it sounded.

"We'll need to talk to him once you have him, Chief."

"Of course," Martin said.

Outside, he stood in the sunshine for a moment before climbing into the Bronco and heading for home. It had been one of those wet weeks, and Martin was glad for the respite. He wanted it to burn the memories of Paulina's death from his mind.

15

When Detective John Cartwell got the call to follow up on a homicide tip, he was sitting in the living room of his two-bedroom ranch, northeast of Capitol Hill. His wife was trying to get him to commit to the idea of having both sides of the family over for Thanksgiving. He wasn't in any mood to listen to her, or talk about their parents, so he welcomed the call from his precinct.

He got into his Chevy and drove toward Chinatown to follow up on a call made to his Anacostia station-house by a New York Chief of Police. The police channel on his scanner was bustling. "They must be bogged down to bug me on a Sunday," he mumbled.

Sunday was usually the best time to attempt something in D.C. The tourists filed out early to get home, and the new batch wouldn't arrive until late that evening or sometime Monday, so there was a visible lull for most of the day.

Getting off Maryland Avenue and swinging around onto Massachusetts Avenue, he made pretty good time to Chinatown. When he reached 118 E Street, the building and its sidewalk looked quiet. The only real sign of life was the lone police cruiser idling next to the curb outside the building's front door.

Inside, a medium-sized lobby held a staircase rising to the top floor of the building. Steel doors locked off the climb and the entrance to the first-floor hallway, but there was a single square window in the upper-center of each door, and Cartwell peered down the first-floor hallway. It was deserted.

A long series of thin, stainless steel mailboxes and a brass call panel were fitted into the wall next to him. Apartment 302's box was jammed to the breaking point with mail.

It was the apartment he was here to check, Cartwell acknowledged, and pressed the button on the panel labeled "Super."

"Yes?" a man answered.

"Police, sir. We received a tip about an apartment in your building."

"What?"

"I need to take a look, sir?"

Cartwell heard the slam of a door down the first floor hall, and he moved back to the window to inspect the approaching man, who looked as though he'd been dragged out of bed.

The steel door opened and a short, round man stepped into the lobby, holding the door as he stood in the threshold. "Can I see some identification?" he asked.

Cartwell displayed a badge fastened to the inside of his wallet.

"Got a warrant?"

"I just want to take a look, sir."

"Which floor?" the super asked.

"Third, apartment 302."

"Only two up there, had to be either 301 or 302," he said, pulling a heavy set of keys from his bathrobe pocket. He unlocked the stairwell door, and began to climb the flight of stairs.

"Who lives in 302?" Cartwell asked.

"Miss Wilme."

"This is the place then."

"I hope she's all right. Real nice looking lady."

Cartwell followed the man to 302, hoping that when they rang the bell, the lady would answer and he wouldn't have to do anything other than look like a dork. But his nose was telling him something else.

The super knocked on the door for a solid minute and then slid a key into the lock and opened the door. A wave of decay rushed at them. Cartwell extended his arm across the short man's chest, pushing him out of the doorway.

"Stay here. I'm not done with you," Cartwell commanded, and stepped into the apartment. A long hallway led into the master bedroom, where a deep gray corpse was lying on the bed, face-up in a small stain of dry blood.

"Shit," he said in a low voice, then looked back down the hallway. The apartment had been ransacked. But it was when Cartwell reached the living room that he had a strange feeling of similarity. Standing next to the entertainment wall unit, he put the pieces together.

"Mitchell," he muttered, and rushed down the hallway back to the spare bedroom. A small personal computer sat on a desk; its hard drive was gone.

The televisions and stereo equipment had been left. The person had only taken information.

Back outside, Cartwell pulled Angela's door shut, took out a pen and notebook, and wrote down the building superintendent's name, telephone, and apartment number.

"Who else lives on this floor?" Cartwell asked, staring down the long hall. There were only two apartments. "Awfully strange they didn't pickup on the smell."

"I don't know that I should be telling you anything about my tenants," the super said, puffing out his chest. "I watch *Law and Order* you know. You need paperwork to violate people's privacy."

"Well, Mr. Must-See-TV, a warrant is pending and if you want to do things this way, I'll be only too happy to show you how far-off base those horseshit shows are," Cartwell said, placing a fatherly hand onto the man's shoulder, and leading him back down the hall toward the staircase.

The superintendent's obstinance seemed to melt away.

"Because unlike those hour sound-bytes, if you interfere in real life I'm allowed to arrest you, throw you in jail, burn you at the stake, and maybe even sacrifice you to the gods of fashion," Cartwell said. "I'd have to check on the last part, but I'm pretty sure it's legal." He was in no mood to debate the Fourth Amendment with a man who wore a pink shower robe.

He called down to the street and told the two officers sitting outside the building to seal the place off, then called Lieutenant Roy Nagel. It was almost the same conversation they'd had from Mitchell's home. Nagel said it was federal jurisdiction if there was reason to believe Wilme's death was connected to the senator's. The FBI would have to be notified and they would check on the relationship, if there was any.

Cartwell clipped the transceiver back to his belt and waited for the Crime Unit to arrive, and on a Sunday that could be one hell of a long wait. First he wished he hadn't stopped smoking, and then he wished he was at home debating his wife about Thanksgiving guests.

When the FBI was notified about the situation near Chinatown, Special Agent Williams and a rookie agent by the name of Grant departed for the scene. It took Williams only five minutes, and a brief discussion with Cartwell, to reach the conclusion that the similarities between the two scenes were too suspicious.

It was late Sunday evening by the time C.S.U. gave Williams their preliminary findings. He reached for his Nokia, and punched out Director Geehern's number with his fat fingers.

"Williams, what have you got for me?" Geehern began.

"Her name is Angela Wilme. D.C.P.D. got the tip from a New York Police Chief. He said she was connected to a suspect in a series of killings up there. It's the same killer as Mitchell, sir."

"C.S.U. confirms it?"

"They're certain."

"So what's the New York connection?"

"No idea."

"Do you think there may be something of value up there in New York?" Geehern asked.

"It's a possibility. It might save us a lot of unnecessary digging."

"So what about this guy connected to these New York murders? Any ideas what his story is?"

"No sir, the information the New York Chief gave the D.C. police was sketchy," Williams said.

"I want you to go up there personally. Find out what they've got, and don't take any flap from them. If you think it's worth something, copy it and bring it back with you. If it pans out for you there, don't be afraid to break out the whole shooting match. Who's there with you now?"

"Grant."

"Good. Take him along. Check in with the New York City office and let them know you're coming. You won't need their help right off, but it's procedure, so call them."

Williams hung up his cellular, slipping it into a blazer pocket as he followed the Crime Unit out of the building. Crossing E street, Williams and Grant walked the short distance to their red Mercury Grand Marquis nestled into a narrow alleyway. The alley descended toward an abandoned warehouse, and the car's roof was just visible from E Street.

Williams was the first to see the two men appear from the seclusion of the building's corner. One was short and stocky, but it was the icy confidence in his eyes that put Williams on guard. The second could have been Williams' twin; the build, the height, and he was no less striking than his companion.

Grant didn't see them until the shorter man had already drawn his silenced pistol and gunned Williams down. Grant went for his own weapon, but a second silenced shot threw his head back also.

The smaller man tucked away his weapon and swarmed over the fallen bodies, fishing for the keys to the Grand Marquis, the agents identification, wallets, and weapons. The taller man opened the lid of a nearby Dumpster and heaved the FBI agents' inside.

The shorter man was named Sampus and was already in the driver's seat with the engine running when the taller man, Dillon, moved away from the impromptu burial and joined his partner in the car.

The Library of Congress was a sea of students, tourists, and grade-school field-trippers, but Senator Braun found an empty terminal in the central room under the towering dome. It was a monstrous place filled with marble and paper, and the creaking of her chair echoed through the room, mixing with the choir of shuffling and whispering.

She looked at the clock on the far wall and gave herself thirty minutes. Fidgeting briefly with her wig to ensure no blond stragglers were showing, she logged onto the Senate Appropriations Committee's main menu and began scrolling through the current docket of the big three subcommittees.

She knew her search would set off the Capitol Hill Watchdogs, a group of Tweens relegated to the bowels of the Capitol Building. Their job was to compile reports on the access of information regarding the use of money within Congress. When she'd first became a senator, it had been a surprise to learn of the group, and the many others, who compile the whos, whens, and whats of information access around Washington. Back then, it had seemed an enormous waste of resources to her, but she had come to understand the usefulness of the reports.

Certain public information is, surprisingly, rarely accessed by the public. Braun wasn't certain if it was because the public didn't know, or didn't care. But it was only in these rarity areas where watchdogs had been posted.

Now, however, she was a bit frightened by them, because it meant that within a very short time, they would see the access of information, and it would be readily apparent what she was after.

She was about to log off when she caught sight of something out of the corner of her eye; a woman standing at the end of one of the stack aisles, just outside the periphery of the central room. It was more the way she was standing: Her hip was almost too relaxed into the shelf; she was almost too engrossed in the over-sized text she was holding.

Braun hastened her log-off and slipped the small pad of hotel stationery into the inner pocket of her camel coat. She double-checked her jeans pocket for the car keys and cash; they were both there. She stopped at an information booth to ask a young man a rhetorical question and hopefully get a good look at the woman, but she was gone. Moving along the periphery of the domed room and toward the exit, Braun caught sight of her again.

She was professionally dressed and had moved to a vantage point where she had a clear view of the exit. Her hand was raised to her mouth and she appeared to be speaking into the same device she'd seen the Secret Service use.

Outside, a rush of cold air hit her in the face, and she shoved her hands deep into her coat pockets, her hand closing around a small canister of pepper spray. She saw him across 1st Street, standing next to an idling gray sedan, the same sedan from the airport. The same man who'd been shadowing her for days.

"How'd they get here so quick," she muttered.

It had to be the Watchdogs or someone eavesdropping on their system.

Then again, maybe she'd never really lost them in the first place. This option made her skin crawl, because it meant they knew she was staying at the Holiday Inn, but she dismissed it. She was convinced her precautions had been careful enough. However, she was still going to have to give them the slip again, and she was less confident now, because the picture of who they were was coming into focus.

Sampus dropped the agents' possessions into a plastic bag and threw it underneath the driver's seat, and pulled two identifications from his jacket pocket. "I thought those two were never going to leave that bitch's apartment," Sampus said, handing a forged FBI badge to Dillon.

Dillon flipped the leather billfold open and inspected the identification bearing his photo and Agent Williams' statistics. "We really caught a break when Williams used his cellular," Dillon said, dislodging the Xybernaut wearable computer from his belt. The device was a fraction of the size of a notebook and just as powerful.

Dillon's had been equipped to eavesdrop on several electronic serial and mobile identification number combinations, one being Special Agent Williams.

"Amateurs," Sampus said. "You better make the call."

Dillon withdrew his own phone and dialed their employer. "Mr. Scaffiotelli?"

"You on a cellular or using a landline?"

"It's stolen, don't worry," Dillon said. "No way anyone could have the ESN."

"I like to worry. So give me only good news."

"The FBI knows about Wilme. What the hell's going on in New York?"

"I need you to go up to that shithole New York town and sort things out for me," Scaffiotelli said.

"Should've involved us from the start, sir," Dillon said.

"Ancient history can't be changed, only learned from."

"We're on our way."

They left immediately for New York. Driving took longer, but there was no paper trail in traveling by car and paying with cash.

———— ·•· ————

Martin was curled up on a basement sofa in his house on Murray Avenue. A dim lamp burned next to him as he slept, illuminating a small table, a bottle of Tylenol PM, and a ringing telephone shaped like Bill the Cat.

He reached over and picked the receiver-tongue out of the cradle-mouth.

"Hello?"

"Chief Martin?"

"Yes?"

"My name is John Cartwell. I'm a detective for the District of Columbia Police Department. You phoned us about a Miss Wilme."

"Yes?" Martin said, sitting up and shrugging off his sleepy disorientation.

"Well, she's dead, all right, and we'd like to have a talk with this mystery suspect. Do you have any information on him at all? We might be able to help you in your investigation."

"Like I told the commander I spoke with, I think he's a physician by the name of Robert Greene. I've got three dead doctors here who were all friends of his, but I don't think he killed them, or Wilme, for that matter. From everything I'm hearing, he just doesn't fit the profile, and to tell you the truth, I think he's being hunted by a professional. But I'm teamed up with the state police, and we're doing everything possible. We'll get him. Thanks for the call, Detective, and the offer." Martin hung up on the man. His response had been sharp but unplanned.

He believed Greene's story, for some reason. Probably because he'd never had a murderer in Goshen before. The residents were just not those kind of people. He could be wrong about Greene, he knew that. He just doubted it.

16

Martin crouched next to the cement patio rising to the front door of 118 Greenwich Avenue, his gun drawn. Officers Light and Gold had their backs pressed against the vinyl-sided wall.

A state policeman was standing on the patio in front of the door with a police entrance hammer. Looking across at the three men, he acknowledged Martin with a nod and swung the hammer's solid metal head against the handle. The door flew open.

Martin rushed in first. The state policeman was right behind him with the Goshen officers taking up the rear. They separated the house into four parts, with the state policeman rushing down a hallway extending from the door to the kitchen, Martin heading up the stairs to the second floor, and Gold and Light splitting in a left and right direction from the entrance.

"Up here," Martin yelled, and the other three men joined him in the threshold of a vault-style doorway. Inside was yet another ransacked room.

There were computers lying on the floor, their monitors' glass either cracked or sprayed across the expensive carpet. Four desks were overturned, and three of them had bullet holes replacing their top drawer locks. Long filing cabinets lined the same wall as the vault door, and they were all open and empty.

"Damn," the state policeman said.

"Were any of the rooms downstairs like this?" Martin asked.

"No," all the men said at once.

"Better do a thorough check top to bottom," Martin said, and moved out of the room. The other three descended the stairs while Martin moved across the second floor and checked a room which was clean and organized. From there, he moved down a narrow hallway to a bathroom and another room.

Both were in order as well.

On the first floor, Martin joined the other men, who reported the same findings he'd discovered upstairs. Apart from the one room, nothing seemed to be out of place.

He thanked the state policeman for his assistance and told Officer Gold to get back on patrol. Then he called the State Police Crime Unit and requested them for the Greenwich Avenue house. Together, Martin and Light sat in the Bronco listening to a Bruce Springsteen song, waiting for them to arrive. The Boss was singing about the way things used to be as Martin stared over the leather-wrapped steering wheel of the four-by-four, across the white hood, at the old Greenwich Avenue Hospital. He was thinking of the past and how Goshen seemed to be some kind of an anachronism.

His department had only four full-time officers, including him. For Myers and Gold, Goshen had been their first and only tour of duty, starting in the early 1970s. They could remember when most places in Orange County were as quiet as Goshen had been up until recently.

Light was the only one among them with any real background. A former Marine and New York City cop, he knew his way around, whereas Martin himself stood with Goshen symbolically. Crime seemed afraid of entrenching itself in Goshen, fearful of the town somehow. Fearful of Ben Robertson, who had been Martin's uncle's predecessor. Fearful of Michael Reeves, Martin's uncle, and for a while, fearful of Thomas Martin.

There were towns and cities in Orange County with rampant crime, and they weren't all that far away from Goshen. Most of them had huge police departments, equipped crime units, and experienced investigators.

Martin was an amateur at the puzzle-solving game, and he was uncomfortable with relying on his friend David McElroy to do so much of his job for him. But Goshen was just as inexperienced. Something evil had come to town, something professional. For the first time, Martin realized the things rural America took for granted. Its attitudes of being untouchable and unaffected were illusory. Security was something to be defended.

He'd failed to do that, and guilt swept through him. There would have to be changes in him and his department. Training, more money, more people. Relying on the state police, who were twenty miles away, was no longer acceptable.

"I let it sneak up on me, didn't I?" Martin asked, and somehow Light knew he didn't really want an answer.

Martin had read once that evil was a seed. Once established, it was like an overfed weed. He didn't want Goshen to end up like the old Greenwich Avenue Hospital, a fading memory. He didn't want his town to be a place where you used to be able to walk at night with no fear, where you could leave your car running outside the store and your windows open on a summer night.

Part of that security had been shattered with the deaths, but as he stared across Greenwich Avenue at the long white brick colonial, he committed himself to restoring the peace.

But first he had to catch this killer.

⸺·⸺

Sunday evening, November 1, found Martin sitting on a wooden chair at his small round kitchen table eating a care package from Georgette Michaels, the owner of the local bed-and-breakfast. His dispatcher Roberta had bent her grandmother's ear about Martin, and the fact that he clearly wasn't eating right. The news had brought both women to his house, armed with sympathy in the form of three days' worth of home cooked meals.

It was true, a lot had lost its allure since he'd seen Paulina in that bedroom, bloody. Cooking and eating were two of the casualties. A thick pork chop, broccoli, and a generous portion of Georgette's famous macaroni and cheese had been scooped out of Tupperware, microwaved, and were now steaming on a plate in front of him.

A large frosted ball-lamp blazed from the ceiling, and an Ahmad Jamal jazz CD was wafting in from the living room. When he finished eating, he rinsed his plate, glass, and silverware before throwing them into the sink.

From there, he went into his office, set the thermostat on sixty-five degrees, and stared wearily at the long-awaited Crime Unit file from the New York State Police.

The first page was a list of the people involved with each of the investigations, their titles, and specific duty. The only person he recognized was Detective David McElroy, New York State Police Bureau of Criminal Investigation Site Commander.

The next part of the packet was broken down into three parts. The first and second were individual assessments of each scene. Since Dr. Dunnelo's body had been found after the lab boys began their analysis, Dr. Strogg and Dr. Delaney were the only victims included in the report. The third part was an overall assessment of the crime and a determination and speculation of the potential suspect.

Martin read through this part first. According to the state police, Dr. Greene's height and weight didn't fit the profile for the killer, which meant he was in as much danger as the other victims had been. It also meant Martin had to convince the man to get himself into protective custody.

Next he began working through the assessment titled "Strogg site."

When he had read everything twice, he pulled a legal pad from a desk drawer and began making lists of things to be done. When he was satisfied he'd offered all he could to the file without further investigating, he reorganized everything. As Martin began to go through everything again, he was interrupted by his ringing doorbell.

"You've got to be kidding me," he said, moving toward the front door, pausing long enough to glare out through a small paned window, at two men in pinstripes standing on his stoop.

"Chief Martin?"

"Yes."

"FBI, sir," The taller man said, displaying a badge with the seal of the Federal Bureau of Investigation on it. "This is Agent Grant, and I'm Special Agent Williams. Sorry to bother you so late and at home. We were wondering if we might have a word with you?"

"No trouble. Come in."

"Thank you, sir," Agent Grant said, as he closed the door behind him. He was short, well dressed, and built like a miniature tank.

"So, what's this about, anyway?" Martin asked as he led them into the living room, motioning for them to take a seat. They remained standing. So did Martin.

"It's in reference to a call you made today to the District of Columbia police. The body of a woman named Angela Wilme was found murdered. How did you come across that information?" Williams asked.

"A man connected to a triple murder here in town called it in to me."

"And when was that, sir?"

"Yesterday," Martin said. "You know, I talked with a D.C. detective earlier today, and he didn't mention that I should be expecting any Q and A. What's this all about?"

"Sir, we need to have a look at the information you've gathered up until now," Agent Grant said. "We understand the state police have been handling the physical end of your investigation, and that they dropped off their preliminary report on the first two killings. Could we see that information?"

"Listen, friend," Martin said, "I don't know where you think you are, but this is my jurisdiction. I'd take a better tone if I were you. We're on the same side, you know?"

"Chief, we can do this one of two ways," Williams said.

"Don't even start with that crap."

"You can relinquish the information, and this can be what I would call a cooperative effort. You can benefit by our presence here. One hand washes the other. Seeing as how we're on the same side and all. But if you want to do it the hard way, we can just take copies of the information, which is fully within our provenance. You would then be interfering with a federal investigation, and I would personally see to it that you are brought up on charges. Am I making myself perfectly clear?"

"Crystal."

"Good. Now let's have that report."

Martin walked to his office, his mind racing. He slid the overall assessment and his personal notes under the blotter, then shoved everything else into the file and strode back to the living room and thrust it in Grant's direction.

"Good. We'd also like to take a look at the crime scenes and the information you have on this case down at your station," Agent Grant said, pulling the file away from Martin.

The drive to the Goshen Police Station was short, and once there, the two men helped themselves to Martin's filing cabinet. Martin sat in a vinyl chair next to Debra Chen, talking about little things that had been reported in the town while he'd been out and about during the day, but his mind was on the two men rummaging through his office.

The men eventually reappeared with armfuls of copied paperwork, walking straight by Martin and out of the station.

"I demand to know what the hell is going on," Martin said as they loaded their Mercury.

"Chief Martin, this is a federal court order," Williams said, handing Martin a piece of folded paper. "Any further involvement by your department, or the New York State Police, pertaining to the investigation of these doctors will be deemed a violation as set forth in this order."

Martin wasn't listening, he was screaming as Officer Light arrived and was getting out of his cruiser.

"We're ordering you to stand down," Williams said. "The Federal Bureau of Investigation is taking charge of this case. Your involvement is over and that is a direct order. Are you hearing me, Chief?"

"You can't do this, just waltz in here like this and make it all better. This town has lost four people. I've lost…" Martin trailed off, his eyes growing harder again. The chance of throttling Paulina's killer was being taken from him and his rage felt like it would boil over.

"We are doing this," Grant said. " Good day, sir." He opened the door to the car and got into it.

"You snide little bastard," Martin said, moving toward Agent Grant's side of the car.

"Let them go," Light said, pulling Martin back from the brink. "I've seen this before. You can't do anything. They have the power to do anything they want."

"They're covering this thing up, plain and simple. You know that, don't you?" Martin said.

"Yes, I do."

"And if that killer is still here, and Greene was telling the truth, and he gets whacked?" Martin asked.

Light didn't answer.

"Then I failed. Failed the town, failed her, failed Greene, and failed to do my fucking job," Martin said, answering his own question.

17

There were four boarded doors tucked underneath the large bowed marquee of the theater, two with broken plate glass and two marred with pellet-gun holes.

In one of the three poster cases recessed on either side of these doors was an old James Bond poster displaying Roger Moore standing on the moon, beautiful woman in one hand, gun in the other. The poster was legible but in bad shape.

The large two-story building was bordered by the Goshen Savings Bank and a tall wooden fence, and could be seen from the center of town. The fence was old and covered with ivy, that, because of the season, looked more like an intricate series of veins and capillaries than a border for a narrow grass walkway. The rear property opened wide, and a small flight of stairs dropped from a cracked cement patio to a basement door.

Dr. Robert Greene descended the staircase, kicking crisp leaves as he went. The back door was unlocked, and he stopped at the basement level to listen, relieved to hear only the traffic of a nearby intersection.

He pushed on the door, and the rusted hinges whined. The now-familiar stench of a decaying building washed over him as he stepped inside and closed the door behind him. It was pitch black. He knelt down and grabbed a candle out of the pile he'd left next to the door. A five-foot circle of bouncing light exploded around him as he struck a match and ignited the wick.

The screeching sounds of small vermin could be heard scurrying along the walls and among the old furniture piled close by. He dropped into a worn chair and held the candle close to his exhausted eyes. He enjoyed the warmth for a moment as the flame jumped.

Greene set the candle down and moved across the room to another candle he'd wedged into a hole in the basement's brick wall. He lit it, moved along the wall and lit another, and another, until about half of the basement could be seen clearly, although dimly. Large wooden beams sagged onto larger wooden stilts that had been planted in the ground long before he'd been born.

Greene had been all over his new hideout quite a few times, and it brought back a lot of good and bad memories. When he was a kid, the theater had been a safe and clean hangout because of the retired policeman who owned it. Greene could remember seeing Clint Eastwood, Chuck Norris, Roger Moore, William Shatner, and Harrison Ford in this theater. He'd had a lot of fun here, and now it was his refuge. His pursuers had followed him to Washington, killed his friends, and then come to Goshen and done the same. He couldn't run from people that powerful and no longer wanted to, and in that regard the theater was also a prison. It was this fact that played into the old stories he remembered hearing about the place when he was little. Stories that the theater was possessed or built on a graveyard. That bodies were buried in the dirt basement.

They were childish scare tactics, but Greene was no more at ease with them now than when he'd been ten. He crossed the basement and headed up the staircase to the first floor, grabbing a candle as he went.

At the theater level, the moldy smell was replaced by heavy dust and rotting leather. The worn carpeting revealed the planked floor in spots. The lobby moaned as he crossed it, heading for the concession stand. He'd cleaned out a small, unplugged refrigerator and loaded it up with ice, bread, lunchmeat, and a six-pack of Coors. It represented what he'd foraged from his refrigerator at home before he'd gone into hiding. He grabbed a beer, the sandwich makings, and let a flood of melted ice flow out. Everything was still cool, but the ice was nearly gone.

He could remember when the lobby was bright and red. Red hotel-style printed carpet, solid red wallpaper with gold accents, and strips of small lights. When the concession stand had been clean and the inside packed with candy bars and popcorn. Smiling faces had been everywhere and familiar soundtracks had played over the loudspeakers.

Across from the concession stand were four double wood doors leading down four wide aisles. The theater was divided into three sections and it had seemed like a day's walk to the screen when he was younger.

The stage was elaborate, and in Greene's youth it had always looked like an actual live performance stage, like those on Broadway.

Now he looked at the long rows of seats and walked down the center aisle with his beer and sandwich in one hand, and a candle in the other. He wasn't impressed. It was in bad condition and he could sympathize.

The building had no running water, electricity, or heat, a point which made the possibility of staying here for any duration impossible. He was grateful the weather had turned for the better. The first day of November had been kind to him, and he was hoping his luck stayed on course.

It was time for him to call Chief Martin again. He was out of options if Martin turned out to be unhelpful.

———————

Inside the Goshen Police Station, Light and Debra Chen were looking to Martin for guidance. The phone began ringing, and Debra welcomed the break in the silence. It was David McElroy.

Martin knew what the call was about. "Hello, David."

"I just got a visit from the friendly Federal Ballbuster's Institute," McElroy said.

"Welcome to the club."

"They walked in, showed me some paperwork, and then proceeded to rifle through all of our material on your case. I've never seen anything like it. So I made some calls to confirm the paperwork, and it's legit. How do you figure that? Then they took down all of our names and addresses, and took that with them. What the hell's this all about?"

"Cover-up, my man. It's like they said to me: It's over."

"You aren't convincing me, Tom. I know you well enough to know that tone. It's the same one your uncle used just before he tried something drastic. What are you thinking, boy?"

"Thinking?"

"I can smell those little educated wheels spinning from here."

"You're imagining things. What could I possibly do that the FBI can't?"

"They aren't going to do a damn thing. They're playing their own little game, and we aren't invited. So don't even think about it."

"Relax. I don't even have a plan yet."

The statement got everyone's attention.

———••———

Greene sprinted across the parking lot of the Goshen Savings Bank and the bustling lanes of Greenwich Avenue, finding his way into an alleyway and along the blue wall of a three-story building. The early-evening sky was growing dark, and the cars moving along West Main Street were already using their head-lights. Crouching next to a Dumpster, he watched the long stretch of sidewalk across the busy street.

There were very few pedestrians, and he considered it a good sign, because he wanted to use the open-air phone booth next to Goshen Hardware, and the fewer people who saw him, the bet-ter. A set of heavy footsteps approached the alleyway and Greene retreated into the darkness.

A short, pinstriped man stopped in front of the alleyway and looked right at the spot where Greene was cowering.

Greene hunched down farther but remained where he could see the man, who was now staring at the two buildings creating the alley. One was painted brick and the other natural. He stared at the windows facing West Main and then back into the alley-way. He moved several steps closer to Greene, and once out of the light created by Village Pizza, he was harder to see.

Greene hunched even lower and now couldn't see the man at all. The steps were close and slow. Greene had never wanted to take off running more in his life. A car stopped, and Greene heard the motor of a power window and then a voice.

"Did you see something?" a husky voice called out.

"No, just curious. I'd like to get a look on top of these roofs," the short man said, and turned. His footsteps softened as he rounded the corner.

Greene stood up and crept to the corner. The man was scrutinizing every building, window, and person he saw. A red Mercury was creeping alongside. The car had three men in it; the driver was huge and had to hunch over to see out the windshield. The two men in the backseat were as mesmerized by their surroundings as the walker.

Greene retreated between the buildings, deciding to jog further up Greenwich Avenue and enter the next alley. He crossed West Main Street, and made his way to the recessed telephone booth. Watching his pursuers round the corner as they began their hunt down Greenwich Avenue, he dialed the police station's number. His heart was pounding in his chest and he thought about his Washington phone booth incident, and fleetingly wondered if this was a mistake, as his call to Mitchell had been. But he was desperate to talk to Chief Martin, and more than ever, he needed help. He was hoping the lawman turned out to be a friend and not an enemy, and he hoped they weren't listening in again.

Debra Chen tapped Martin on the shoulder. Her face was anxious.

"Hold on a minute," Martin said to McElroy. "What is it?"

"It's Greene," she said.

"Call you back David," he said, and switched to the other line.

"Chief Martin?" Greene asked.

"Doctor Greene?"

"I'm glad you figured it out," Greene said. "I have to be brief. Things have taken a turn for the urgent tonight."

"What do you mean?"

"Please, Chief, let me run the damn conversation. Did you call Washington?"

"Yes."

"And?"

"And she's dead, just like you said. Now you're a suspect in four murders. The D.C. police department, not to mention the FBI, is very anxious to speak with you."

"Well, this is a change. The last time we talked, you were accusing me of doing it. Now you sound almost sympathetic."

"I don't think you did it, Doc."

"What changed your mind?"

"I was asking around and you're just not the type. Of course you could be one of those closet whackos who hides his true personality from everyone, but I don't think that's the case. I know it in my gut."

It was obviously what Greene wanted to hear. A slight sigh came through the receiver. "I'm glad I have someone I can trust. I can trust you, can't I?"

"Yes, but I don't know that it's going to do a whole lot of good. I was officially relieved of any connection to the trouble you're in."

"What are you talking about?"

"The FBI came knocking today and took us off the case. They took all the records, everything."

"Are you saying you're not going to help me?"

Martin swallowed hard and stared at the wall as though he could see through it. Greene's statement hurt him. It hurt him that officially, he couldn't do anything without jeopardizing himself and his career.

"Chief, are you there?"

"You're a resident of Goshen. I took an oath to serve and protect you. I was serious when I took that oath. Why don't you just come on in? Just come in so I can get you into protective custody."

"First things first. The killer is still in town, and I think I saw four of his henchmen just a few minutes ago. They're looking for me. Second of all, as far as I know they've killed five people, not four."

"Five? You mean Paulina Orange." Just saying her name out loud made his chest constrict and his grip on the receiver tighten.

"No, not Paulina. I'm talking about United States Senator Byron Mitchell."

There was a long pause before Martin said anything else. He was confused and felt more and more in over his head. That was the second time Washington D.C. had come up. Greene had gone to medical school in D.C. and was obviously still connected to it somehow.

"What are you mixed up in?" Martin asked.

"They must have killed him the same night I found Angela." After a long silence Greene said, "Oh my God," as though he'd seen something horrific. "They're here. They're coming right toward me."

"Greene, where are you? We'll come get you." Martin stood up. He could hear traffic in the background.

There was no answer.

"Greene?" Martin yelled into the receiver.

Martin slammed down the phone, grabbed Light by the shoulder, and ran out of the station, heading for the Bronco.

"Where are we going?" Light asked.

"To stop a killing."

18

Senator Braun decided not to return to her rental car, and instead walked to the Capitol Building. It was the safest bet, in her mind; after all, it was her building, and she knew it better than her pursuers did. She went over the sequence of events in her mind. Capitol tour groups began on the front steps each half hour, and they were always groups of about fifty, which meant there would be at least a hundred people milling around, between the group starting and the one finishing. Following a U.S. park ranger's introduction and a brief description of the exterior architecture, the group would move single-file through the metal detectors and gather inside.

There was enough time for her to pull off the same maneuver she'd managed in National Airport yesterday. There was a staircase off the main hallway to the right, and as long as there was enough distance between them, and she could reach it before her pursuer rounded the corner, she would be home free.

As she reached the paved elliptical that circled the building, she feinted to her left, but she'd lost sight of the man. She stopped and scanned the area around her. Pedestrians were everywhere;

dog walkers, joggers, tourists, government suits, but he was gone. Her heart was counting seconds twice as fast as her watch. There were only nine minutes until the next tour started. She suddenly felt like she was walking into a trap.

"This isn't going to work," she told herself, as she reached the steps of the Capitol Building. "Where the hell is he?" she muttered, scanning the area again before beginning her ascent. The wind was so strong that she suddenly envisioned her wig lifting off her head, exposing her identity to everyone.

She pulled her purse around and quickly rifled for her keycard. Her escape route was off the tour path, and it was controlled by a keycard. She was again conscious that anyone watching the computers would know she was back in the building.

She moved through the metal detector, made her way to the hallway and stairwell, stopping only a moment to look over her shoulder before she slid the card across the slot. The lock disengaged, and she stepped through, pulling the door tight behind her, sighing. A long set of dusty cement stairs angled straight away from her. She was in a hurry to reach the bottom hallway, which, after three turns and two more doors, would lead her up and onto Constitution Avenue.

She was twenty feet into the hallway when she heard the pop of the lock disengaging behind her and the sounds of heavy footsteps descending behind her. She took off running. She was a gangly sight, all flails and bad angles, but she was quick. The FBI didn't have keycards for down here, she thought, and the Secret Service was only interested in tunnels during inauguration time, which was three years off.

The footsteps hit bottom, and their pace increased. She patted her side pocket, relieved to find her canister of pepper spray; it was her only chance. Rounding right and then immediately left, she came to the second door and fumbled with the keycard. The lock popped and she bolted through, slamming the door behind her. Making her final turn, she came to another door, where a single blue bulb illuminated the exit. Using the butt of the canister, she broke the bulb, and the hallway grew dark.

She heard the release of another lock and more quick footsteps, which abruptly halted as the man rounded into the darkness. She could see the man's silhouette against the light of the other hallway. He was breathing hard, and it sounded like something other worldly, inhuman.

"Bitch," the man hissed, walking into the short hall.

Just a little closer, Braun thought, her mind racing, her heart trying to pry itself between two ribs. Her hand was sweaty and the canister was slippery, and she was horrified to realize she'd never tested the thing, not once since she'd bought it. Was it pointed in the right direction? Did it stream out or mist? How close did she have to be, and was it even real pepper spray?

She was watching the outline of his head. He was close.

When the man's shoe found the broken shards of light bulb, he instinctively looked down, right into the pepper spray Braun was shooting from her crouched position.

"Fuck!" the man screamed, tearing at his eyes.

Braun kicked her leg like she was attempting a fifty-yard field goal, and her pursuer dropped to the floor. She was immediately over him, feeling along the floor for his keycard, certain he'd been carrying it, ready for another door.

She found it next to his foot. She stood and blindly felt for the door, her own skin burning from the spray. She could taste it in her mouth and feel it in her lungs. The hall burst bright, and she turned to see him. He was scruffy and lying in a fetal position, whimpering. She could see the butt of a pistol in a shoulder holster. She knew a government employee when she saw one, and this was something else entirely.

Pushing the door closed, Braun locked her pursuer in the bowels of the Capitol Building. Constitution Avenue seemed different, crueler, as she hailed a taxi. She would have to be a lot more careful. They knew she was still in Washington.

Greene was standing next to the telephone when the short man appeared from around a corner three blocks down West Main Street. The red sedan mimicked his action, crossed the lane of traffic, and parked next to the sidewalk.

As its headlights extinguished, the short man got in, and Greene could see there were no longer four men inside. Exhaust plumed from the tailpipe as he moved away from the recess in the building and walked down the sidewalk away from them.

"They're just sitting there," he thought as he glanced over his shoulder, making his way back to his sanctuary. Crossing through the intersection of West Main, his attention was fixated on the line of cars parked along each side of the street, but he could no longer distinguish the red car.

Focusing his eyes forward, he stared down the short distance to the movie house and caught a glimmer coming from the rooftop of the blue building he'd just hidden next to; it stopped him in his tracks. It was one of the men from Washington, staring right at him. Something was attached to his face, some sort of binoculars, and he suddenly took them off and began speaking into a transceiver.

For reasons Greene couldn't explain, he took off running full tilt across the intersection and found himself bombarded by sliding cars. Horns blasted, brakes screamed, and he saw the lights of a car ignite exactly where the red sedan had been. It burst into traffic, its engine roaring as it sped toward him.

Greene ran faster, dodging one of the sliding cars. The grille of an Audi slid toward his kneecaps. He raised his legs high, cleared the hood, and landed on the ground, barely breaking his stride. He felt lightheaded and out of energy. He wished he'd eaten more than one of those sandwiches before he left the theater.

Hollow ringing sounds pierced the pavement and the sheet metal of the cars behind him. He tried to run faster but was topped out. Cocking his head, he saw the sentry standing on the roof firing a long rifle. Light erupted from the barrel of the weapon as the sentry pulverized everything between himself and Greene.

Greene dove behind the line of the cars waiting on South Church Street for the light to change. Bullets shattered windshields, side windows, tore through sheet metal. Passengers screamed. Greene sprinted into the darkness of Presbyterian Park lawn, and the gunfire stopped. He turned to look for the man, but the roof was clear. The red sedan however, was coming around the corner of West Main and into the intersection. Its tail end flew sideways and struck another car, rupturing one of its brake lamps. Plastic sprayed the pavement as the tires squealed, trying desperately to fix themselves back to the pavement.

Greene began running again. The park was big, and it was a long way to the church, too long. If he made it, what would he do? Would the Reverend be there this late?

The car crossed the street and hopped an old slate curb, landing on the church lawn. They had misjudged his direction, but with a slight turn of the wheel, they'd cast their halogen headlamps right at him. He couldn't hear anything but the car. He dove behind a large tree and crouched in the darkness.

The sedan slowed.

It was getting closer and closer, zigzagging over the stretch of lawn where they thought he was. The headlights landed on the tree, casting a long shadow on the grass.

The car came to a halt. The engine idled.

A car door opened, and he heard hushed voices. He clenched his eyes shut. Sweat was pouring off his forehead and his heart was pounding.

Then, to his joy, the door slammed shut and the car swerved around the tree, jumped onto the church's driveway, and accelerated until he could no longer hear it.

The world crept back into his senses. A stiff breeze made him shiver, and he could hear an approaching siren. He saw the Chief's Bronco fly by the church on Main Street. It was chasing the sedan. Greene tried to call out but couldn't. He couldn't even move. He was frozen to the tree with fear.

———

Turning from an extension avenue connecting South Church Street and Main Street, the red Mercury retreated alongside a large brick building, stopping underneath an overgrown tree separating the Surrogate Court Building and a restaurant called Oliver's. The four men had an ideal view of most of the church and its park. They heard the sound of a loud siren pass on Main Street and then grow faint.

Dillon, the man who had been on the rooftop, now stood outside the car. He spoke with a New England accent, walked with a calculating confidence, and was never mistaken for a warm personality.

A gun was tucked into the small of his back, and he held a pair of night vision goggles, through which the dark world turned lime green and very visible. The streetlamps made him squint, but he tirelessly searched the grounds within his field of vision. Moving behind the car and walking backward down a driveway, his view expanded.

The short man, Sampus, grabbed the receiver of a Motorola portable out of an open briefcase sitting on an empty half of the backseat. He engaged the source scrambler, dialed his boss, and put it on speaker.

"Yes?" the voice asked.

"Mr. Scaffiotelli, we found Dr. Greene, sir. He was leaving a telephone booth in town. He'd just made a call to the Chief of Police."

"Is he dead?"

"We missed the opportunity, but we have his general location. He's in a church park. We're outside there now. Dillon's on recon, we'll nail him."

"I'm very disappointed." There was a short pause. "Did you record the telephone call?"

"Yes. We're tapped into the Chief's line."

"Let me hear it."

Sampus used the laptop fastened next to the Motorola to replay the conversation.

"The Chief knows everything?" It was posed as a question, but none of the men answered it. "He'll have to be eliminated. Keep Dresden involved as much as possible. Dillon has free rein and can fill the rest of you in on what should be done."

Scaffiotelli had barely finished when Dillon opened the door and got in. "It's Dillon, sir. I've located Greene. He went into the basement of an old theater across the street from the church park. What are your instructions?"

———— ·○· ————

When Officer Light and Chief Martin backed out of the police station in the Bronco, they headed for the five places where Martin knew a person could use a public phone during an evening hour. He'd heard background noise that sounded like traffic so he ruled out the one in the lobby of the local Burger King.

Martin drove around the police station and got onto West Main Street, heading toward the highway. There was one phone outside the Village Diner and two more outside the local supermarket. From West Main they crossed over a side street and turned onto Greenwich Avenue. The road ran in front of the diner.

There was no one at the outside booth.

From the diner they swung around into the parking lot of the supermarket situated right behind the diner.

Both were empty.

Martin was abandoning the supermarket when Roberta Michaels, who had just taken over as night dispatcher for Debra Chen, called him on his transceiver.

"Tom, someone just reported gunshots in the town square. They said motorists have been shot," she said. "I can hear them from inside the station."

"Oh, Jesus. Roberta, get GOVAC down there on the double. We're on our way," Martin said.

Light held onto the truck door's armrest as Martin jumped a curb and cut across the grass of the diner to make the journey back to Greenwich Avenue less time consuming.

The Bronco's emergency lights reflected off the bare trees and the sirens broke the quiet still of the night. Faces were pressed to the windows of the diner as patrons watched the Bronco speed toward town.

Martin was glad he lived in a town where volunteering was such a big deal. In no time there would be thirty people in the square who were trained to deal with a crisis situation. Even though it was usually a fire-related crisis, they would still be calmer than ordinary civilians.

The speedometer on the Bronco climbed above sixty miles an hour as they crested the small hill before the center of town. They could see at least ten cars in the intersection and a mob of people.

Martin jammed on the brakes and slid to a standstill. A young resident, who he knew quite well, rushed to his truck. The boy had a red welt rising on his forehead as though he'd head-butted an oak tree.

"Jim, what the hell happened here?" Martin asked as he stared at the boy's classic Mach I, whose front end was imbedded into the rear end of a Saab.

"Some fool was shooting an automatic rifle from the roof of Lipman's law office. There was another guy running across the square," Jim shouted, pointing to the blue building perched over Goshen's town square.

"Greene?" Light interrupted.

Martin nodded in agreement.

"He ran behind that line of cars and the man kept firing." There was a row of punctured cars sitting at the South Church Street traffic light.

Martin looked at the cars lined up at the light to his immediate right. Glass and plastic were everywhere. Steam was pluming from radiators and people were slumped against driver's door panels or steering wheels.

"Jesus, not here." Everywhere he looked, in all directions, all he saw were people running around, screaming in horror. Some were lying on the ground because they were too frightened to move or they were wounded. It was pandemonium and it was in his town.

"Which way?" Light asked.

"They went across the church lawn over there and then out onto the street." Jim's voice slurred and Martin knew he was going into shock from his collision. Martin told him to back away from the truck and he did. From all directions Martin heard sirens and saw the flashing lights of Goshen's volunteers. They were in for the shock of their lives, he thought.

"What kind of car?" Martin asked.

"A Mercury," Jim answered.

The Bronco negotiated the center intersection and then roared down Main Street away from the crowd. The make of the car didn't set off an alarm for Martin or Light.

───

When Greene regained enough composure he turned away from the protection of the tree and looked back at the center of town. He saw people running and screaming, and cars with emergency lights and sirens pulling up to the crowd. To his right, on the corner of South Church Street and an extension avenue, two garage doors were opening on Goshen's volunteer ambulance building.

He could also hear the sounds of fire whistles going off and diesel trucks starting up. Goshen, he realized, had mobilized in an attempt to clean up the situation he'd caused.

Greene looked across the park lawn toward the church and in the direction the sedan had gone. He couldn't see the car or any suspicious people moving in on him. Once the GOVAC ambulances had passed, the direction away from the traffic light was dark and quiet. He ran down the long lawn toward South Church Street, across which lay the temporary safety of the theater.

He would sit out the transpiring panic and count himself lucky he hadn't been a victim of it.

He'd escaped his pursuers again, but now more than ever he had to get to the Chief and tell him everything. He had to make it right, especially considering what he'd brought down upon Goshen. He was a doctor, and death seemed to follow him as though it were a shadow. A dread swept over him and he somehow knew he was still less than safe. He ran faster.

Crossing the street he moved down the narrow strip of grass between the theater and ivy covered fence. He turned the corner and descended the cement staircase. Pushing the door open he went inside and closed it behind him. He picked up another candle and lit it. The room was empty, dark, and he could see only the small portion around him the candle illuminated.

He slid a heavy piece of furniture against the basement door and then backed himself toward the desk he'd set in the middle of the dirt floor. He sat down and waited, contemplated.

His senses were heightened, and even from the sealed basement he could hear muffled cries coming from the center of town. He closed his eyes and cringed. He was a doctor, he was a fool, and he was frightened beyond reason.

19

Black spent Sunday night sprawled on a queen-size bed with pillows propped against the headboard so he could watch television. The 8 o'clock movie had just come on, but he wasn't paying it too much attention. The chaperone's leather case sat open on the bed next to him and he really wanted that inner phone to ring so he could evacuate Goshen.

It was generally accepted that forty-eight to seventy-two hours after a murder, most killers wouldn't be apprehended. It was sheer stupidity to hang around the crime scene after killing someone, when flight very often equaled freedom.

He had always acted according to those considerations, but now he was being careless, and it was Dr. Robert Greene and Black's code of professionalism holding him in the town.

On the television, Brian Dennehy was playing a wild tempered basketball coach who could save his career, his life, simply by winning the big game. Black began to fade as a commercial came on. Reaching for the remote, he turned the television off and turned onto his side. He moved a pillow from its propped position and brought it under his head. He was sound asleep in seconds.

At 8:45 the odd pulsing tones of the phone sounded. Startled, Black sat up and let the phone ring four more times before he answered it.

"Mr. Dresden?"

"Yes."

"We've located Dr. Greene." There was a finality to the man's voice.

"How?"

"We've had the whole police station Echomiked. He called there tonight and gave the Chief his location."

Black didn't answer right away. He was eager to ask Scaffiotelli how the hell he got his hands on a piece of laser hardware that was supposed to be more fable than reality. He also had doubts about the capability of the two trunk residents to handle such sophisticated hardware, but was in no mood to debate his suspicions "Where? I'll go take care of it and get the hell out of this town."

"There's another problem. The Chief of Police knows everything. He'll have to be taken care of."

"You're kidding me, right?"

"He's meeting Greene at nine-fifteen. They'll both be at the same place at the same time, an abandoned movie house on South Church Street. It's near the center of town."

"I think I know where it is," Black said. "I'll be leaving your sedan in the rear of the hotel. Your two shadows are in the trunk of their car. They'll need medical attention. It's your responsibility."

"That won't be a problem."

"Goodbye, Mr. Scaffiotelli. I'd like to say something positive, to end things on the right note, but I can't."

"Tonight should totally free us of any further problems."

Black hung up the phone and left the hotel. He took the first interstate on-ramp, traveled south for one exit, and then got off the highway, doing his best to avoid the center of town.

The back roads criss-crossing the periphery of the rural town were lined with both old Victorian and colonial homes, and more modern developments. The streets were dark and the temperature had dropped.

The moon was just a faint, hallowed ball hiding behind thick clouds, and as he coasted over the crest of South Street, heavy snowflakes began to blur the bright amber lights of the intersection just ahead of him. New York had gone from a spring-like, autumn day to winter in a span of hours. Getting caught in the snow in a strange place would slow his escape.

He engaged the windshield wipers, pushing a coat of slush from the glass, and made a left turn onto South Church. The center of town was deserted except for a police cruiser sitting at the traffic light. The signal turned green, and the car moved through the intersection, turning left and disappearing. The snow became heavier. He parked on a side street two blocks from the theater and left the warmth of the car. The wind was picking up at about the same rate as the storm and it whipped the heavy powder against his face.

When he came within sight of the theater, he moved off the sidewalk and into the shadowy darkness surrounding the old houses of South Church Street. He was moving at a good clip when he heard a noise which made him instinctively drop to the ground.

A church's property across the street was a blanket of white, save the blades of grass tall enough to poke through like a five o'clock shadow. He could see no prints in the snow as he scanned the area. An extension avenue connected the main artery of the town and South Church Street. It was dark and deserted also. He reached for his light-gathering scope, but it wasn't there.

"Dammit," he said, and cupped his hands over his eyes so that even less light could reach his pupils, in order to further adjust them to the lack of light. In seconds, and through the slim cracks of his fingers, his vision began to adjust and sharpen. Removing his hands, his vision was briefly acute and he saw the outline of what looked like steam coming from a pine tree against the backdrop of a brick building, about halfway down the extension avenue.

The wind was whipping naked branches together in a haunted chorus and made it impossible for Black to focus his hearing on the steam. His heightened vision deteriorated as his eyes readjusted. The steam, the tree, and the building disappeared. Panning from where the steam had been, and across his entire field of vision, he saw nothing, and heard nothing. He looked at his watch and saw it was almost 9 PM. Goshen was preternaturally quiet and he decided to continue.

"Just a laundry vent, or something," he muttered, turning the back corner of the theater to see a staircase leading to the basement level. He again looked over the surrounding property and again there was nothing.

He descended the stairs slowly and pushed on the door. He took out his pistol, disengaging the safety, and ignited a bright flashlight, holding the gun parallel with the light so he could fire on anything he saw. There was nothing.

Closing the door behind him with his heel, he crept across the dirt floor, moving the beam around the room. It was warmer inside by about fifteen degrees and it seemed like all the heat in the world. A small table littered with empty beer cans, a dead flashlight, and a pile of candles sat in the center of the room, but Greene was nowhere to be seen.

Black's light finally hit the doorway leading to the floor above. He aimed the beam of light up the staircase and saw Greene's bloody body fastened to an upper door.

A single shot had been fired into his forehead. It was fresh, and Black understood all at once what was happening. The oldest saying in his profession flashed across his mind again as he turned to retreat. The first rule of assassination was to always kill the assassin.

The beam of light jumped between the floor and walls as he sprinted toward the door. When it landed on the timer fastened to the brick wall just above his exit, he stopped in his tracks. It was displaying the number 4, and then the number 3. He was out of time.

Shining the light along the wire running from the top of the timer, he came to a ball of plastic explosive and more wire, then more explosive and more wire.

2 flashed on the timer's display.

He fired his silenced 10mm at the wiring coming from the box, attempting to break the connection.

1.

Senator Braun eased into a secluded booth of Chadwick's Tavern on K Street in Georgetown. She asked the waitress for a Corona and then called an old friend on her new cell phone. She was staring at the Eberhardt & Ober Brewing Company poster above her as she listened to the chiming rings. Of all the bars in Washington this was her favorite, good food and enough of a beer selection to keep you on your toes.

Shannon Fallon was a former N.Y.P.D. detective from back in the days when Braun was a prosecutor in Manhattan. It had been too long since they'd spoken, and Braun was embarrassed.

"How's retirement?" she asked.

"Susan Braun, is that you?" Fallon began. "Retired? Hell, I'm in private practice now, busier than I ever was. You're not back in New York, are you?"

"Wish I was."

"What's up, trouble find you again?"

"This is a whole new level for me," Braun said.

"Tell me."

Braun told her old friend all of it.

"You have to blow the lid off, Susan," Fallon said.

"I'm not going to throw away thirty years of work."

"So be smart about it. Didn't you tell me one of those Watchdogs had a crush on you once?"

Braun hadn't realized until this very moment that Chadwick's had been James Redfield's favorite watering hole. She quickly looked to the bar and saw that Liz was still tending. There was a good chance James still came in every night to check on his sister.

"So maybe he could help you out. There's not a whole lot I can do from up here."

"That was years ago, besides…"

"I know, he was too boring for you, just like the rest of them. Not everyone can be Charles A. Braun, Susan."

"He was an accountant for the GAO back then, but I doubt if he even lives in the District anymore. He took things pretty hard when we split."

"What was his name?"

"James Redfield, why?"

"Well hold on a minute," Fallon barked. "James Redfield of 1430 Newton Street, Washington D.C., receives General Accounting Office's dedicated service award for 2003, sound familiar?"

"The address is right, the rest is new," Braun said. "Aren't we Miss Marbles these days."

"Grade-school stuff. Listen, if you ask me, I think an accountant who happens to work for GAO is too good a chance to pass up."

"I think I'm the last person he'll want to see."

"He proposed to you, didn't he?" Fallon said. "He'll help."

"I better go, Shannon," Braun said as the dinner crowd began filling the booths around her. "Thanks for listening."

"You better stay in touch."

"I will," she said, and slipped the cell phone back in her pocket, and ordered another drink and some food. The wait for James Redfield might be a long one.

———

Dr. Benjamin Tafton, the Orange County Medical Examiner, lived on an old seventy-acre horse farm, complete with yellow farmhouse, stables to match, two large white barns, and a lake.

Tafton was sitting on a worn recliner in a small reading room to the very rear of his home, laboring over a thick leather-bound Henry Miller novel.

From the front of the house, light was barely visible through the crescent-moon windows in the upper section of the front door. The red Mercury Grand Marquis seemed to float over the snow-covered driveway. The car's headlights were off, and two men sat somberly in the front seat.

They stopped between a side door of the main house and the long stable. Incandescent light blazed through an open door. The men went inside the stable first, finding six disinterested horses settling in for the night.

Dillon then headed for the front of the house, while Sampus moved toward a side door. Both pulled ski masks down over their faces.

They found Dr. Tafton, basking in the glow of a fire. They left him beaten within an inch of his life and lying on the floor of his country home. In the kitchen, they found what they had come for—a complete set of keys to the county morgue, just as Tafton had confessed.

After Sampus had rummaged through the large refrigerator, extracting a jar of zesty pickles, the two men went back to the car.

⸺•⸺

Goshen seemed devoid of civilian presence as Martin and Light made their way back into the station. Windows were dark and the streets were deserted, save the reinforcement units he'd enlisted: Select fireman were guarding each intersection within the village, while Officer Myers, Officer Gold, and seven state police cruisers patrolled Goshen.

Martin could almost feel Goshen cowering from the square's earlier horror.

"So there has to be more than one of them in town now," Light said.

"Greene said, *they*, on the phone. *They* had found him. And that he'd survived a week with a professional killer after him."

"So odds are we won't find him, either," Light said easing into a chair.

"Not unless he wants to be found. You should hear him on the phone. Jumpy and paranoid. One thing I can't figure is what he would have done to get in this kind of shit."

"He was into something mammoth."

"Yeah, but what? I mean, he was involved with this local group of doctors, had a few extramarital affairs, but was basically quiet, right?"

"Right."

"Those members were all killed because of something they knew—"

"Or to flush Greene into the open so they could kill him," Light said.

"Right. And then he calls us for protection, and they nail him."

"You said he told you Angela was killed by the same people killing the local doctors. So Washington happened first, and then they followed him here. They must have missed him in D.C."

"So the prick runs back home and brings his problems with him," Martin said.

"He's gotta call, or we're up the creek. If he's the last one they have to take care of, then it's all sewn up," Light said.

"We're not supposed to be doing anything, remember?" Martin said.

"The good old FBI. Leave it to them to decide when something should be covered up, and to be total pricks about it."

"I'm not going to let this thing get honeyed over by a couple of federal numb-nuts. I've got physicians dropping like Ebola patients. Paulina was…" Martin trailed off, and his face grew paler. "Now automatic gunfire in the square. Do they expect me to just forget about what's gone down here? I'll go to Washington and fire up a shit storm before I roll over. I'll kiss my career goodbye, I don't give a damn." Martin got up and paced the floor. "Sometimes vengeance is the only cure."

He was standing beside the window and staring at the dark and empty parking lot behind the police station, when the windowpanes shook before his face. A roar reverberated through the station, and Roberta burst through the office door almost simultaneously.

"What the hell was that?" she bellowed.

Another shock wave swept against the station and was followed by recurring earthquake-like jolts. An explosion of light flashed over the rooftop Martin could see from his office window. He could also hear several of the surrounding building's alarms being triggered by the jolts.

"Artillery." Light had his eyes closed, as though he could better sense what the sound was with them shut.

"What?" Roberta asked in disbelief.

"I know artillery when I hear it, and that's it!" he exclaimed.

"Come on. It came from the militarized zone," Martin said. Light followed him past Roberta and out of the station. Before they could get the Bronco started, a call came over the transceiver that the theater had just exploded, covering its neighbors and South Church Street with debris. Goshen was no longer quiet.

As Martin turned the corner onto South Church, he saw a burst of brick and light fly from where the theater had once stood. The shock wave made the Bronco jump from the pavement as it skidded to a stop some distance away. Martin could hear firehouse alarms sounding.

Martin stared at the theater in disbelief. He'd driven by it earlier in the day, and now it was demolished.

"You figure this means they found Greene?" Light asked as state police cruisers and firemen's personal vehicles began crowding the scene.

"That gets my vote. There won't be anything left to find, though," Martin said. "No evidence, no worries."

"Then it's all sewn up for them," Light said, his voice sinking.

"Hardly." Martin said.

The young volunteer charged with guarding Goshen's main intersection rushed the burning house, his strong shoulder burst through the front door, and the bright beam of his flashlight could be seen through smoky windows as he searched for people. The explosions had caved in the entire side of the house bordering the theater, and fire was sweeping through its second and third floors. The volunteer appeared back through the front door with a man over his shoulder. A state trooper rushed over and began CPR on the man. An infant began to cry inside the house as a flame swelled across the front porch, cutting off that entrance.

Light took off running for the far corner of the house, almost losing his footing on the dusting of snow.

Dillon slid the pilfered brass key into a lock and opened a rear door of Arden Hospital. Sampus made his way to Dr. Tafton's office and cleaned out all the files concerning the three men who had been killed in Goshen over the last week.

Dillon proceeded past a door labeled "Examination," and entered another labeled "Morgue." It was large and dominated by stainless-steel drawers fitted flush into the walls. Dillon slid each of them open and examined the tags attached to the corpses' toes. Dunnelo, Delaney, and Strogg were on the second wall he rummaged through.

Sampus returned to help Dillon load the bodies onto a gurney and strap them down. The two men wheeled the cart down the hallway and out into the bitter night. The snow had turned to sleet, creating large black splotches on the white-draped parking lot. Unstraping the three men, Sampus rolled them off the gurney and into the trunk of the Mercury. Before he could close the lid, Dillon's heavy foot was required to get the stiff bodies into the compartment.

The tires of the car spun on the soft snow as the car sped out of the rear lot and disappeared.

Paddock Estates was a condominium development not far from Arden Hospital, and Matthew Light called it home. He pulled his aging Corvette into the small garage and out of the freezing drizzle. He was thinking about the infant he'd found in the house and left in the capable hands of a local EMT. But mostly he was thinking about Martin and Goshen, and how wrong he'd been about the quietness of both.

It was dark and he was reaching for the condo door when the butt of a pistol struck his brow, dropping him to his knees. It was after two hours, and once Light had endured what no man should have to, that he unknowingly told his assailants that Martin had gone to Washington to put things right.

"It's too late. You don't have a chance," Light spit at the taller hooded man.

"Is that so?"

"You've awakened something you shouldn't have."

"We were right here in his town all along. Why is he running in the wrong direction?" the shorter man asked. "Because he's a coward, a failure."

"I have a feeling you'll be seeing him real soon," Light managed, even as the corners of his vision disappeared like a closing aperture. "If only I could be there to see him rip off your fucking heads."

"Not a chance in hell, cop." A burst of white light and the force of a bullet striking his temple were the last things Matthew Light ever knew. His body was left on the hallway floor of his new home, in his new town.

20

Thomas Martin stepped from his 1969 Camaro onto the slushy paved driveway that winded its way through Rosewood Cemetery. It was raining now, and the light snow that had fallen was disappearing.

There was very little light at this hour, but he found the headstone easily. He was uneasy that he hadn't been here in over a month.

Michael Reeves
Goshen Chief of Police, Orange County, New York - '57 to '90
Beloved Son, Brother, Uncle
Born 1930/Died 1992.

"Sorry I haven't been here in a while," he said, kneeling down to clean around the stone. "I really need your advice Uncle Mike. I feel like I'm being pulled in a hundred different directions."

Martin stood and ran his hand through his soaking hair. "FBI came to town, I'm sure you've been watching. They told me to back down and forget about everything. I just can't let it go, guess that's your doing, huh? If you were here you would have them cuffed and stuffed already."

"I have to go to D.C. and find out what the hell's going on, because I don't have a clue. Except that D.C. has come up once too often. Myers, Light, and Gold can hold down the fort. Besides, they've got your old compatriot McElroy to watch their tails," Martin said, stuffing his hands deep into his pockets.

"I have to set it straight, not just for the town, but for those doctors, for you and me, and for Paulina. You were right about crime and violence. I turned my back and it crept up on me, grabbed Goshen by the jugular. I wasn't paying attention I guess. I suppose I should've seen it coming. I should have been able to save her, don't you think?"

"I'll sort all this out," Martin said. "I promise."

——————

When Thomas Martin left Goshen it was early Monday morning, November 2. He'd left Officer Gold in charge and ordered his three cops to cease and desist all investigations into the local killings. He was sure the killers had fled Goshen and there would be no more problems. He'd also arranged for a few Troopers to patrol in town, so that the exaggerated police presence would remain twenty-four-seven.

Goshen had been blanketed by its first snow, but as Martin reached the state highway, he saw the road was clear. He cringed at the thought of his car getting wet, but going on a reconnaissance trip to Washington in the Bronco wasn't very covert; the light-bar and emblems would be an announcement that he was there, disobeying the FBI. Taking the Packard out in this kind of weather would make his uncle roll over in his grave; besides, he doubted the thing would've made it. So he'd pulled the Camaro from under its heavy cover, out of its heated garage, and was now heading south, for Washington D.C.

The car was a throaty cameo white convertible with orange racing stripes. When he reached the New Jersey state border, the roads had dried and there were no signs it had snowed at all. He was conscious the car was already dirty and began to look for a truck stop. They had all-night washers, and cleaning the classic would distract him. It was pure vanity, and Martin knew it, but the quirk didn't bother him, and he didn't care if it bothered anyone else.

The inside of the wash bay was big enough to hold a tractor trailer and he stood watching two middle-aged men baby his baby. They were all-night employees and had offered to hand-wash the car for him, instead of using the machines. Martin accepted the generous offer and used the extra time to go over his intended route to Washington. Four tractor trailers were lined up behind him and all four of the drivers stood near the entrance to the wash bay. She was an eye-catcher and Martin begrudgingly realized it was going to stick out as much as the Bronco would have.

When at last he reached the Capitol he was barely awake and stopped at the first lodging he saw, the Hill Motel. He planned on looking over the Wilme crime scene in the morning, and try to piece together what had gotten Greene killed, along with his three friends and Paulina. He would start with Angela and then move onto Senator Mitchell's widow. Matt Light had come through in providing the politician's address, and Martin hoped he would get some sense of where to go after he had seen Mrs. Mitchell.

———•••———

Dillon and Sampus could hardly believe their ears when they heard about Martin's southern crusade. Light was their final stop in sewing things up, and Martin's willfulness was going to enrage Scaffiotelli. They were confident they had convinced the man to back off, confident he'd been convinced they were the FBI.

Dillon took out his cellphone and dialed Chicago. Scaffiotelli couldn't believe the news.

"I want you and Sampus to bury those bodies and then fly to Washington. Hunt the little shit down," Scaffiotelli began. "Split the other two members of your team up. Send one here with all the physical information, and the other to D.C."

"Light wasn't quite clear about the hotel, but he mentioned a couple where Martin had stayed in the past," Dillon said. "It's a place to start anyway."

"Get to it," Scaffiotelli said, and hung up.

After catching a flight out of a local airstrip called Stewart Airport, Dillon and Sampus reached Washington just ahead of Martin. Two large men were waiting outside the Arrivals Terminal of Dulles Airport next to a gray Lincoln Town Car. Dillon and Sampus got into the car and began to search for a white 1969 Camaro convertible.

At 6:20 AM the Lincoln left the parking lot of a cheap motel called The Hubbit Inn, and pulled next door to check the Hill Motel. They hadn't found the car at either spot.

———•••———

Martin reached over and set the alarm clock so that he would get eight hours of sleep, and then rolled onto his side, gripping the cool sheets close to his neck. Memories of his last conversations with Paulina and Greene were replaying in his head.

It was 6:40 AM.

21

Martin stepped from the Hill Motel and stared at his breath pluming into the heavy sky. He pulled the door to his room tight behind him, turning the handle to double check its security.

His car was backed into the spot directly in front of his room, and once inside he began pumping the gas pedal, enticing the protesting engine to turn over. Waiting for the old car to warm up took a few minutes, so he passed the time by unfolding and studying his map. His route involved Pennsylvania Avenue, which would lead him to E Street and Angela Wilme's apartment.

The sidewalks were crowded with pedestrians, and with the streets clogged with buses, trucks, tourists, and residents trying to get through the afternoon traffic, the trip turned out to be longer than he'd anticipated.

He parked on E Street next to a building marked 134.

Wind swept the street toward him, blowing litter and stray leaves. The stretch of Washington he could see didn't resemble the typical tourist photograph. The sights were cold, gray, and average. It looked like any other city, in any other state, no better and no worse.

The building at 118 E Street was easy to spot from the District of Columbia police officer standing outside the entrance. After his last run in with the federal government's finest, the intention was to avoid making contact with the police or the FBI, so he waited to see if the officer was checking for identification. It was only a few minutes before a delivery girl entered the building, unchecked.

"Easy enough," he said, and walked straight by the officer, and into 118 E Street.

Martin stepped around the cleaning supplies stacked near a busy custodian and climbed two flights of stairs and entered the third-floor hallway. The spring-loaded hinges slammed the door behind him and shut the hallway off to the street noise.

Quiet as a church up here, Martin thought, noticing that Angela's apartment door was defended by a strip of yellow police tape. When he turned the knob, he was surprised to find it open.

Too easy, he thought, and turned, half expecting to find someone standing right behind him, asking him what the hell he thought he was doing. To his relief there was no one.

The long corridor had only two apartment doors and an exit doorway at each end. Angela was sharing the floor with only one other resident. "A lot of space," Martin said, and ducked underneath the police tape.

Her apartment didn't tell him anything he didn't already know, and he was growing more and more uncomfortable by the minute. His fear of getting caught and having to answer a lot of questions forced him from the apartment, and his apprehension was confirmed when he closed the apartment door, and heard the sounds of quick footsteps on the stairs. To his right was another staircase. He took it.

Between the first and second floors he slipped and grabbed at the railing for support. The third-floor hallway door burst open, and a man leaned over the railing.

"Got him," the man said, and started down the flight of stairs at a rate that shocked Martin.

Instinctively Martin sprinted toward the door that led down the first-floor hallway, and back to the front of the building, back to his car. He threw the door open, stopping only long enough to find another man staring through a glass window in the door at the opposite end of the hall.

The far door flew open and a second man sprinted toward him.

"Shit," Martin said. He didn't know who they were, but he knew they weren't cops, there were no commands to halt, freeze, or stop. They had something much more mortal in mind.

———⊶•⊶———

Senator Braun kissed James Redfield, their tongues and hands exploring as they said their goodnights. She came away from their Chadwick's meeting, which had migrated to his townhouse in Brookland, charged with a sense of a future filled with possibilities. His love had never waned and the predictability which had once turned her off now seemed a requisite quality.

She got into her rental, which he'd retrieved, and made her way back toward Georgetown. She had enough of the puzzle put together to feel somewhat confident of her conclusion, but it was her N.Y.P.D. detective friend Shannon Fallon's second phone conversation, that brought to light a host of new questions. Questions which might fill in the remainder of the picture.

Fallon had told her about a rural New York Police Chief named Thomas Martin, who, among his other qualities, seemed to be a bit hardheaded, and perhaps, conveniently naïve. Martin's town in New York had been besieged by a killer, who Fallon believed, for reason's she couldn't adequately convince Braun of, might be connected to Mitchell.

But Braun saw an opportunity in Martin, an opportunity to steer someone in the right direction, a direction which would conveniently skirt her involvement to a great extent.

Stopping at a deli along the way for provisions, she found a secluded spot to watch Mitchell's estate on R Street, and waited for Chief Martin to make his appearance. She was hoping Mitchell's widow would be a logical place for the cop to begin his search, and she was hoping it wouldn't take too long.

Martin felt the small of his back and panicked. His revolver was locked in the glove box of his Camaro. The man descending the stairs turned the corner of the second floor and was almost within arm's reach of him. Martin turned and raced through the building's rear door, down a long flight of cement stairs, and into a parking lot. The door slammed behind him and then whipped back open, colliding with the building's back wall. Martin could feel his senses heighten and the world close in around him. He heard the silenced gunshot as he sprinted underneath the carport and in between a Mercedes and a Ford. It felt like a hornet dive-bombing his head.

He could also hear two sets of footsteps. They were heavy but weren't gaining on him.

He vaulted the hood of the Ford and, with a sturdy foot on

its quarter panel, he vaulted the chain-link fence serving as the barrier for the parking lot. Another shot burst the glass of the Mercedes and another skimmed by his ear, loud and chilling.

The protection of the cars was inadequate, and the men soon had another clear shot. They didn't take it, opting to climb the fence in pursuit. Martin knew this was his last chance. His legs were aching, and his heart felt as though it would burst through his chest. As he turned the corner of the building, a bullet landed in the brick, spraying him with stone and grit. He burst across 9th Street for an alley diagonally across from the one he'd just exited. There were two side doors ten feet into the dim and narrow alley. The second was unlocked. He entered. It was pitch black.

He stumbled into another door and, with some fumbling, managed to open it. A dim corridor stretched before him. He couldn't see anything very well, never mind a viable exit. It was too risky to try, and suicide to go back. He was trapped.

It was much darker at this end of the corridor, so he backed against the wall and crouched next to the floor behind the open door, hoping he would stay hidden.

The alleyway door swung open and two men entered, breathing heavily.

Martin was holding his breath the best he could. His heart was pounding and sweat was beading down his face. When the men rounded into the corridor, he could barely see them.

"Where the hell did he go?" one of them said, gasping for air.

"He's too damn fast."

"Big-time football hero. Running from a fight like a little

girl." The men rushed down the corridor and burst through another door. "C'mon."

An abundance of light flooded that end of the hallway, and as the door closed, the hallway grew dark again.

Martin coughed the stale air from his lungs and tried to catch his breath as he got to his feet. He made it back out onto 9th Street and decided to head to F Street and get a cab. He'd have to come back for his car later. He realized he was leaving his baby, and he also realized, at that moment, he didn't care one bit about the damn thing.

"To 515 R Street," Martin said once he'd hailed one. "That's in Georgetown. But, first I need to stop at the Hill Motel. That's on—"

"I know where it is," the driver interrupted.

Martin needed his backup Smith & Wesson before he did anything.

———

During the trip to Senator Mitchell's house in Georgetown, Martin thought about the near scrape he'd just survived. If this was what Greene had endured for a week, he'd been the better man. The side of his face was stinging hot from the spray of brick wall.

Who the hell were they? he wondered. How'd they find me so fast?

They'd been shooting at him in broad daylight. They didn't care if they got caught, and it was obvious they wanted him dead.

It was also obvious they thought he knew what the hell was going on, that he was as much a threat as Greene had been. Now they were hunting him, and he was tearing himself up inside because he couldn't put the pieces together.

He had to find out what was going on, and quick. It was no longer just a matter of putting things right for the sake of Goshen. He had to save his own ass. He couldn't just pack up and go home. They would simply follow him back to Goshen and he'd fall victim to a scene out of a Francis Ford Coppola movie. He was furious that Greene hadn't been able to talk longer on the phone that night. He might have said something useful, or he might have turned himself in and told him everything.

By the time the cab reached 515 R Street, Martin's mind was racing. He got out of the cab, told the driver to wait, and approached the callbox affixed to a brick privacy wall.

"Mrs. Mitchell?"

"Who's calling please?"

"My name is Tom Martin and I must speak with her," Martin said.

"I'm sorry, but she isn't available."

"Please Mrs. Mitchell," he said, assuming it was her. "I'm a Police Chief from New York, and I traveled all this way to speak with you. During a recent investigation I came across a man who knew your husband. I believe he was killed by the same people who murdered your husband."

There was a short pause followed by the sounds of motors warming up as they began opening an entrance gate crested with a large *M*. The fifty-yard driveway arced upwards among maple trees and a groomed property. Mrs. Mitchell was standing in the front doorway, looking at him as he approached. The door was open only the width of a whiskey tumbler, and Martin could see the heavy chain securing the door. She was still being careful. He waved and smiled to put her at ease, but she opened the door no wider.

She was younger than Martin had anticipated, and attractive.

"I'm very sorry about your loss and for barging in on you like this," he said, extending his badge. His courtesy caught her off guard, and there was a look of misjudgment on her face as she unlatched the door and let it swing open.

"Now, what can I do to help you?" she asked, leading him inside. Her voice was soft and hoarse.

In the library, Martin took a seat next to her on the sofa. "The first thing I want to tell you is that I'm here unofficially. I really have no right to talk to you, but I was hoping you could clear up a few things for me."

"I thought you mentioned you were investigating a killing?"

"Yes, I did, but I was relieved of those duties." He was playing into her hands and hoping she could deduce his purpose. She was the widow of one of the most powerful men in the country, and she had to know something, which was a hell of a lot more than he knew at this point. Indirect and cryptic comments seemed a good ploy to get her curiosity up.

"Relieved by whom?" she asked.

"The FBI."

"What? Why?"

"They waltzed in, confiscated everything, and left me to twist in the wind."

"Well, what are they doing about it?"

"I would be the last to know. I got the feeling they weren't going to do anything further."

"Well, the FBI has been no real help to me. The president called me last week to tell me how sorry he was, and that he was going to personally keep an eye on the investigation. But aside from that, I haven't heard anything. I just took it for granted they would keep me informed, so I don't know how much help I'll be to you."

"Mrs. Mitchell, I come from a small town where I personally know ninety percent of the people I protect. People dying on my watch is unacceptable. I can't sit idly by and wait while this gets swept under the carpet, hoping the FBI will call and let me know what is going on. I have to find the culprit."

"You seem like an honest man, Mr. Martin, but I've been in this town for longer than you've been alive, and I constantly see the underbelly of people. People who can outperform any Hollywood legend; who, at will, can produce the kind of naïve heart you're displaying. Besides, I don't know you, and if I could help, I don't know that I would."

"I'm not a politician, Mrs. Mitchell, or an actor. I'm just a guy who came an awfully long way for a few answers."

She took a long time to consider him.

"Please," he said, thinking of Paulina again.

"All right."

"Who found your husband?"

"I did, a week ago this evening."

"Could you describe the house when you found him?" Martin asked.

"A disaster area. The painters, carpenters, and cleaning service just got the place back into order Friday. I'm going to sell it."

"Do you remember what was missing?"

"Nothing, really. Paperwork, computer stuff, and photos. They were the most valuable things stolen. Photos are memories."

"They took the same kind of stuff from all of the doctors killed in New York."

"They were looking for something, and when they couldn't beat it out of Byron, they ransacked the house for it. That's what I think," she said.

"They beat him to death?"

"Yes." A tear welled in her eye, but she summoned her strength, and it dissipated.

"Do you have any idea what they were looking for?" Martin asked.

"None. I think the FBI had some ideas, but they wouldn't tell me anything. I'm still a suspect, you know. Ridiculous."

"Would it be too painful for you to tell me a little bit about your husband?"

"No, that would be fine. What would you like to know?"

"Start with his professional life."

"He was born and raised in West Virginia, and he became their Republican senator in 1964. He hasn't left Capitol Hill since. Although last year was a close race for him. It wasn't a good year for incumbents. There are many, many freshmen on Capitol Hill this time around. It's rare to have this many new faces around town. It's also rare for the Republicans to still control Congress, what with the president being a Democrat and all. That was another thing Byron had to worry about."

"I'm not sure I follow you," Martin said.

"If the Republicans had given up their control of Congress, as they should have, then he would have been booted from his committee positions as well. I guess you could say everything up there is new."

"Including the president," Martin said.

"Byron hated him. Anyway, he founded a committee assistant scholarship program in the seventies. That got him in the news, which was probably the only reason he did it. Then he was appointed to Appropriations a few years later."

"The money committee?" Martin asked.

"That's right."

Martin was silent as he mulled over the new pieces of information. The committee part might be important, but he couldn't figure it.

"Anything else?" she asked.

"Do you know of any enemies he had?"

"Nope. FBI asked me the same thing."

"What about the name Dr. Robert Greene? Mean anything to you?"

"No, I don't think so."

"Dr. William Delaney?"

She shook her head.

"How about Dr. Peter Dunnelo?"

Again, no.

"Dr. Eric Strogg?"

She was still shaking her head. Martin had reached a dead end.

"Were they the ones killed in your town?" she asked.

"Yes."

"And they were all doctors?"

"Yes."

"Odd, and horrible."

"Well, I can't think of anything else. Thanks for your help, though," he said, a bit resigned, extending his hand. "Good luck with the house."

As Martin began to open the front door, Mrs. Mitchell said something in a quiet voice. "You might check with his mistress."

He looked at her, but she had already turned away from him. "What?"

"She was a scholarship recipient, an intern. Check with George Washington University. She's a student there. I didn't mention it to the police because I wanted to protect Byron. I hope I haven't made a mistake with you."

"What's her name?" Martin asked.

"Don't know."

"No one knows of this? Not even the feds?"

"No." She began to climb the tall staircase, hugging the right wall of the foyer. "Good luck, Mr. Martin."

Outside it was growing dark, and a slight glimmer of orange appeared on the horizon. Martin walked through the open gate at the bottom of the driveway and got into the cab. The mistress was now the key and there was still time to get to the Capitol Building and try to get an answer. If that didn't work he'd have to go to George Washington University and get a list of the people who interned during the semester break.

When Dillon and Sampus burst through the building's lobby,

they ran down a set of stairs and onto G Street. Sampus sprinted to the intersection of 9th where he saw heavy streams of pedestrians and motor vehicle traffic, but no sign of Martin. Dillon sprinted to the intersection of G and 10th streets, but saw nothing different.

After thirty minutes of searching, they were standing on a corner of E Street, watching their red Mercury Grand Marquis speed toward them. Monroe had finally caught up with them.

Monroe slid up to the curb, and Dillon and Sampus got in. "So what happened?" Monroe asked.

"He went to Angela's apartment, just like we thought, but we lost him," Sampus said.

Monroe swerved in and out of cars, negotiating the insanity of E Street until he reached Pennsylvania Avenue. "Lost him how?"

"He's a quick son of a bitch," Dillon said.

"Well, the bug we have at the Mitchell place picked up faint voices, which our girl in Chicago beefed up and analyzed. Martin's in the house talking to the wife," Monroe said, still accelerating.

"The boss called you?"

"Yeah."

"What else did he say?"

"Kill the bastard before he uncovers everything."

"Why's he worried about one cop?"

"Because Martin talked to Greene, and he's smart enough to put it together. The FBI is still compiling an all-inclusive who's-who of corruption on the Hill. The boss says they'll never find anything, but Greene knew what was going on and he talked to Martin. I guess it's reason enough."

The Mercury weaved through the winding bends of R Street

and began a deep descent toward Mitchell's property in time to see a yellow cab pulling away from the curb. Monroe, Dillon, and Sampus agreed that it was Martin sitting in the back seat.

When a bullet shattered the rear passenger window, the cab-driver took heed of Martin's commands and began to pull away from the Mercury. Bullets rang against the sheet metal of the cab as Dillon leaned out of the car firing a silenced automatic pistol.

When a revolver appeared through the broken glass of the cab, Monroe tried to move the Mercury away from Martin's line of fire, but two quick shots landed in the windshield, splintering the glass so that he couldn't see. A third shot missed the Mercury altogether, but the fourth punctured the glass and struck Monroe in the neck. Dillon leaned back into the car and grabbed at the steering wheel, but the car had already exaggerated too far to the left. It jumped a tall curb and began spinning out of control. Sampus braced himself with outstretched arms against both rear door panels. The Mercury came to rest when it collided with a tree, sending all three of its unsecured passengers throughout the car's cabin.

22

On Tuesday, November 3, Director Geehern sat in the back seat of a Lincoln Continental, en route to the FBI's headquarters via Pennsylvania Avenue. The driver of the silver car made the habitual trek around the National Mall and in front of the Capitol Building.

It had been over a week since the death of Senator Mitchell, and his crew of senior investigators, whom he'd hand picked for the task of bringing both the culprit and financier of the crime to justice, still had very little to show for their efforts. They had a long list of people who hated the man enough to want to kill him, but it was at best inconclusive.

The drive along the Mall was quiet and bare, and the press, who had long ago figured out Geehern's early-morning schedule, were waiting for him at the entrance to the Hoover Building.

"Who did it?" they all seemed to asked at once.

"Are there any significant developments in the case?" another asked.

Geehern assured them everything was being done that could

be, and that was the only comment he was prepared to make. He pushed his way through the crowd and entered the building.

Geehern entered his office with secretary in tow. As he hung up his jacket, booted up his computer, and adjusted his window blinds, she ran over the man's long schedule for the day, and paraphrased the several calls which had already come in for him. The messages were from satellite agencies around the country with significant information regarding cases being solved or new problems arising. None of the messages were from Special Agent Williams, and Geehern was disappointed.

Standing next to his secretary, he looked over his schedule list for the day and moaned at its length. He also grieved at the sight because he noticed the expectation of a call from the president about Senator Mitchell.

"President Hanland in the White House doesn't make me sleep well at night. But, if I didn't have to meet with or listen to the son of a bitch, I probably wouldn't mind that much," Geehern said, getting a smile out of his secretary.

"Heading back to Chicago again today, I see," she said.

"I'll drag that field office into the Twenty-First Century whether they want to be there or not."

She left him logging onto his computer, but her voice came through the intercom almost immediately. Agent Tobin was calling with news of some importance.

"Sleep is a good thing, Tobin. What's so important that you're calling me at 6 AM?"

"The D.C. Police found Special Agents Williams and Grant in an alleyway Dumpster near Chinatown this morning. Looks like they've been dead about seventy-two hours."

There was a long pause.

"Do you know what they were doing down here, sir?" Tobin asked.

"Yeah, I sent them to check out a tip about a dead woman, allegedly connected to the Mitchell case. Then they were heading to some town in New York to check on the origin of the tip and try to verify the extent of the connection."

"Well, they never made it," Tobin said.

"I appreciate the call, Agent Tobin," Geehern said, ready to hang up, but Tobin had more questions.

"What are you going to do about Williams' slot?" he asked.

"I'll assign someone, and I'll tell whoever it ends up being to come and see you. You're in charge of this mess now, and it'll be up to you to bring his replacement up to speed."

"What about New York?"

"Later," Geehern said. "We have field offices in New York and they'll have to take care of it now. Square that situation away and get back on the Mitchell investigation," he added, and hung up.

"Williams," he said, leaning onto his desk with both hands. "Poor bastard."

He asked his secretary to get him the closest field office to Goshen, New York, and in short order, his telephone began to ring.

A cool, practiced voice answered. "This is Agent Connole. How can I help you?"

"Connole, this is Director Geehern in Washington."

"Yes, sir?" the New York agent said.

"We're currently looking into the death of a United States

senator, I'm sure you got the memo. Well, we received information concerning a possible connection to that case from a Chief of Police Martin in Goshen, New York. How far is that from your office?"

"Twenty minutes," Connole said.

"This Martin character has a series of unexplained deaths and they may be connected with Senator Mitchell. I'm faxing you a short summation," Geehern said.

"The murders over in Goshen have been the top news story up here, sir," Connole replied.

"Well, we had dispatched a special agent to Goshen last week to check in with the Chief, but the agent was killed before he could leave Washington. We believe the agent was killed because of the information in the possession of the Goshen Police Chief. I want you to get down there and go through all of the material they've compiled so far, and I want you to courier a copy of everything to me in Washington, by this afternoon."

"Yes, sir."

"I know this sounds simple enough, but stay on your toes. Caution is the name of this game, Connole," Geehern said, and then hung up the phone.

Martin left his motel early on Tuesday morning to search for Senator Mitchell's mistress. He'd changed his mind about traipsing around Capitol Hill after the events of R Street; he'd waited almost three hours the previous night before he felt it was safe enough to pick up his car. Then he'd driven around for another hour making sure he wasn't being followed.

The main arteries flowing by the Capitol Building were all jammed, but he found a parking space on Madison Drive, and walked across the National Mall. He climbed the long set of stone stairs to the building and walked inside. Employees and tour groups were bustling about the large entranceway and Martin negotiated the crowd and approached an obvious employee.

"Can I help you, sir?" the employee said, speaking with a slight southern accent.

"I'm looking for the personnel office," Martin said.

"Which house?" The man's tone changed when he recognized Martin wasn't a tourist. The new tone was tired and sharp.

"Senate," Martin said.

"That's in the Senate Office Building. There are two of them over there. It's the one on the corner of Maryland and Constitution," the man said.

"Thank you."

Martin walked back toward the front of the building and exited. He could hear the man reverting to the pleasant and quiet tone of voice as another potential tourist approached.

Outside the air was heavy. Beyond the Capitol Building's dome was a stately blue sky, but over the National Mall a curtain of black storm clouds was pushing toward him, engulfing the clear day and threatening rain or snow.

Martin walked the several blocks to the Senate Office Building, enjoying the cold air. Deliberately passing the Supreme Court, he waited for the traffic on Constitution Avenue to thin out before he crossed and entered the building.

The two buildings, separated by 1st Street, were twins of one another. Martin entered the large, stone giant perched on the corner of Maryland Avenue, and walked toward the reception desk and a heavyset woman.

"May I help you?" Her tone was sharp. She was skipping the pleasantry stage altogether.

"The personnel office, please."

"It's on the second floor. Go through this security check," the woman said, pointing to a man standing next to a metal detector. "When you get off the elevator follow the hallway to the left. It's at the very end, room 230," she said, handing him a clip tag, while pointing toward a log book he was required to sign.

"Thank you," Martin said, clipping the tag on his jacket and signing his name to the log. He followed her instructions and got on the elevator. When the door opened onto the second floor he headed for room 230.

Through the door a counter blocked the entrance into the office. A slim, handsome man sat at the only visible desk beyond the counter, typing on a computer at a lightning pace.

"Be with you in a moment," he said, not looking up from his keyboard. His long fingers were tapping the keys so quickly it was almost mesmerizing. He finished typing, turned away from his desk, and approached Martin.

Martin withdrew his wallet and flashed his New York badge. "I'm investigating a homicide in conjunction with the FBI, and I was wondering how I would go about getting a list of interns who served in the Senate over the last semester break."

"I don't know if I'm allowed to give out that information, sir," the man answered.

"Who would I have to speak to, then?"

"I'm just a temp. Everyone's at a retirement breakfast downstairs. Maybe you could come back."

"It's just routine."

The man stood, considering Martin.

"Don't worry about it, I just wanted to confirm my information on her, anyhow," Martin said, preparing to leave.

"Which senator?" the man asked.

"Mitchell."

The man's expression changed. He appeared more ready to help.

"Which university?"

"George Washington University. I think she's a graduate student."

"You have to be, to intern with a senator. They don't allow underclassmen anymore. You said the student was female?"

"Yes."

The man was typing on the computer again and a printout rolled from a printer across the room. Walking over, he ripped the paper from the machine and handed it to Martin.

"There you are. There were seven of them last break."

"A lot," Martin said, looking at the list.

"So she's on there?"

"There she is," Martin said, flicking the sheet with his finger and folding it in eighths, slipping into a hip pocket. "Thanks for the confirmation."

George Washington University was located a few blocks from the Potomac in a neighborhood of Washington called Foggy Bottom. It was too far from the Senate Office Building to walk, so he headed back to the car.

He drove along Pennsylvania Avenue until he reached Washington Circle, where he picked up 23rd Street and drove onto the campus. Cement sidewalks and blacktop streets divided the university's stone buildings. He found a parking spot in the visitors' lot and then spent some time searching for the university commons.

The commons building was on the other side of the campus, but once he found it, getting the location of all seven females who had interned on Capitol Hill was a snap. Anne, a young woman of the nineteen persuasion, was the only one working the records office, and with a little effort in the charm department, Martin got what he wanted from her. Martin was thinking of one of his favorite Stephen King lines which summed up their encounter nicely: *At 9:58 she came, at 9:59 she came around*, or something to that effect.

By noon Martin had trekked across the campus four times and had even walked six blocks off campus to locate Mitchell's mistress.

The last address on his list was 2514 I Street and a student by the name Joanne Temus owned the entire row house. In passing, Martin thought of how similar Foggy Bottom and Georgetown looked. The distinct way two-story town houses lined shady streets was a dead giveaway you were in Washington, D.C.

Martin climbed the slate steps toward her bright red door and noticed that the house had new windows and fresh paint on its black shutters. Dead, soft, and vibrant leaves lay pushed into the corners of the porch step and a harsh breeze was blowing at Martin's back as he pushed the buzzer. When Joanne Temus answered the door, he knew he'd found the right woman.

She had grief in her eyes. It had become easy enough for him to spot.

"Miss Temus, could I talk to you for a few minutes?" Martin asked, displaying his badge. She really didn't look at it.

"What about?"

"Senator Mitchell and the relationship you had with him."

"We had no relationship," she managed. She was clearly out of tears, but his bluntness was a rabbit punch.

"Please, you could help me find who did this."

"How did you find me?"

"The college gave me your address."

The answer disappointed her. "They're not supposed to do that," she said as she opened the door and instructed him to enter.

"Thank you," he said, skirting the statement concerning the university's indiscretion. He was just as sure the Senate personnel employee wasn't supposed to divulge what he did, either.

"So, what's your name?" she asked.

"Thomas Martin," he said as they both sat down. The room was small and packed with comfortable antique furniture. He waited for the James Bond comparison, but it never came and he was grateful.

"So, are you with the FBI? You know, I read the paper every day, and the reporters say you don't know what you're doing. But now you've found me, so I guess you're digging up stuff."

"I'm not with the FBI. I'm a Police Chief from New York," he said.

"New York?" she asked. "But your badge?"

Martin pulled his identification again and she examined it closely this time.

"There was a man involved with the senator, a resident of the town where I work in New York. They were both killed by the same people, and I'm trying to find out who did it."

"All by yourself? Why don't you go to the FBI?"

"Like you said, they don't know what they're doing."

She studied him for a moment, considering his answer. "Bad blood, eh? So why do you think I can help you?"

"I don't know if you can or not, but I'd like you to try."

She nodded her head. "Fire away."

"When did you begin to work for Mitchell?"

"This summer. I started in June."

"And what did you do for him?"

"Well, I'm studying to be a tax consultant, so I worked with his accounting team."

"He had an accounting team?" Martin asked. He didn't quite understand why a senator would need a team of anything.

"Well, he had a pretty large staff, and five of them are accountants."

"What did you do on this accounting team?"

"I was a gopher basically, adding figures, double-checking arithmetic and chart layouts, picking up the takeout."

"And when did the relationship begin between you two?"

"I told you there was no relationship. Who told you that?"

"Mrs. Mitchell."

Joanne was silent for a moment, staring at the floor and then at Martin. Finally, she began to speak again. "Byron and I spent a lot of time together, but he was way past the point of any kind of physical involvement. He was a romantic and an intellectual, and we enjoyed talking. When you've been around as long as Byron had been, you know an awful lot, and you've seen a lot of things you'd rather forget. I was interested in those things," Joanne said. She was a petite woman, perhaps twenty-five, blond, and very beautiful in an angular, mathematical way.

"So when did the two of you extend your contact beyond Capitol Hill?" Martin asked.

"In July, I guess. We met over dinner or coffee until late September."

"That's into the semester, isn't it?"

"Byron wanted me to stay, so he arranged it with the university."

"Did the two of you ever have one of your talks in this apartment?"

"Yes. Byron liked it here. He bought me this building, and we decorated it together. He loved auctions, and he loved buying me things."

"Did Mitchell keep a room here?"

"I told you, it wasn't that kind of setup."

"No, I mean an office."

"Yes, he did. Why?"

"Could I see it?"

"I suppose." She stood and motioned for him to follow her. Martin didn't know what to make of her, and he wondered if power really was an aphrodisiac for some people. Joanne seemed smarter than that.

The office was papered in a flowered design, and the floor was dark hardwood. The furniture was early-American colonial and in impeccable condition. A roll-top desk sat under a pane window overlooking a very small backyard. The drawers were stuffed with meaningless papers, pens, and mail, but as Martin pulled out the chair to sit down, he saw a fireproof box underneath the desk. He looked at Joanne and pulled it out, setting it on the desk.

"Do you have the key for this?" he asked.

"It'd be in the desk, if anywhere," she said.

Opening a drawer above the writing surface, he found a single key emblazoned with an *F*, which unlocked the box. Inside were spreadsheets, campaign lists, audio tapes, and bundled folders filled with paperwork.

"Paperwork," Martin mumbled so that Joanne didn't hear him.

Together, the two of them mulled over the contents until the daylight had faded from the office window and was replaced by the amber lamp illuminating the walkway leading into the back yard. Large lazy flakes of snow fell past the lamps and onto the now dusty white ground.

The spreadsheets were detailed accounting records of both recent and dated proposals on which the Senate Appropriations Committee had voted favorably. They outlined the amounts of money to be granted to each proposal and when.

The campaign lists were long and stapled into sections: *Contributions for 2005 election, Contributions for 1999 election, Contributions for 1993 election*, and so on.

The latest list held the greatest interest for Martin, because Dr. Robert Greene's name was on it. The list was in alphabetical order and next to the murdered man's name were three initials: PSR.

Martin flipped through the list until he came to the letter P, and then skimmed through the page until he saw the physician's organization acronym. "PSR, contribution of $25,000,000 received on May 30, 2005. Contact Dr. Robert Greene, Greenwich Avenue, Goshen, New York."

Martin stared in disbelief. If his jaw had been resting in his lap he wouldn't have been a bit surprised. The local organization had been high speed, but they weren't that big of a deal. There was no way four local physicians could come up with that kind of cash. He checked the list for Strogg's, Dunnelo's, and Delaney's names but they were not on it. Then he checked the list for Angela Wilme's name. It was there. "Angela Wilme, R.N., see PSR contribution."

Martin was beginning to think the other three physicians, who had been killed because of Greene, either knew what was going on and wanted to keep a low profile, or the more probable possibility, Greene and Wilme were using the organization for their own ends, and the other three physicians didn't know squat.

"Does the name Angela Wilme mean anything to you?" Martin asked.

"No, why?" Joanne asked.

"What about the name Dr. Robert Greene?"

"Nope. Do you want to tell me what's really going on?"

"That wouldn't be my first choice. Plus, it would take forever."

"So how about a quick version?"

He picked up the piece of paper and showed her Angela's name on the list. Once she'd read it, he flipped through the sheets to the PSR line and let her read that.

"The PSR is an organization in Goshen, New York, where I work, and it's run by four doctors. Dr. Greene was one of them. All four were killed in Goshen by professionals. The same ones who killed Mitchell, at least according to Greene, and I'm starting to believe everything the man said. He was having an affair with Angela Wilme here in Washington, and she was killed around the same time Mitchell was. So Greene runs home and the killers follow him. Now I'm in Washington trying to piece together what the hell happened here, so that I might run across who did the killings in my town. That's the short version."

"You're in over your head," she said.

"Maybe, maybe not. I found you before the Feds. You said so yourself."

"Regardless. Because of this list, you're in over your head."

"What?"

"Well, your doctor and the woman are on it, and they're dead. That's a little more than coincidence."

"The list would seem to prove someone's knocking off campaign contributors."

"Looks that way to me."

"So that sort of puts me out of my element, according to you?" Martin asked.

"Sort of. Wilme and Greene are the only names on the list associated with the PSR and they're dead, right? You said she was killed here in Washington and he was killed in your town. Well, then the killers got pissed off at these two, but they missed Greene in Washington. So they followed him to Goshen, and when they saw the PSR was in your town, they killed everyone associated with the organization. They must have had one of these lists. They were just playing it safe, being systematic." She held the campaign list in her hand.

Martin knew she was right.

"You have to tell the FBI what you know," she said. "This could really help them. It might be the one missing piece to the puzzle they need to solve this thing."

"It's probably the proper course of action, but if I had time to give you the long version, you'd see why going to the FBI is the last thing I want to do with my life."

"I'm right, and you know it."

"You know, if Mitchell was as smart as you say he was, then some of it rubbed off on you."

"Thanks for the insult. He was a wonderful man, but I'd like to think I was cranial to begin with. He might have sharpened me up a little, but no more than I did him." Her self-confidence was reassuring.

When Martin left her home, there was a dusting of snow covering the yard, street, and his car. He opened the trunk and dropped Mitchell's fireproof box next to the spare tire, and removed a pair of gloves and a rag. He spent several minutes wiping his car windows down, then got in and started up the engine. He waited for the heat to come on and tried to find a weather report on the AM radio.

———— •◦• ————

Agents Dean Connole and Lisa Donalds drove their Ford Crown Victoria out of the parking lot of the Newburgh, New York, field office of the FBI and toward the small town of Goshen. A thin trail of snow lined the dry county road stretching through Orange County. They arrived at the converted railroad station serving as the Goshen Police Department building to find only an unmarked state police cruiser sitting in the front parking lot. Stepping out into the swirling gusts of snow blowing off the station's roof, the two agents made their way into the building and were met by Dispatcher Debra Chen.

"I'm Agent Connole, and this is Agent Donalds. We're with the FBI's Newburgh field office. Where can we find Chief Martin today?" Connole asked.

The dispatcher leaned back in her chair and pounded on the thin wall behind her. "Detective, would you come out here for a minute?" she barked, then returned to her work, ignoring the agents.

"Well, well, well. Do I have a bone to pick with you," McElroy said, physically backing the two agents into a corner as he began his rampage through the account of what had transpired over the past few days.

"And I'll tell you this, Mr. and Mrs. Federal Bonehead. If something doesn't happen right quick to rectify things, I'm going to personally start detaching appendages," McElroy concluded.

"Can I have a moment, Detective?" Connole asked, squeezing passed the man and withdrawing his cell phone.

Under the frightening glare of McElroy, he finally got through after a very long wait. "Sir, this is Connole with the Newburgh field office. We spoke this morning."

"Yes, I remember," Geehern said. "I'm not senile yet."

"We're up here in Goshen, and it appears that two men disguised as the agents you dispatched already took all of the material from the local and state police departments."

"What?"

"They had the necessary paperwork, sir. I'm looking at it now, and it sure looks legitimate to my eyes. They also had Special Agent Williams' and Agent Grant's identification."

"Great, just great. Where's this Martin character? I want to talk with him."

"He's missing, sir. The men posing as agents apparently killed an officer and put the local medical examiner in a coma he'll be lucky to wake up from. Chief Martin is nowhere to be found."

"So what happened to Martin? Do they think he's dead?"

"They think he might have gone to Washington."

"Here? Why would he come here?"

"From what the people here say, he's not the type of guy to let something slide. The fake agents told Martin and the state police we were taking over the investigation, and that they were to stand down or face federal prosecution."

"That's great, just terrific. Thank you Agent Connole, you've been very enlightening," Geehern said, and hung up.

23

Kori Svenson continued to spend a lot of her time in the bowels of the Chicago headquarters. She sat at a large countertop beneath a wall of video screens and audio recording equipment. The whirling sounds produced by the room's sheer amount of electricity was the only sound, aside from an occasional moan from her swivel chair.

Svenson was staring at a section of the wall, where a series of CD drivers were stacked. Drawer numbers eleven and twelve had been programmed to monitor a police station in Goshen, New York. Both drawers had been recording all day, but when she enabled the speaker in order to listen to what was presently being recorded, she wasn't prepared for what she heard.

Throughout the day, Svenson had listened to a lot of the calls coming from the tapped lines, and from the Echomike which was programmed to pull everything else from the air including conversations and cellular calls. Each time she simply let the system run its course, forgetting about it, but this time was different and Svenson knew it. She had managed to put two and two together by accessing information from Goshen's local newspaper. She'd become convinced her boss had ordered the death of three physicians there, but she couldn't quite put her finger on the bigger picture.

A conversation began to come over a speaker, a conversation between a New York field agent of the FBI and Director Geehern himself. The sound of the man's voice drained the blood from her face. She was afraid. They were discussing Martin and the fact that he was either dead, or had journeyed to Washington, D.C. to try and piece together what had happened in his small town. They also discussed that there had been two men in New York who'd posed as federal agents, confiscated evidence, and killed quite a few locals.

When the conversation was over Svenson left the room. Her boss was out on a limb, too far out. She would have to take care of herself or become a casualty of the situation. She chose the former, and the first step was to shed her loyalty to boss and company, and disappear.

<hr/>

John Scaffiotelli walked the length of hallway leading from the empty security room to an elevator, slipping the CD of the New York field agent's conversation into his pocket, and wondering why his chief of security wasn't where she was supposed to be. He stepped off into his upper-floor office, which smelled of wood oil.

A brass button next to the door ignited a desk lamp, chasing out the darkness created by the drawn velvet curtains. The wall clock chimed twelve noon.

He sat in that low light for a long time, staring at the telephone, dreading what he knew he had to do. Pressing a button on his telephone labeled "Mr. Nivinson," he listened to the pulsing rings, and when a voice answered, he lifted the receiver and began to tell the New York story.

"Not over the phone," Nivinson interrupted Scaffiotelli's recital. "This is too important for me to merely relay to the others. You'll have to appear."

"Appear? Why?"

"They'll want to hear it from you. We'll all want to hear what went wrong, and what you plan to do to rectify the situation."

"Yes, of course," Scaffiotelli said, his voice low and reflective.

"3 PM John. We'll be waiting."

John eased the receiver back into its cradle and eased back into his chair. He could hear the stiff movements of the wall clock and could feel his options slipping away from him with each tick.

Tick.

Tick.

Scaffiotelli spent the better part of that afternoon on the telephone, screaming at the people who were searching for Martin. There were ten of them looking under rocks, and it was mystifying to him they weren't tripping over one another. Yet somehow the small-town Chief had eluded them since the Georgetown incident near the senator's home.

Three PM sped toward him, and everything he'd spent his life attaining felt like it was sliding through his fingers. The group to which he reported hadn't a history for great tolerance, and he knew his handling of the Mitchell situation had been far from exemplary.

Walking into the outer area of the floor his office was located on, Scaffiotelli stopped in front of his private elevator. He inserted a thin key into the lock next to the stainless steel door, stepped inside the bare compartment, and descended to the lobby of his Chicago headquarters building.

White clouds were rolling across the brilliant blue sky as he walked the several blocks to South Wacker Drive, to Mr. Nivinson's building. The skyscraper reached out above him as he stepped onto the shadow-gripped quad leading to the main entrance. The sweet smell in the air seemed to be mocking the magnitude of the largest building in America, as well as some of its most powerful men waiting on his arrival.

Inside an upper floor, a wide hall lined with elegant trimmings and thick pile carpeting stretched out before him. Polished doors labeled with an individual's name lined each side of the hallway. Some of the names he recognized, like Mr. Nivinson's, while others he didn't. He crept past those closed offices, toward the conference room. As he entered, he saw the group seated at a long polished table, waiting for him.

The six brothers grim, he thought, descending a set of three wide stairs onto the main floor of the room.

An empty chair was tucked under the far end of the table, and Scaffiotelli made his way around to it and sat down. The reflection he saw staring back at him in the table's mirror-like finish was filled with fear. I look as bad as I feel, he thought.

The room was bright and sparing in its elegant decoration of glossy maple and dark leather. The room and the men were intimidating to Scaffiotelli. He couldn't remember a time when he felt more self-conscious.

"Let's have it, John," Douglas Nivinson said.

"We've been unable to find Martin, and it looks as though we may not," Scaffiotelli said, his voice cracking at first.

"And what exactly does Mr. Martin know?" another man asked.

"He talked with Greene in New York. It wasn't all that informative, but I guess he learned enough from it to decide to go to Washington and poke around."

"And the first thing he did was talk with the senator's widow?" the man asked.

"Yes."

"And now the FBI has been alerted to his presence in Washington and are probably searching for him as well?"

"Yes."

"And why is that, do you suppose?"

"They found the two federal agents' bodies in Washington that we killed. It was probably just a routine call to New York that alerted them to the fact someone had marched in there and helped themselves to all of Martin's evidence."

"That we killed?"

"That I killed," Scaffiotelli corrected himself.

"So now they're focusing on the connection between the events in Washington and New York?" The man continued to be the only person to speak, and Scaffiotelli didn't even know his name.

"Yes."

"And if they hook up with Martin, what do you see happening?"

"They might be able to put it together."

"How could this have happened, Mr. Scaffiotelli? It seemed a simple enough plan."

"I—"

"The position you have put us in is unbelievable," Nivinson said. "How do you plan to rectify this situation, John?"

"Killing Martin should plug the last remaining hole, especially if he hasn't gone to the Feds yet. We have all of the information connecting us with New York and there's nothing all that conclusive, and the gentleman who did the killings for us is dead."

"You hope you've gotten all the information. And if Martin's gone to the Feds?" the unknown man asked.

"Then I don't believe it can be rectified," Scaffiotelli answered, his voice sinking.

"Then we have a situation that can't be contained and an investigation that will lead right to our doorstep," said a board member named Calaberi. "Personally, I don't think killing the man is going to do it. Too many people at the FBI know New York is the focal point. They're under the gun to point a finger at someone, and that someone will be us. Hell, it doesn't take a genius to figure the situation out."

"So what would you recommend? Turn ourselves in?" asked another board member, addressing Calaberi.

"Of course not," Calaberi said. "It was young John here who was entrusted to solve our little problem with the senator, and he fucked it up three ways to Sunday. He must take responsibility for his actions, and if that means apprehension, then so be it."

Scaffiotelli stared around the room. They were all nodding.

"There can be only one course of action at this point, one that will ensure the president's legislation dies as it should, as we intended from the start. Kill the son of a bitch," Calaberi said.

"Excuse me?" Scaffiotelli asked in disbelief.

"You see, John, if you had done as you were told, then the senator would have died, and the FBI would have either declared the case unsolved or pinned it on someone they wanted to bust anyway. Whichever, the senators we have in our hip pocket wouldn't have had the balls to try a stunt like Mitchell was trying to pull off. We would have had the illusion of being beyond the law, as we've always had, and that would have been the end of it."

"But it became very apparent there were other parties involved," Scaffiotelli said. "It was a judgment call, but you can't blame me for killing Wilme or Greene and his compatriots in Goshen. Mitchell was never just the end of it, and you know it."

"Squabbling over this now is pointless. This is the only avenue open to us," Douglas Nivinson interceded.

"But killing the president?" Scaffiotelli asked Nivinson. "That's not just something you decide to do one day."

"It's always been an option, and we've planned for it to the tune of millions of dollars," Nivinson said.

"What?"

"We had hoped it wouldn't come to this; we don't want it. But there's a threat to our collective future, including yours—"

"You'll never pull it off," Scaffiotelli interrupted.

"Not us, John, you," Nivinson said. "Things are moving fast now. We need to have confidence and conviction."

"Impossible. President Hanland has had two attempts since he was elected. He's hot, and the Secret Service knows it, and Mitchell's murder made everyone in D.C. heighten their security. It's impossible."

"Anything's possible. Jesus, you're naïve. This has been planned to the last detail. We have people inside the Secret Service, the military, and the White House," Nivinson said. "We even have them in the FBI, and have been paying some of them for years. Some have never been used, never done a thing to earn their fat accounts, but it's time for them to start. Hanland arrives back at the White House tomorrow, and shortly thereafter, on national television, he'll sign that damn bill of his into law. He's verbally approved the changes Congress made, now all that's left is the formality. That cannot happen."

"How?" Scaffiotelli asked, his mind was racing like a doped Kentucky Derby stud.

"You don't have to worry about the details. You've put us in a very delicate position, threatened our very existence. We want the satisfaction of knowing what we set out to do has been accomplished. That should be understandable."

"Yes, I suppose."

Calaberi stood and walked toward Scaffiotelli. Placing a heavy hand on his shoulder, he whispered into his ear. "Use Sampus and Dillon. I hope you realize that getting busted is the least of your worries right now. We're all family here, and you can't get away from your family, John. They're always with you, around you, and part of you. Understand? I hope you do, because if you botch this up, I'll delight in watching someone rip your heart out through your asshole. But only after I've seen your wife and beautiful children brutalized and butchered."

"You're dismissed," Nivinson said, and Scaffiotelli left the room.

————•————

When Martin at last heard something about the weather, it was a forecast depicting a grim future for Washington over the next few days. They were expecting more scattered snow for Wednesday followed by freezing rain and high winds for the remainder of the week. He turned the knob on the radio to a music station and pulled the car away from the curb.

At the intersection down the street from Joanne's apartment, a bright amber street lamp was illuminating the snow on the pavement. It also lit the backseat of his car so well, that when Martin stared into his rearview mirror, he could see someone was there. The low-backed front seat provided inadequate concealment and he could discern the straggling fibers of hair against the backdrop of white scenery through his car's rear window. Sweat beaded up on his forehead and his earlier incident flashed through his mind. He swallowed hard and could feel his pulse rate climb.

Slipping the car into park and reaching for his Smith and Wesson revolver, he swung in his seat and brought the gun to bear against the ear of his passenger.

"Don't shoot, for Christ's sake. You'd be killing a senator," the woman exclaimed. "Please drive. They're looking for me also."

"Get the hell out of my car," Martin said, still holding the gun against her head.

"The men you ran off the road in Georgetown, in front of

Mitchell's house, they're hunting high and low for both of us. Please, I need to talk to you."

Martin reached forward and switched on the dome light so he could see her better. "Get up in the front seat where I can keep an eye on you," he ordered, and she climbed around the passenger seat and eased into the front.

Martin put the car back into drive and moved straight through the intersection, coming to a stretch of road that was just wet. The Camaro picked up speed and the granular sounds of sand and salt could be heard pinging beneath the undercarriage.

"Who the hell are you?"

"My name is Susan Braun. I'm a senator from New York."

"You wouldn't have any identification to convince me of that, would you?"

"You don't recognize me?" she asked, displaying a New York driver's license. "I'd feel better if that gun weren't jammed in my face."

"Well, it makes me fell better having it jammed in your face. That license doesn't say anything about your being a politician."

"Would you please?" Braun said in a near-commanding tone. "Guns make me very nervous."

Martin lowered the weapon until it rested on his leg. "Well?"

"Well, what?" she asked.

"Well, why the hell are you in my car, Miss New York?"

"I've been trying to figure out what happened to Senator Mitchell, and when I did, I tried to figure out who I should tell."

"And you came up with me? Brilliant choice. Why?"

"Because you're disconnected enough."

"What?"

"You're not from Washington."

Martin noted that Greene had said almost the same thing. "How did you know who I was, what I was in Washington for?"

"Do you think everyone is stupid, or should I feel honored?" she asked, sounding offended.

"Maybe you should feel honored. Yes, I recognize you, I do know what my senator looks like. But, I don't believe a word of what you're saying," Martin said as he headed toward his hotel, veering every once and a while to throw his passenger off. "How do I know you're not feeding me some sort of line?"

"You have to trust me."

"Why is it that everyone wants me to trust them?" he asked under his breath.

"What?" the senator asked.

"Sorry. I don't." He was still keeping a close eye on the woman and a grip on his revolver. "Due in no small part to your occupation."

"Did you find anything about the PSR when you were inside with Joanne, or were you discussing the curriculum at George Washington University?" Braun asked while looking out the passenger window at the dusting of snow covering the scenery.

"What?" Martin asked. "Now how the hell do you know about that?"

"I have connections, but I've been keeping a low profile, so I don't have the whole picture. At least where you're concerned."

Martin swerved the Camaro to the side of the road and shut off the engine. "We're not moving until I get some damn answers out of you," he said. "How do you know my name, and how'd you know what I came to D.C. for?"

"It isn't safe to sit out in the open like this," she said, looking out the windshield of the car.

"Too bad."

"I have connections, like I said before," she said, being as cryptic as ever.

Martin leaned over and pulled on the handle for the passenger door. It swung open. "Get the hell out of my car."

"One of my connections is associated with the Department of Justice. They told me about a possible link between Mitchell and a small town in southern New York," she said, pulling the door shut.

"Go on."

"They also said someone from New York was possibly in D.C. snooping around. It wasn't hard to figure out the rest. I just waited and watched Mitchell's house like a hawk. I figured the widow was a safe bet, and she was, because you showed up. By the time you found Joanne, my connection had identified you for me."

"I've been staying at a motel just outside Washington. It's a flea trap, but no one has come looking for me there yet, so as traps go it's safe," Martin said, restarting the car and easing the revolver between his right leg and the vinyl seat.

"Good, let's go," she said.

The motel room was warm but hadn't been cleaned, and Martin felt somewhat self-conscious about having a United States senator here. The bed was still turned down, and the sheets were pushed into wavelike disarray. A small, cluttered table and two chairs sat beside the window.

Martin moved all of his belongings from the table and sat

down, while Braun took up position across the table. "So, do you want me to fill you in first, or do you want to begin?" she asked.

"I'm afraid you'll have to give me something more to go on. I don't plan on rambling on for an hour to someone who may or may not be pulling my chain."

"Dr. Greene and Angela Wilme met while they were at Georgetown University, and they've been lovers ever since. How's that?"

"Okay, I'll start. That way you can give me the full story, with the benefit of what I've told you," Martin said.

"Good," she said.

He ran through the story quickly. "So once I reached Washington, I questioned Mrs. Mitchell and the senator's mistress, and then you pop out of the woodwork, and here we are," Martin concluded.

"Do you realize how close you are to the answer already? All that's needed to explain your killings is in what you've just told me."

"So why don't you enlighten me, Senator," Martin said.

"What was your impression of the PSR?"

"What are you talking about?" he asked.

"What did you think of them?"

"They contributed twenty-five million to the Mitchell campaign fund, and I just didn't get the impression they were that well off."

"So you mean they were middle men?" Braun asked.

"Give the Socratic methodology a rest and just tell me what you know."

"The PSR is a medical organization with a philosophy that happens to be discordant with the traditional medical outlook. Of course, in theory the medical profession is there to serve the people, but that's a very naïve belief to hold as truth."

"Sure, I'll buy that, with the amount of money doctors make," Martin said.

"When Greene was at Georgetown University Medical School, he established a charter membership of the national organization called the PSR."

A questioning expression fell over Martin's face.

"That's right," Braun said. "Your four musketeers didn't invent the thing. Now, it was no surprise that the organization wasn't real big with the medical students, because of its conflicting philosophy, but it was big with the nursing students at Georgetown, because they are more committed to the patients. Enter Angela Wilme, who represented the nurses belonging to Georgetown University's charter of the PSR. Now, I don't want you to think of the PSR at GU as some huge animal, because it wasn't. It was an organization in direct conflict with the medical students and always met with great resistance. So you're correct to think the PSR in Goshen could never have had that much cash squirreled away. But when Wilme and Greene graduated, she remained in Washington while he returned to his hometown. Angela stayed in D.C. for a reason."

"What are you getting at?"

"Angela was killed because of her involvement with the PSR, here in Washington. Their goal of the moment was to help President Hanland pass his Health Care Bill. They were interested in this because the bill was the single greatest representation of a core philosophy, providing quality, affordable health care. The PSR was the holding tank for the cash they were using to influence Congress, in an attempt to get the bill passed." Braun paused a moment and stared at Martin. "Who do you think would stand to lose the most if Hanland's Bill were passed?"

"It regulates cost and everything, right? So anyone associated would lose, the doctors, the insurance and pharmaceutical companies."

"Some would call that socialized medicine."

"Some would call it long overdue."

"Okay, who represents the doctor's interests and has seen to it that they've been so prosperous for so long? Who wouldn't want to see the present health care institution tampered with?" Braun said.

It has to be the flip side of the PSR, but who would oppose them? Martin thought. Then the answer was so clear that he felt ashamed he hadn't seen it before. "The AMA," he concluded, slapping his hand on the tabletop.

"Very close guess, but no," Braun said.

"You lost me, then."

"The American Medical Association has the power and wealth to do something like this, and they're one of the largest and richest lobbies in Washington. But that's infeasible, isn't it? That an entire organization is responsible? But if there were an association within the AMA; a group of people who were in the right position to utilize the organization's power and wealth? A group motivated by a strict obligation to further the financial and public relations status of the American physician, and to preserve the status quo of the American health care system? An association radical enough and willing to do anything to stop the bill from passing into law, even murder?"

"Who are you? How did you come up with this? I mean it's clear that you believe it, but how on earth? And why the hell didn't you go to the Feds, get into protective custody? You're as crazy as Greene was," Martin said, astonished.

"Protective custody? Senator Mitchell was killed because he was taking money from the PSR and the association found out about it. They hired someone to do it, or they did the killing themselves, and somewhere along the line, they found out about the connection with your local doctors, so to be safe, they killed everyone."

"But how did you know?"

"I'm a member of the Appropriations Committee, and I'm in hiding because I figured if they were willing to kill one of us, why not more than one? At least I thought that initially."

"You lost me again."

"Senator Mitchell established a conservative voting block within the Appropriations Committee, and he kept us well re-warded for voting as a block. I was being paid to vote a certain way; we all were. We never knew where the money came from or what deals Mitchell had made to get it. He told us how to vote, and he lined our pockets. It was always done in such a way we'd never jeopardize our conservative position, either."

"Democracy in action," Martin said in disgust. "So why kill Mitchell, then?"

"He must have been planning to have us green-light the Health Care Bill. Killing him took away our block's majority position. Without Mitchell's final voting decision, known to the group, the senators in the Appropriations Committee whom the association already exercised influence over would guarantee the bill wouldn't see one red cent. Simply because it's a liberal piece of legislation, and because the president is the author, meant we would vote against it."

"So why not kill more members of your secret little group?"

"Who knew what kind of people would replace us? We were more useful scared than dead. Killing Mitchell was enough to destabilize the voting block, that's all they needed."

"Joanne was right. We have to go to the FBI. We're in way over our heads."

"But I thought you didn't trust them? Didn't you say they were going to bring charges against you if you pursued this?" she asked.

"Doesn't matter. This goes way too deep for me. I don't know what I was expecting to unearth down here, but it sure as hell wasn't something like this."

"I can't be a part of it if you're going to proceed with this course of action," Braun said, standing up.

Martin grabbed her by the wrist. "What do you mean, you can't be a part of it? You're the most important part," he said, and leveraged her back into the chair. "Did you think I was just going to start arresting people? Listen, I'm not real fond of the FBI, you're right, but they're the only ones that can deal with a situation like this. I stand to lose everything by going and talking with them. All I have is police work. It's all I've ever done. It's what I am. It may not seem like losing a lot compared to someone like yourself, but it's everything I have, everything. You have to come and set things right. Besides, with the amount of shit that's going to fly about this thing, your role is insignificant. They'll make you a deal. If there is one thing I've learned from the media during the last week, it's that when there are bigger fish to fry, they don't give a shit about you. After all, you're the one bringing the culprit to light."

"You're quite a convincing man, Mr. Martin. In an ordinary situation I'm sure your schoolboy forbearance gets you most things you want, but this is extraordinary, and I won't overextend myself for you or them. I'll help put the FBI on the right course, but no more. I'm not going to commit professional suicide without some assurance of special consideration. Contrary to what you think, I am a big fish. As big as they get, and when either the authorities or the press get the chance to bring down a government official, they make the most of it. I won't throw away what I've accomplished for anything or anyone. If you want to be the genius who figured out this great puzzle, that's fine, you be that genius. My help will be minimal, and in the end it will look like your discovery and not mine. I hope you can see my point of view and why I must insulate myself to some degree."

"I don't understand at all. I can't believe the way things operate down here. I actually feel worse now than when I left Goshen. I never would have thought that was possible, congratulations. I don't see a whole lot of corruption where I come from but I'm educated enough to tell the difference. You do what you have to do, and so will I. Your showing up and helping me nail these pricks might just be taken into consideration later. People take it for granted that politicians are corrupt, so when it's confirmed by the media, it's no real surprise to John Q public. But, I have to say this political awakening has made me nauseous. You play it anyway you want. I'm not interested in whether you're on the take or whether you get caught. I've found the people responsible for the murders of five of the residents I swore to protect, and I intend to put their collective asses in a sling. After that, your life is your own business."

"I'm so glad we understand each other."

"There's only one thing I do understand and that is I'm not letting you out of my sight, so get comfortable. We'll hit the Feds tomorrow, and then you can tiptoe through the tulips, for all I care."

"Good enough," Braun said, curling up on the bed.

Martin remained in his chair.

He dozed off but didn't dream.

24

John Scaffiotelli leaned against the wall of the elevator as he ascended the several floors to his office. When the doors opened he walked the length of the hallway and entered his office, closing the door behind him. He slumped into his high-backed chair and stared at the telephone, paranoid the association was, through the aid of audio and video devices, hanging on his every word and movement.

Looking around the room he wondered how many audio or video devices there were. He wondered if he was just being listened to, or whether they were watching him as well. He glanced at his phone. Eleven short numbers and a quick order away was the death of a United States president. His hands were sweaty as he leaned forward in the chair and picked up the receiver.

Dillon answered.

"Have you been able to locate Martin?"

"No, we haven't."

"He's no longer the solution, Dillon, stop hunting," Scaffiotelli said. "I'll be e-mailing you an encrypted information packet. In it you'll find detailed instructions on a contract I want you to carry out. After which, your services are no longer required, and as an old friend, I would suggest that you get lost. As lost as possible."

"Who's the contract for, sir?" The man's voice was edgy.

"I don't want to say over a landline. Just confirm your receipt of the packet and your acceptance of the assignment immediately."

"Message understood. I'll be waiting for the information."

"I want you to send Sampus across the river to Fort Myer. A man by the name of Marson will meet him there in one hour. He'll be in a military vehicle near barracks Seventeen. Have Sampus make out a list of all the equipment you'll need. He's knowledgeable about that sort of thing so let him take care of it. Marson will leave the requests with another insider. The instructions I'm sending will give you the rest of the details."

"Understood sir," Dillon spoke with his characteristic seriousness, and it was reassuring to Scaffiotelli that he could trust those men to accomplish the goal.

Scaffiotelli had made a judgment call to go outside the association with the earlier killings in order to keep everyone as far removed as possible. That turned out to be a bad call, especially when he had several able and experienced killers working for him. Hindsight was useless now, because he was convinced there would be no second chance for him. He would either be turned over as a patsy or killed. Whichever way, he was the association's Oswald, yet he set it in his mind to accept his fate and remain a professional. He accepted the responsibility for his actions because it was his nature to do so, because there was his family to think about, but it didn't mean he was happy about it.

"Good luck," Scaffiotelli said, then hung up.

Dillon turned to Sampus, who was lying stretched out on one of the beds.

"Scaffiotelli wants you to go to Fort Myer."

"Why? Did they find Martin?" Sampus asked.

"No. Circumstances have changed."

"Why?" Sampus said, moving toward Dillon's notebook computer, which was signaling the arrival of an incoming message. "What's the plan now?"

"I'll let you know in a minute," Dillon said as they stared at the security window. ENCRYPTED was the only word that was legible. The rest of the screen was gibberish until Dillon began pecking at the keyboard, and slowly most of the characters melted away, leaving only—

Target: President Hanland

Location: White House

"Now I understand why he said we're on our own after this. He told us to disappear."

"No shit," Sampus said, staring over Dillon's shoulder at the computer. It was an obvious thing to do after killing a president.

"There will be a man by the name of Marson waiting for you in a military vehicle near barracks Seventeen. Give him a list of everything we'll need to pull off the hit. And bring back something to eat."

"What are you talking about?" Sampus began. "But…"

"No questions now. I'll fill you in later. Just do it," Dillon said, and typed a short encrypted message of acceptance. "Hey, you don't have a problem with doing this do you?" he called after Sampus who was leaving the hotel room.

"No."

———⋅⋅———

Fort Myer was a good distance from The Hotel Washington, but when Sampus made it through the main entrance and to the barracks, there was Marson's Hummer parked beside a chain-link fence. He could see the man behind the wheel leaning forward, staring at the license tag.

Headlights flashed and Marson pulled onto the road running the perimeter of Fort Myer's property. He coasted down a slight grade until the entranceway was out of sight, then pulled back to the side of the road and stopped.

Pulling next to the rear bumper, Sampus got out and walked up to the opened passenger window. "You Marson?"

"Get in," The man said, and Sampus did. The Hummer pulled off the grassy roadside and moved further down the road. "So let's have it."

Sampus began to go over the list of equipment needed for the contract. Just about the time Sampus was finishing with his rendition, the truck was pulling to the side of the road opposite his car.

"There won't be a problem. Look for a large nylon bag with yellow straps. Now get out," Marson said, while looking out the windshield.

Sampus got out and crossed the street. He stood inside the opened door of his car watching Marson climb the hill.

He'll probably get it right out of military supply, Sampus thought.

He eased onto the seat, started the engine, and pulled off the grassy roadside, heading for a pizzeria he'd seen on the other side of the Potomac before he'd crossed the Theodore Roosevelt Bridge for Fort Myer.

———•———

Wednesday morning creeped into existence for Martin because he'd been staring at the Hill Motel's ceiling most of the night. He'd managed some sleep, but it couldn't have been more than an hour's worth. He'd been going over the senator's story all night and the more he thought about it, the less sense it made. He'd be glad to talk to the director of the FBI, and get the whole story off his chest.

He stepped out of the shower and onto the cool tiles of the bathroom floor. He dried himself off and slipped into a pair of jeans and a sweatshirt. He combed his hair, brushed his teeth, and then relinquished the room to Braun, whom he'd handcuffed to the radiator while he cleaned up.

"You didn't have to do that you know?"

Martin just looked at her; a night of thinking and not sleeping had softened his opinion of her a bit. He was tired.

"I wouldn't have gone," She continued.

"It didn't cross your mind?" he asked. "You told me what you knew. You could have vanished, left me to fill in the Feds."

It had crossed her mind, but there was something energizing about Martin to her. His attitude and honesty was contagious, and she found herself thinking about doing the right thing, and thinking about James Redfield. What would his opinion of all this be? What would his opinion of her be, if she skirted this somehow and everything got missed, or worse, swept under the carpet. She suddenly found taking advantage of Martin's naïveté unthinkable, but there had to be consideration on the part of the FBI. After all she was blowing the whistle, and it had always accounted for a lot when she'd been prosecuting. It had to count big time, this time.

Braun was slow to get out of the shower, and it was past ten when she appeared. They sat facing each other, staring at the telephone on a bureau between the two beds.

Martin picked up the phone and called the operator, who gave him the number of the FBI building in downtown Washington.

He dialed and gave the receiver to Braun. It was agreed she would have a better chance of getting through to the director. She was, after all, a United States senator.

"Could I speak with the director, please?" Braun said. "It's Senator Braun calling. Yes, he's expecting the call. Thank you. The Mitchell investigation." Braun handed the phone back to Martin.

He waited a few long minutes and then a man began to speak to him.

"Senator Braun, how can I help you?" the man asked.

"With whom am I speaking?"

"This is Director Geehern. Who is this?"

"This is Thomas Martin. Does that name mean anything to you?"

"Jesus, where the hell have you been hiding? We've been looking high and low for you, boy."

"Looking for me? Why?"

"You need to get in here right away, son. There are handfuls of men looking for you, and they all want your hide stuffed and mounted on a wall."

"Yeah, I know people are after me, but I'm still around."

"Tell us where you are, and we'll come get you."

"Not so fast. You pricks did an awful lot to piss me off last week."

"The two men you're referring to, the ones who ordered you to back down, they weren't federal agents."

"What the hell are you talking about?"

"I ordered two agents to go to Goshen and speak with you, but they were killed before they ever made it out of Washington."

"Just hold on a minute," Martin said, trying to slow the conversation down a bit so he could think straight.

"There's no time. Tell us where you are and we'll come and pick you up. We have to talk to you about why those men were so interested in what was happening in your town."

"Listen, I've got Senator Braun here as well. She's a casualty of the situation, and she has just as much to offer as I do."

"We'll come and get you both. Now where are you?"

"I want you in the car that comes and gets us."

"Impossible, that's completely against protocol," Geehern said, sounding impatient.

"Come again?" Martin asked.

"I have no way of verifying—"

"Who I am," Martin finished the director's sentence. "Spare me the security lecture. Don't screw around with me. Just be here, in the car, that's the deal."

"Where are you?"

"The Hill Motel. It's on—"

"I know where it is. You two stay put," Geehern said, and was gone.

Martin returned the receiver to its cradle and stared at Braun. It was a long wait before they heard the squealing tires of two sedans on the Hill Motel's parking lot.

———◦◦◦———

On the third floor of The Hotel Washington there was a light knock on the door to room 300. Dillon moved away from the large plate glass window overlooking the White House and walked toward the door.

Looking through the security lens, he saw Sampus. He unlatched the chain bolt, opened the door, and his partner walked past him.

"Have you memorized the material yet?" Sampus asked. "I need to know what the hell this is all about."

"Piece of cake," Dillon said, returning to his notebook computer after closing and re-bolting the door. He moved a briefcase so Sampus could set the two large brown pizza boxes down on the table.

"So let me hear it."

"At 6 PM, President Hanland lands on the South Lawn in Marine One. At 7 PM he's signing a bill into law on national television, and that's what we're preventing. We'll never get him inside the White House, so that means the chopper. Following the last two attempts on Hanland, the new SOP allows for pilot's discretion where Air Force One lands, and the route Marine One takes to the White House. That means we have to be in the house prior to his arrival. In order to be in position on the roof of the White House, it will take us, at minimum, one hour to get by the Secret Service and to the security room located in the basement. Mr. Marson will arrange to have the equipment near the easternmost basement door, located underneath the staircase leading out onto the South Lawn. We grab the stuff from there and disable the Communications Net, as well as disarm the top-floor security system. Then we'll have to allow another hour in order to hit the Secret Service shift change, so that we can get to the top floor unseen. That shift change occurs at 5 PM. So in order to be in position on the roof in time to meet Marine One, we would have to be at the front gate of the White House at, let's say, 2:30 PM," Dillon said.

"Sounds a little too neat," Sampus said, taking a steaming slice of pizza from the box.

"Someone went to a lot of trouble to get all the information in this packet," Dillon said. "There's a page-long employee summary on everyone posted at the White House. Then there's Secret Service shift schedules, structural and security system schematics, weaponry inventories, and a hundred things telling you everything about the White House. What is there, who is there, when they're there."

"Scaffiotelli didn't come up with this," Sampus said.

"There's no way in hell," Dillon affirmed.

"So getting in is a cake walk?"

"With all this intell, anyone could waltz in there and pop Hanland."

"Not knowing who's behind the intell adds an element of

unpredictability," Sampus said with a frown.

"There would have to be some key players at the Justice Department, an awful lot of risk in attempting something like this. We could disappear now and leave Scaffiotelli out in the wind," Dillon said, pulling a slice of pizza from the box for himself.

"You know me better than that. My allegiance to Scaffiotelli is as strong as yours," Sampus said. "I gave up on this country long ago, just as you did, when they left us to swing in the wind. I went dark and I'm not turning back now."

"They left a lot of us out there, my man. Besides, I've been a soldier all my life, and the only thing that's changed is who's calling the shots."

"This is what the Corp trained us for. This profession is volatile by nature, any day could be our last. I think it's a hell of a way to go out. The ultimate kill for a Marine sniper is the high ranker, it's worth the risk," Sampus said.

"With all this information there's a hell of a good chance we'll walk, just like we've been walking away from shit-storms our whole careers. That started in the sixties, when we survived hell without a scratch. We're charmed," Dillon said. "Even when death seems inevitable it isn't, we're living proof. Besides, I've never walked away from anything in my life, and I'm not about to start now. But this is the big time, make no mistake about it."

"If you have to go, better it be on the field of battle. I'm in."

"How was Mr. Marson?" Dillon asked, getting back to the business at hand.

"Corrupt, but connected. I don't have any doubt he can get the shit."

"So we're set?"

"So long as the stuff gets into the White House, we'll have all kinds of toys to play with," Sampus said, and reached for the computer. As he ate his food he began to scroll through the material.

"You see the part about the roof personnel?" Dillon asked, grabbing another slice of pizza.

"Cherries, don't worry about them." Sampus said, after moving to the proper page and reading what Dillon was talking about.

"Don't be so sure."

"They'll be dead before they know what hit them," Sampus chuckled, folding the pizza slice in half and taking a generous bite off the end of it.

Dillon had every page of the material memorized, and out of all of it, only three things worried him. The first was they were going to kill a United States president. The second was two former United States Army rangers were part of the Secret Service's Special Tactics Unit guarding the roof later that day. Lastly, that the Special Tactics Unit would turn out to be less armed than rumored. The rooftop arsenal was fabled to include a next generation version of the Stinger Missile Launcher, as a means to deter an air assault.

It was part of the plan to get to the roof, disable the Special Tactics Unit, and shoot Marine One out of the sky as it came across the South Lawn preparing to land. But if the Stinger wasn't there, this would be the shortest offensive of his life.

By the end of their meal neither of the men showed any apprehension about what they were about to do. They were both talking and laughing.

At 2 PM they got into a gray Chevy sedan, preparing to leave for the White House.

25

Martin pulled the motel curtains aside to see two dark brown sedans angling in behind his Camaro, and six men dressed in dark suits pouring from them. Two of the men moved to the rear of the cars toward the parking lot entrance. Another moved down the thin cement walkway in the direction of the motel office, away from his room's door. A fourth man stood next to one of the sedans rear passenger doors, his hand outstretched behind him, resting on the door handle, his eyes darting around the parking lot.

An older man, who looked more like a regular patron of an expensive country club than a federal agent, was escorted by a hulking black agent. All six of the men looked like agents of the Federal Bureau of Investigation.

There was something prototypical about their seriousness and mannerism that had been lacking in the men who visited him in Goshen. Martin was embarrassed he hadn't picked up on it when they'd come to his house, but then again he didn't know a federal agent from a hole in the ground until this very moment. Everything about them screamed government agent.

A loud knock on the motel room door was followed by a man's voice. "Thomas Martin, it's Director Geehern."

Martin swung the door open and inspected the proffered identification.

"It's good that you came," Martin said, shaking the man's hand.

The large agent gave a quick glance toward his fellow officers and when all four of them nodded, he turned back to Braun, Martin and his boss. "Okay, let's go," he said, and ushered them toward the safety of the cars.

Once inside, two men climbed into the front seat and sped away.

The large man withdrew the set of keys he'd taken from Martin and got behind the wheel of the Camaro, while the other agents piled into the second sedan.

At the corner of the Hoover Building, the three cars turned off Pennsylvania Avenue onto 10th Street, coming to rest in front of an E Street entrance. Two men met the car on the street and walked the group into the building and to a rear elevator. When they reached the third floor and were safely off the elevator, a relieved look swept over the faces of all the men who'd participated in the transportation effort. Anyone who seemed to know anything about Mitchell was ending up dead, and they were glad to have someone in protective custody.

The group of chaperones dispersed, and Geehern, Martin, and Braun moved into a conference room filled with perhaps a dozen people.

"This is Special Agent Kerrigan and Agent Tobin. They're leading the investigation into the murder of Senator Mitchell.

Terry Rabinowitz is a special technical adviser for us," Geehern explained.

"We've been hunting high and low for you, Chief. Both here and in New York," Tobin said.

"New York? Why would you still be looking for me there?" Martin asked, but Tobin didn't answer. "Surely if you bothered my department enough, they would have cracked." Tobin still said nothing.

Geehern began to speak, "An officer by the name of Matthew Light and a county medical examiner by the name of Benjamin Tafton were found by your police department. Light was murdered and Tafton is in a coma, fighting for his life."

Martin was speechless. He stared at Geehern for a few long seconds and then his gaze fell to the tabletop. He swallowed hard as two vivid memories came back to him displaying the last time he'd seen both men. He cringed at the thought of Light running away from New York City only to get killed in a rural town.

His voice shook with anger as he tried to respond, and he was required to clear his throat in order to do so. "How?"

"Both were beaten," Geehern said. "Tafton survived it somehow."

"Beaten to death?"

"None of your local personnel or the state police had any idea where you'd gone. Quite honestly, we all feared for the worst," Tobin said. "A state police detective by the name of McElroy wasn't positive whether or not you actually came to Washington. He told us you weren't the type of guy to let something rest, but he wasn't sure."

"They were trying to find out where I had gone," Martin mumbled.

"Who was?" Tobin asked.

"Tafton is family," Martin said, pained.

"Who was trying to find you?"

"The men who killed my friends."

"Maybe you should tell us why they were willing to kill in order to find out what had happened to you," Geehern said.

"Maybe you should tell me how the hell guys with forged FBI credentials can just waltz around doing whatever they want, killing whomever they please?" Martin barked, but got no answer.

He didn't trust any of them, but in the pit of his stomach he knew what they had said about Light and Tafton was true. He also knew he was in over his head and they were the only people to whom he could turn. "How detailed should I get?" he asked.

"It's imperative you tell us everything you know, as well as everything you think. Just start at the beginning," Geehern said, leaning forward.

Martin began telling the group about the apparent connection between Goshen and Washington. He was staring down the long table, past the men seated at the other end and into space. His stare was blank, as though he could see it all happening again as he spoke.

After a few minutes, he began speaking to Geehern, ignoring the rest of the table. He explained about the murders in his small town, his conversations with Dr. Greene, and how he'd been pointed toward Washington by the physician.

Martin described Angela Wilme's apartment and how he'd interviewed Senator Mitchell's widow.

"It's got to be the same people," Tobin said. "They followed this Greene to New York, and then they followed Martin back here to D.C."

"Sounds like it," Geehern agreed. "Please go on Chief."

"Mrs. Mitchell then told me her husband was having a summer affair with a young graduate student who'd been interning for him on the Hill. I found out who she was, where she lived, and spoke with her on Tuesday. She unknowingly had detailed files in her possession that Mitchell had stored in her Foggy Bottom apartment."

"Files, what kinds of files?" Geehern asked.

"Mitchell's campaign contributions. The PSR was listed, and supposedly they donated twenty-five million dollars to the senator." Martin said.

"That's presidential proportions, not senatorial," Agent Kerrigan said.

"Well there's no way the PSR had the resources to donate that kind of money. It just wasn't that kind of place. Not that high speed, if you know what I mean?" Martin stated back to Kerrigan.

"Where are these files now?" Geehern asked.

"Locked in the trunk of my Camaro."

"Douglas, Johnson, get down to Martin's car and fetch those files and get to work on them," Geehern commanded.

Two men rose and rushed out of the office.

"Go on," Geehern said to Martin.

"When I was back in my car, I found Senator Braun cowering in the backseat." Martin then looked at Braun, who was sitting next to him.

She looked as though she intended on being as tight-lipped

as she'd threatened. Martin thought it insane for her to follow him around, hide out in his car, spill her guts about some wild conspiracy, and then stride into the FBI headquarters only to take the Fifth.

"You've all but implicated yourself as it is. It can only help your situation by spilling," Martin said into her ear.

The group crowded around the table watched them with interest as they whispered to each other.

"I want to come clean, that's why I came here," Braun said, fidgeting. "Somewhere along the line, I lost touch with the reason I came to Washington. Before I begin, I have to know that what I say will be weighed in my favor at a later point."

"It will," Geehern said.

"I'm a member of the Senate Appropriations Committee, and I'm a Republican. Until the death of Byron Mitchell, the conservatives comprised a secret majority pact within the committee, and we ensured that any legislation needing approval was strictly up to us. We either approved it or we flushed it. Mitchell was in charge of this pact, and we were well compensated for our unwavering and unquestioning support. This pact has been around for decades, and it has always voted according to our political persuasion. Mitchell never accepted any influence outside of our political party, so we were still voting our conscience and serving our conservative constituency, from a certain point of view," Braun said.

Martin was amazed at her level of honesty. She was burying herself.

"When Mitchell was killed, the majority position we had over the committee was jeopardized. We no longer had the power.

In fact, its polarity changed sides. Why did someone kill Senator Mitchell? Because they knew about the pact and how it would vote on the president's Health Care Bill." Braun continued to explain the scenario as she'd done with Martin the night before.

"There's only one problem. As Chief Martin said, even with Angela Wilme's assistance, the PSR could never get their hands on twenty-five million dollars to turn over to Mitchell. There's no way."

"So who, then?" Geehern asked, but got no response from the senator. "You're certain about all this, the PSR, and this association? You're positive?"

Again Braun refused to answer.

"It figures," Tobin said.

"And are any of those a radical faction of physicians, pharmaceutical and insurance company representatives buried inside the AMA?" Geehern asked Tobin while still staring at Braun.

"Nope," Tobin said.

"So, who do you think is behind those PSR funds, Senator?"

"Who do you think it is, Chief?" Braun asked, staring at Martin.

Martin shrugged off the question.

"Humor us, Chief." Geehern was growing impatient.

"Agent Tobin looks as though he has an idea," Martin said, staring across the table at the agent. Martin and Braun were playing an old game with the FBI, letting them paint in at least some of their own conclusions. They were backing away from blaming who they both suspected, out of fear and out of respect.

There was a calculating look in Tobin's eye. He believed the senator's story, and from the look of it, had a good idea of who was behind it.

The whole table was looking at Tobin, but it was several long moments before he said anything.

26

By 4:30 PM Senator Braun had long been taken into custody for admitting that she'd accepted bribes in return for voting for the legislation Mitchell supported.

Seven of the key people involved with the Mitchell investigation were sitting around Agent Tobin's cubicle, discussing the information they'd just gotten from the IRS. Martin was seated next to a young agent with a law degree in taxation, trying to follow what the man was saying. Tobin was in front of his PC, entering information or searching for it, as the young agent read through the IRS printouts. Director Geehern was wedged in among them, as was Kerrigan, two other female special agents and another tax attorney.

As Tobin typed and his younger counterpart analyzed, the picture became clearer and clearer. The PSR owned a great deal, including a business called the Talbot Corporation, which for all intents and purposes was a bank account at a Manhattan branch of Citibank. It had an elaborate front, but upon further checking, via the computer, it was discovered their headquarters in New York City was nonexistent. The PSR, and its Talbot Corporation front, had a current balance of five million dollars, which didn't include the twenty-five million the Mitchell pact had received in exchange for a favorable vote on the president's Health Care Bill.

But the initial problem still existed. The PSR was only a middle man. The organization itself was half phantom, and there was no way it could account for 30 million dollars.

It was 5 PM when Tobin and his computer finally tracked down a company by the name of Eagle Development, and their deposit of thirty million into the Talbot Corporation's bank account. Eagle was another fallacy, only this one turned out to be an offshore account belonging to the Hanland family.

The president was funneling money to the PSR, and in turn they were lobbying Congress, including the bribing of Mitchell's pact on the Appropriations Committee.

"I'll be a son of a bitch." Geehern's face dropped when they uncovered the truth, but he could believe it. On the several occasions he'd met the man, and come away from the experience feeling shaken that the fate of the most powerful nation on earth was in the hands of a fruitcake, he'd never equated the man as cunning. "Looks like you were right, Tobin," Geehern said, breaking the heavy silence in the room.

"I'm not thrilled with the accomplishment," Tobin said.

"Looks like you and Braun pretty much had the thing nailed down," Geehern said, turning to Martin.

"So now what happens?" Martin asked.

"Well, there's enough to make me suspicious about this Chicago association, as Braun called it, being behind the murders of all of those people. The special agent-in-charge of the Chicago field office will take care of that part. But seeing as how the President and the Appropriations Committee are involved up to their necks, that part gets handled a little different, I'll have to sit down with the Attorney General tomorrow. It's all over though." Geehern said, reaching for the telephone on Tobin's desk. He dialed Chicago's number from memory, and gave the SAC a brief synopsis, knowing she'd begin filing the necessary court paperwork to allow her to bust the physicians, pharmaceutical, and insurance coalition wide open.

"I don't think it's over, sir," Kerrigan stated as Geehern's hand dropped the receiver back into its cradle. "Why not just kill the president in the first place?"

"What?" Geehern asked, turning toward the woman.

"If you didn't want the Health Care Bill passed, then why not simply eliminate its writer? I mean, if it was that dangerous to the association's way of life."

"The ball was probably already in play. They didn't really think it would pass. But when they found out Mitchell and the Appropriations Committee were planning on giving it the green light, they panicked. They figured they could send a clear message through Congress, and the pact, by killing one of the most powerful men on the Hill, Mitchell. When they realized the extent of the situation they decided to clean up the mess, plug the holes causing dissension against the association," Tobin said.

"So if they were willing to go to all that trouble to stop the bill from passing, why would you say it's over, sir?" she pressed Geehern.

"Well, the bill did pass, didn't it? Didn't they rush it through because of the upcoming holiday? They'll break for Thanksgiving soon, and won't be back until the new year. As I understand it from the news, Congress made all kinds of changes, but the president approved of them. The association failed in their task. It's all sewn up," Geehern said, smiling.

"I'm not so sure. It just doesn't add up in my mind. It's too simple. Just for the sake of argument, what happens to a piece of legislation when it's altered from its original form?" Kerrigan asked.

"It goes back to the author, so they can read the new draft and either accept the changes or reject them," Tobin said.

"And who has the final say in either vetoing or accepting a piece of legislation after it's been through and approved by the Senate and House machinery?" she said.

"The president," Geehern said.

"But, that can be gotten around by a congressional override."

"That's academic," Geehern added. "What's your point, Kerrigan?"

"Who's the author of the Health Care Bill?" she asked.

"Hanland. So?" Martin asked. They were all staring at each other, and at Kerrigan.

"So, I saw on CNN this morning that Hanland's signing his bill into law tonight on national television, at 7 PM. What if they were to kill the President before he had a chance to officially approve the changes Congress made by signing it tonight?" she asked.

"It's my understanding Congress got dragged into it kicking and screaming, didn't they? They might just let it die," Tobin said. "But that's a big hypothetical."

But it made a kind of weird sense to all of them. Hanland

was out of the country for a brief Middle Eastern conference and due to return that night. The association's killers were in Washington, D.C. trying to kill Martin. It all added up.

When Geehern picked up the telephone, he called his secretary and instructed her to patch him through to the White House. The group of people at the cubicle stared at him as he held the receiver next to his ear. "I'll just get a hold of someone over there and confirm that nothing is going on. Considering the attempts he's had already, this seems ludicrous. I know for a fact the Secret Service has stepped up their game more than enough. So we'll just put even more protection on him. No problem, though, it's not even six yet."

The phone rang and rang. The White House wasn't the type of place where someone didn't answer the call after the first ring. It was as if no one was at the switchboard.

The phone rang and rang.

"How the hell can that be?" He hung up, called his secretary back and asked for the number so that he could dial it himself. "Dolores must've dialed the damn number wrong," he mumbled under his breath.

The phone rang and rang.

The next call was to Edwards Air Force Base, and after a brief exchange of clearance information, it was confirmed that Marine One had already left, en route for the White House, ETA 6 PM. Geehern demanded to be put through to the chopper, but the response to this request was a short lecture on procedure and his lack of clearance.

Geehern hung up the phone and glared at his watch.

It was 5:40 PM, and rush hour.

He relayed the information to the small group of people and they all knew the death of the president might only be twenty short minutes away.

"Tobin, get on the phone and call upstairs. Have those helicopters ready to go ASAP," Geehern commanded.

"They're not on site, sir," Tobin said. "You loaned one out to Treasury last week, and the other blew a fuel pump or something last night."

"Are you kidding me?" Geehern barked, looking down at his wristwatch and shaking his head. "All right, we do it the old-fashioned way."

Within five minutes, Geehern had put together a team of thirty agents, including the FBI's Special Tactics Team, stationed in the building.

Martin ran out the back of the building and got into his Camaro. He pulled at one of the bezel vents and the blind frame came out with a set of keys attached to it. In seconds he was on Pennsylvania Avenue, passing sedans with federal plates. He took a position behind Geehern's lead car and ahead of the large van carrying the Special Tactics Team.

In the half-dozen or so blocks between the Hoover Building and the White House, there were hundreds of cars caught in gridlock.

The convoy of federal cars came to a crawl as the minutes slipped away.

In Martin's rearview mirror he could see the Capitol Building, but outside his windshield, all he saw was brake lights and pluming exhaust.

27

Dillon and Sampus pulled their sedan to the top of the driveway, passed the front garden fountain, and parked off to the west side of the White House between two news vans.

A small group of reporters and their accompanying vans were being searched inside and out by two Secret Service agents as Dillon and Sampus got out of their car. The cold November air whipped through the tight aisles running between the vehicles, and Sampus flashed Agent Grant's FBI badge toward an agent's suspicious glare. The man simply smiled and returned to his other duties.

The duo walked into the White House and approached a desk where a single agent sat keened to his surroundings. Without uttering a word he regarded the two men and then studied their badges, finally pushing two identification cards across the tabletop. The names Agent Grant and Special Agent Williams were typed with bold letters on the laminated tags.

The words "Department of Defense/Electronics Analyst - Bold 1 Clearance," were printed underneath their names.

"Bold 1 will allow you to go where you want. Keep your FBI identification out of sight at all times. The bag is where it's supposed to be," the agent said, and then pointed behind him. "Go down this hallway to the fourth door on the right. Take the staircase to the basement. The central hallway will be in front of you; take it all the way to the southend of the house. The large opening at the end has three doors leading out onto the South Lawn. The bag is inside the easternmost door. Head back north until you reach the second door on your left; that's the security room. Tell the man he's relieved and to report to the front desk for instructions. Show him your identification and ask for the situation change log. Both of you have to sign in the agents' names and enter their clearance number. Got it?"

Dillon and Sampus clipped the DOD tags onto their lapels and removed their badges, folding them in half and stuffing them into their pockets so they couldn't be seen.

"Thanks," Sampus said, and the two men walked past the Secret Service agent and down the wide hallway, heading for the fourth door. The hallway had three chandeliers hanging from a carved marble ceiling.

Dillon was thinking of how much the house had been through since it was built. Burnt down and rebuilt, gutted and reconstructed; there was a lot of history and a lot of changes. With each new president the style and decor was uprooted and replaced with a more suitable one.

The carpet was dark red and the walls were Spanish white. Marble laced painted walls and several pieces of famous furniture lined the expanse of the hall. At the far end was a huge pillared doorway guarded by two large ferns, and at the fourth

stained oak door Sampus was waiting for Dillon. He stood looking back at his partner, who was enthralled by what Sampus considered to be an exuberant waste of his tax money.

Another Secret Service agent stood guard on the other side
of the door leading off the hallway.

The central basement hallway was shallow and the stone walls
were close. There were a multitude of wooden doors leading off
to the left and right. At its terminus were a set of double doors
and an arcing pane window.

Sampus turned to the left when he entered the foyer and
approached the easternmost door. It was clear that the doors,
which at some point long ago had led out onto the South Lawn,
were no longer meant to be opened. The corner of the wall was
pitch black, and even though he couldn't see anything, he took
it for granted there would be something there.

He reached down and felt along the dirty base where the
wall met the floor, and it was obvious this particular corner of
the White House was neglected by the cleaning staff. He hunched
over and continued into the darkness until Dillon, who was waiting at the entranceway to the foyer, couldn't see him.

Sampus reappeared toting a long black duffle with yellow
straps, and Dillon could tell the bag was heavy by Sampus' posture.

The two men headed back down the hallway together, entering the second door to the left. They went through the routine
as the agent had instructed, and the security officer left the room,
heading for the front desk and new instructions.

It was 3:05 PM. They were ahead of schedule by twenty-five
minutes.

The security room of the White House occupied over a hundred square feet and was dominated by video display screens and audio equipment. A single computer keyboard sat on a short table. Taking his Palm TX handheld computer from his breast pocket, Dillon began scrolling through screens until Scaffiotelli's packet of information appeared. Placing it on the table next to him, Dillon took up his position. He returned the White House computer to its menu mode and a selection of options appeared on one of the screens before him. Sliding the mouse down along the tabletop until the words "Third floor" were illuminated, he pressed the mouse key, and more selections came onto the screen.

He proceeded in that manner until he found the code that would let him isolate the audio and video system components that would track their route to the roof. Breaking from the main menu, he copied the short program from the Palm that would provide a brief and uneventful cycle for each leg of their ascent. The screens would display the false picture for only a few moments, after which they'd return to the actual sights and sounds. But Dillon knew it would be plenty of time for them to reach the roof, as long as everything went according to procedure.

Once he was finished with that, he broke back into the system and began to search through the files for information dealing with the communications NET.

The White House had two distinct communication systems comprising its NET. The first network provided the security personnel inside the property the ability to communicate free from signal interception, thanks to the miracle of encryption. The house also had conventional telephone lines, but each system fed through the central computer and were just as controllable.

It was 4:50 PM when Dillon moved away from the keyboard, and he was glad they had arrived earlier than scheduled, because as it turned out, he needed the time. It had been ages since he'd been required to do computer related tampering, and the White House's system was state of the art, which turned out to be a tough but conquerable challenge.

During the time Dillon spent typing at the keyboard, Sampus had donned a pair of latex gloves and sprawled all of the equipment onto an empty table in the security room. He was scrutinizing the MP5s and their ammunition, as well as the Colt Commanders and their ammunition. The rounds were a now illegalized brand of explosive tipped penetrators. He had taken a round from each clip and inspected it.

There were two MP5s, two Commander pistols, and four clips for each weapon. The clips for the submachine guns had been modified so they could hold an extra large capacity.

There were also two M24 Sniper Systems. The 7.62mm weapon was the preferred choice of special military teams such as Army Special Forces and Navy Seals. The modified Remington rifles were disassembled and lying in large metal cases. Each of the pieces, including the magazines and Leupold scopes, were tucked into molded gray foam, and secured with cloth straps. They were fresh off the press. It was the way the system was shipped, and Sampus had been correct about Mr. Marson liberating it from military stock.

Sampus assembled the two sniper rifles, realizing that fine tuning of the calibration would be required once they reached the roof. He was a crack shot and could hit a target at twelve-hundred yards with the gun. Dillon was quite good in his own right, but Sampus was excellent.

Once he was satisfied Marson had delivered on everything they had requested, he separated the gear into two piles. Sampus slipped his arms through a black-fitted coverall vest designed for military and police use, and slipped a pair of night vision goggles, a portion of plastic explosive, detonators, and wiring in each of the included back packs. He tucked one of the Colt pistols into a fitted holster on his vest and clipped a strap, securing it into place. The MP5 had a slide holster fitted into the chest portion of the coverall.

In short order, half of the remaining equipment was separated into each pack. Standing, he tested the weight of the pack. It wasn't even noticeable, and he returned the duffel and the two metal rifle cases to their hiding spot, satisfied.

It was 4:45 PM and Dillon was finishing up on the computer work. Sampus bent over and grabbed his sniper rifle and slung it over his left shoulder. He briefed Dillon on the equipment he'd requested; he was familiar with all of it.

As Dillon suited up, Sampus stowed his eight replacement clips.

They were ready by 4:55 PM.

They left the security room as they had found it and walked to the southwest corner of the house, staring up through the long series of stairs leading to the third floor. There were very few cameras and even fewer White House workers in this far-removed corner of the house. They were invisible.

At 5 PM they heard distant footsteps heading down the basement's central hallway, stopping at and turning into the security room. The agent relieving the first shift would find a situation change log telling him that two technicians from the DOD had performed a computer check on the security of the White House and found no problems; that they had dismissed the agent and left the room unattended at 4 PM. The second shift security agent would find nothing odd about this, because once a month, for as long as he'd been working in the bowels of the White House, it had happened precisely as it did today.

Dillon and Sampus ascended and opened the door leading into the main third-floor hallway. Although empty, they could hear the voices of men just around the corner of each end of the hall. The shifts were changing as Dillon and Sampus stepped out onto the bright cream-colored carpeting, unseen.

Even though it was only ten feet to the door leading to the roof, it felt like ten miles. All any one of the Secret Service agents had to do was poke their head around a corner.

Dillon and Sampus opened the door and closed it behind them just as the voices silenced.

In the hallway, an agent stepped into view and began to adjust his earpiece. Another agent walked the length of the hall and took up position next to the door Dillon and Sampus had just passed through.

The men were staring at each other, motionless. Both had been chosen for third-floor duties because of their ability and commitment. They would die for Hanland. It would be a decision they'd make without thought, without remorse.

Dillon and Sampus stealthed up the wooden staircase to the roof, not making a sound for the men in the hallway or on the roof to hear.

Cold air rushed in on them as Dillon opened the door to the north side of the roof. Because of the wind and the sound of the front fountain, the Special Tactics Unit member did not turn from his eastward position when they stepped through the doorway and onto the flat perimeter of the roof itself. It was tar and stone, the least favorite possibility Dillon or Sampus could have hoped for.

Sampus closed the door behind him and crept west along the island wall rising off the center of the roof.

Dillon slid his M24 off his shoulder and moved snakelike toward the man standing by the carved marble railing running the edge of the roof. He wedged himself against an exhaust duct where it was impossible to see him. He lowered the Remington rifle even with a piece of the ductwork, silenced end pointing east, Leupold scope displaying the man's belt. He calculated the proper vertebra, estimated the location of the man's spinal cord, and waited. He would give Sampus a few minutes to get into position and then fire, causing the man's body to fall backward and onto the roof, instead of forward and over the edge of the house.

Sampus' shoes made very little sound as he moved along the island toward the west side of the roof, but he thought it was all the noise in the world. The other member of the roof team was on the southwest corner, six feet away from the edge, and could withstand a head shot without falling to a noticeable death. Sampus swung the M24 rifle off his shoulder and leaned around the corner of the island, pointed the silenced end of the weapon at the man's head, and fired. The man fell forward, landing on his AR-15.

Dillon fired a simultaneous shot into his prey's spinal cord, just below the skull, and he stiffened, and fell hard onto his back.

Dillon and Sampus met on the south side of the roof.

Fitted into the island portion was a protrusion of marble and glass. Under the marble and past the glass, against the wall of the island, were a metal door and an electronic keypad.

Dillon entered Special Agent Williams' clearance number on the keypad, and the door hissed as it popped open. Sampus grabbed the edge of the steel door and swung it open even wider. Two SIIML missile launchers and several missiles sat inside a checkerboard-like series of cubby holes.

Sampus grabbed one of the launchers and slid it out of the hole. He held the piece of military hardware so that it rested on his right shoulder.

Dillon breathed a little easier, seeing that the fabled Stinger prototype was really there.

It was 5:10 PM.

Geehern placed another frantic call to the Secret Service number at the White House. There was no answer. It was as though the White House were gone.

The traffic in front of his car inched forward as his pulse and blood pressure inched higher. He placed the call again. Nothing.

He turned to look at Chief Martin, who had taken up position behind him. The man was looking around as though he were plotting something. When his driver's door swung open and Martin got out, Geehern knew his intentions.

Martin leaned into his Camaro and retrieved his pistol from the glove box, slid it into the small of his back, and slammed the door shut, looking back for a moment at the FBI's Special Tactics Unit sitting in the van behind him. Then he looked forward at Geehern, who was staring right back at him while bellowing at his driver.

Martin began to run with all his might down Pennsylvania Avenue in between the lines of cars. He moved around the hood of one of them, through a cloud of thick diesel exhaust, and onto the sidewalk. In front of him, he could see 15th Street and Pershing Park. He was almost a block away from his car when he heard Geehern calling out to him. The director of the FBI and two other agents were right behind him, so he waited for them. A block behind them the side door of the van slid open and men armed to the teeth jumped out and followed.

When Geehern and the other two agents caught up with Martin they resumed their sprint, but Kerrigan and Martin pulled away from the other two again. They didn't wait for Geehern and Tobin to catch up.

Off to the right of Pershing Park and across Alexander Hamilton Place, a deserted Treasury Department Building stood in the shadows of dusk. Martin crossed 15th Street and sprinted up the park's slight grade of green grass and brilliant flowers. He could see the east gate of the White House and its Park Police booth.

Martin and Kerrigan reached the East Gate with hungry expressions, as though they expected to see something horrifying.

It was 5:50 PM.

It was quiet.

28

The Park Police officer stationed at the east gate of the White House knew nothing about what Martin and Kerrigan were saying. As far as he knew, the communications network within the White House was operational.

When the agent tried to call his supervisor and got no response, he began to realize that what Martin and Kerrigan were telling him might have merit.

By the time the police officer was leading them up the driveway toward the White House, Geehern and Tobin had caught up with them. Concealed by a thick canopy of autumn, the five of them moved toward the east wing of the White House.

The Special Tactics team, dressed in dark uniforms emblazoned with the FBI emblem printed in bold yellow lettering, were yelling at pedestrians, or just knocking them over. Despite the amount of equipment the team was trying to cart down the sidewalk with them, they were speeding toward the east gate of the White House.

The traffic on Pennsylvania Avenue had come to a complete standstill and several of the commuters and tourists were standing outside their vehicles looking at the entourage running down the sidewalk, automatic rifles drawn, pistols visible, and various cases and back packs swinging from shoulder straps.

"We have a breech in security," the Park Police officer said into his scrambled transceiver, the only Com device outside the Net's control.

An agent moved from behind his security desk when he saw Geehern, Kerrigan, Martin, and Tobin approaching the east wing staircase where he was posted. Behind him, two Secret Service agents heard the broadcast through a nearby Park Police officer's transceiver, and began jogging east, down the long hallway.

The agent next to the security desk drew a Beretta pistol and moved behind the safety of a thick marble pillar. He fired two quick shots at the Park Police officer moving through the east wing doorway, then turned his attention to the two agents sprinting toward him.

The Park Police officer fell backward in mid-stride, and ended up on the ground, gripping his shoulder. Kerrigan grabbed Martin and threw him out of the line of fire, her weapon already drawn, and firing two cover shots into the wall next to the agent.

"Thanks," Martin said.

"Try not to get yourself killed," she said. Getting to her feet she crossed over to the other side of the doorway, hoping to get a clearer shot at the man.

The two agents who had been running down the hallway managed to wound the corrupt agent and were moving in to subdue him.

Martin and Kerrigan could hear the Special Tactics team behind them. A score of Secret Service agents had also moved around to the east side of the house, spreading across the lawn, beginning their lockdown of the property.

Above them all, Dillon was at the edge of the roof, MP5 in hand, aiming for the running men. The quick pops from the weapon were like eruptions as he targeted three of the men at locations where their body armor didn't protect them.

Martin and Tobin ran into the White House, down the hallway toward the large Jefferson Room, while Kerrigan and Geehern moved toward a set of stairs.

"We've got to get to the roof," Kerrigan called out to Tobin. "Get to a Secret Service agent, fill him in, then get up there."

A few short seconds later, three agents were rushing Martin and Tobin, their guns drawn and barking commands. Waving his badge and doing some barking of his own, Tobin gave them a short rundown, and two of them headed to inform other agents while Martin headed for the roof.

———※———

Dillon moved away from the edge of the White House and joined Sampus, who was backed away but facing the South Lawn. The sound of Marine One's heavy rotor engine could be heard approaching the White House. The sky was gray and Dillon's wavy hair was being blown in the stiff wind. His breath funneled out of his nostrils like the quick puffs of a steam engine's exhaust.

"Well?" Sampus asked, as Dillon moved alongside his compatriot.

"Feds, Secret Service, who knows. But they know we're here and what we're up to," Dillon said. The helicopter was getting louder by the second.

"So much for the element of surprise."

"Unavoidable," Dillon said.

"But unfortunate," Sampus said, refocusing his concentration from what Dillon was saying to what he saw through the SIIML's scope. The electronic display was equipped with weather hardware that eliminated most of the cloud cover and fog hanging in the air. "Hanland doesn't know yet, he's still coming like nothing's wrong."

"Then they haven't found out why the NET's offline yet."

"Amateurs. You'd think one of them would be clever enough to use their cell phone. One call to the Secret Service agents on board and this is all over."

"There are no protocols for an attempt from within the White House. It will never cross their minds."

"Had to be the Park Police accelerating things. They're the only ones we couldn't control. Still in the Dark Ages with those damn transceivers."

"Cops," Dillon said.

"Amateurs," Sampus said. "I'm going to have to fire this thing at the chopper manually. The tactical identification system won't allow me to shoot down a friendly aircraft. When I shut down the tactical system, the thermal guidance will go with it."

"How?"

"This green key-up switch next to the trigger guard engages the automatic systems. But I'll wait until the last possible moment. It would be like trying to see through the secondhand smoke screen of this town, without the weather hardware," Sampus said, showing his partner in case he became incapacitated. "There, I see it."

The rotor was growing louder now, and the sound waves it was producing could be felt, but the helicopter was still invisible to Dillon's eye.

———•———

Kerrigan opened the door leading to the roof, and with Geehern close behind, she bolted up the stairwell, bursting onto the north side of the house. That part of the roof was empty.

She sprinted across the graveled rooftop and hunched next to the island, toward the south side of the house. When she came around the corner, Geehern was right next to her. She saw two men, one with a missile launcher and another with an MP5. She raised her pistol and moved into the openness of the south end of the roof.

"FBI. Put down your weapons," Kerrigan shouted.

As Dillon turned to see what the hell was going on, two shots burst from Geehern's weapon, landing in Kerrigan's back. She fell onto the roof.

"Jesus Christ, Scaffiotelli," Dillon said.

"The boys in blue are close behind. What's taking so long? Let's get the hell out of here already," Scaffiotelli said, approaching the two men.

"Twenty seconds, Mr. Director. Keep your pants on," Sampus said.

29

Martin didn't bother to wait for Tobin to finish explaining what the hell was going on to the Secret Service agents. He sprinted the wide stairway Kerrigan and Geehern had just climbed, and found the set of stairs leading to the third floor. He was using his arm muscles on the banister to propel himself up the stairs faster.

The staircase opened into the third floor's central hallway. It was bright and sparse. Down toward the other end of the hallway stood an open door, and he headed for it. His Smith & Wesson revolver was drawn, and he stepped to the side of the threshold.

Jutting his head around the corner of the door frame, he saw the empty staircase. Taking two steps at a time, he burst through another door at the top of the flight and rolled onto the roof of the White House. His eyes darted around the roof. The portion he was lying on was deserted, save the dead body right in front of him.

He could hear the president's helicopter; he could feel it. It sounded like it was right over him. Looking up, more out of habit, he saw nothing but dense cloud cover.

He got up and crouched next to the island portion of the roof and approached its corner. He jutted his head into the line of fire and then back to safety again. Kerrigan was lying motionless on the stone roof.

He felt light, steely drops of rain hit his face as he exhaled, and watched his breath rise upwards. Past Kerrigan were Geehern and two other men standing next to the edge of the roof looking out over the South Lawn.

Martin thought about Geehern with grave disbelief. "Son of a bitch," he muttered, his thoughts straying to Paulina. The association was no longer a faceless enemy.

The sound of gravel being displaced from around the corner startled him from his raging. He poked his head around again.

Kerrigan was alive. He grabbed at her ankles and yanked her around the corner.

Geehern and Dillon heard the noise and swung their weapons around, firing on Martin's position. Kerrigan had just made it around the corner of the island when bullets imbedded themselves into the roof, kicking up tiny stones where she had just been.

"They have a Stinger. Kill the man with the Stinger," Kerrigan pleaded.

"Too many people have died over this, so don't," Martin ordered.

"Just try not to get yourself killed," she said.

He jumped from the island's protection and saw that Dillon and Geehern were almost on top of him. Martin got off a clean chest shot to Dillon, who fell back while expending a stream of rounds from his MP5.

Geehern fired and hit Martin in his left shoulder. Martin swung his gun away from Dillon and fired his second shot into Geehern's stomach.

Geehern fell to his knees, clutching his abdomen, and Martin kicked his weapon away in time to see Marine One appear through the dense fog. To Martin, it seemed as though there was no world beyond the White House rooftop. The fog was being pushed in odd swirling patterns with the help of the helicopter's main and tail rotors. The rain was getting heavier. Martin squeezed the trigger on his pistol.

Time seemed to slow to a standstill. The blast from his gun seemed to come seconds after he had squeezed the trigger.

The bullet landed in Sampus' upper back, which caused him to misfire the Stinger. Martin sprinted toward the man as the missile ejected from its launcher, contacting with the tail rotor of the chopper. Martin heard the pitch of the engine change, signaling the pilot had seen the inevitable coming, but there was nothing he could do.

The tail rotor exploded, and the helicopter began to spin at an angle toward the ground. Martin could see each rotation of the main rotor from the corner of his eye, but his focus was on Sampus.

Sampus had dropped the launcher and turned toward Martin. There was a look of surprise on Sampus' face. He hadn't heard the confusion going on behind him; he'd been engrossed in what he was doing and nothing else. He'd expected to see an FBI agent or at least the Secret Service spoiling his plans, but it was the local cop, a nobody.

Sampus produced his pistol with such speed it was almost magical.

Martin and Sampus fired simultaneously, each landing a shot in the other's chest. Martin was halted in his tracks, falling onto the roof of the White House, while Sampus was hurled over the edge of the roof and down onto the South Lawn.

Time returned to normal for Martin. He could see the dense gray smoke coming from the chopper mixing with the fog, and he could hear the sounds of Marines and Secret Service agents yelling as they crowded the helicopter. They were removing the president and getting him to safety. At the front of the house he could hear cars climbing the driveway and endless sirens.

He was flat on his back staring at the sky, which seemed to be so low that he could have reached out and touched it. The rain was heavy and soaking his clothing, but he couldn't feel it. He blinked, trying to keep the rain out of his eyes so he could see the sky. The multitude of drops sounded like tap-dancing on the gravel roof next to his ears.

The last thing Martin saw or heard was that rain dancing, and Agent Tobin standing over him exclaiming, "Oh my God!"

30

From the relative safety inside the White House, a frantic CNN cameraman was talking into a cell phone, telling his news studio what was happening, as it happened.

———◆◆———

Inside a newsroom, the cameraman's interpretation of the events transpiring on the evening of November 4 was being sent to affiliates across the country.

———◆◆———

It was December when Martin's doctors agreed he was at last fit for travel. Washington was cold, and outside Dulles, it was raining. Tobin and Kerrigan both extended him a firm handshake and saw him off.

His American Airlines flight took off on time, but when he reached his own airport, heavy snow was causing delays. He took an old copy of *The Washington Post* from his coat pocket and read the headline again.

New York Chief of Police Thomas Martin
Thwarts Assassination Attempt

Martin left the Stewart Airport terminal in Newburgh, New York, to find his Camaro, which the FBI had freighted back from D.C., waiting for him. The engine turned over and he made his way back to Goshen and to some well deserved rest, relaxation, and paperwork.